Deep into Mani

other books by Peter Greenhalgh

Early Greek Warfare (Cambridge)
The Year of the Four Emperors (Weidenfeld)
Pompey: the Republican Prince (Weidenfeld)
Pompey: the Roman Alexander (Weidenfeld)

Deep into Mani
Journey to the Southern Tip of Greece

PETER GREENHALGH
AND EDWARD ELIOPOULOS

First published in 1985
by Faber and Faber Limited
3 Queen Square London WC1N 3AU
Reprinted in 1986

Phototypeset by Wilmaset
Birkenhead, Merseyside
Printed in Great Britain by
Ebenezer Baylis and Son Limited
The Trinity Press, Worcester and London
All rights reserved

Text © Peter Greenhalgh, 1985
Photographs © Edward Eliopoulos, 1985

British Library Cataloguing in Publication Data

Greenhalgh, Peter, 1945–
Deep into Mani.
1. Mani (Greece)—Description and travel
I. Title   II. Eliopoulos, Edward
914.95′2   DF901.M34

ISBN 0–571–13523–4
ISBN 0–571–13524–2 Pbk

Library of Congress Cataloging in Publication Data

Greenhalgh, P. A. L.
Deep into Mani.

1. Mani (Greece)—Description and travel.
I. Eliopoulos, Edward.   II. Title.
DF901.M34G74   1985   914.95′2   84–25916
ISBN 0–571–13523–4
ISBN 0–571–13524–2 (pbk.)

This book is sold subject to the condition that it shall not, by way of trade
or otherwise, be lent, resold, hired out or otherwise circulated without the
publisher's prior consent in any form of binding or cover other than that
in which it is published and without a similar condition including
this condition being imposed on the subsequent purchaser.

Contents

Illustrations	page 7
Preface	13
Introduction: The History of Mani	17
1 Yíthion, Passavá and the City of Ares	44
2 Caves, Churches and a City of Towers	60
3 Mézapos, Tigáni and Cávo Grósso	78
4 Yerolimín, Boularií and the Unhappy Bride	106
5 Kipárissos, Váthia and the Bay of Quails	128
6 Poseidon, Ténaron and the Sunward Coast	143
Bibliographical Note	164
Index	167

Illustrations

between pages 32 and 33

1. Looking north across Yíthion harbour towards Sparta and the distant peaks of Taïyetos
2. Looking down on the island of Kranaï from Koúmaro in the spring
3. Kranaï's lighthouse and fort at dawn from near the little church
4. Ploughshares replacing swords beneath the north-eastern ramparts of Castle Passavá
5. The bare cone of Kouskoúni frowning over the entrance to Inner Mani
6. The Castle of Kelefá commanding the Bay of Ítilon
7. Looking south over the monastery church of Dekoúlou to Ítilon Bay and the distant road that zig-zags up to Areópolis from the harbour of Liméni hidden behind the first headland
8. The beautifully carved and painted iconostasis in Dekoúlou church
9. A fresco from Dekoúlou depicting the righteous Melchisedek, King of Salem, who blessed Abraham and received his tithes (*Gen* 14. 18–20; *Psalm* 110.4): St Paul made him the precedent for the eternal priesthood of Christ (*Hebrews* 7.3)
10. Petróbey Mavromichális (1765–1848), the last Bey of Mani and hero of the Revolution of 1821
11. Looking north down to Liméni and across the Bay of Ítilon to the Pentadáktila, the town of Ítilon and the pass into Messenian Mani
12. Anna Petrochílou with the innkeeper and his dog who discovered the Alepótripa caves
13. (a) and (b) Some of the beautiful formations of stalactites and stalagmites in the Díros caves
14. The dilapidated church of Trissákia with its three chambers – an improbable repository for great works of art
15. The Last Supper, a fourteenth-century fresco from Trissákia, and part of the adjacent Betrayal in the Garden of

Gethsemane, where the soldiers are dressed and armed like contemporary Crusaders
16. The grandmother replies to the *miroloyístra* at the funeral of the little boy killed by a hand grenade
17. St Barbara's at Érimos (*c.* 1150), one of the most beautifully proportioned and disgracefully neglected Byzantine churches in Greece

between pages 64 and 65

18. St Theodore's, Vámvaka (1075), and a ruined tower that once dominated the village below
19. The cloisonné decoration of the grouped window above the south door of St Barbara's, Érimos
20. Some of Nikítas's marbles and the founder's inscription round the west door of St Theodore's, Vámvaka
21. Looking eastwards to 'many-towered Kítta' below the saintly mountains of Áyia Pelayía and Áyii Asómati
22. 'Tourlotí', the beautifully restored twelfth-century church of SS Sergius and Bacchus near Kítta: the intricate cloisonné masonry of the upper parts is as effective from close up as the great T-shaped crosses from a distance
23. Walking out along the handle of the 'frying-pan' to the medieval castle of Tigáni
24. A Sássaris from Mézapos passing the eastern side of Tigáni's crag
25. The thirteenth-century church of Odiyítria perched half way up the cliffs between Tigáni and the Lion's Head
26. The Archangel Michael from Odiyítria – evidently no armchair general despite his gorgeous Byzantine clothes
27. Boats moored in mid-air in the secret harbour of Mezalímonas under the Lion's Head
28. Áyia Eleoússa, 'Our Lady of Compassion': the hermit's church and tomb in the cliff wall of Cávo Grósso
29. The twelfth-century church of Episkopí overlooking Mézapos Bay and Tigáni
30. Frescoes from Episkopí: (a) the Nativity, a composite scene showing the bathing of the Christ-child below the manger scene in which the Magi offer gifts and a shepherd-boy plays the recorder while Joseph looks on; (b) the uncomfortable fate awaiting ladies of easy virtue at the Last Judgement
31. A northward view over Vlachérna (twelfth century), the poet's church above Mézapos Bay

Illustrations

32. Our Saviour's at Gardenítsa (early eleventh century) against the barren cone of Mt Áyia Pelayía
33. The thirteenth-century church of St John at Kéria
34. (a) and (b). Ancient marbles and tombstones, used solely as building materials, studding the walls of St John's, Kéria

between pages 96 and 97

35. The twelfth-century church of St Nicholas with its nineteenth-century campanile against a background of the towers of Koúnos and the most westerly ridge of the Cávo Grósso
36. Three girls standing on the south-facing cliffs of Cávo Grósso above Yerolimín and looking down the coast towards Cape Matapán: they came there every year to remember their father on the anniversary of his death
37. The Mantoúvalos tower at Boularií as repaired after the feud with the Mavromichális clan that ended in a marriage-feast
38. The early eleventh-century church of St Michael nestling in its high valley above Upper Boularií
39. Frescoes from St Michael's, Boularií: (a) one of the two scenes of the Healing of the Paralytic ('Take up thy bed and walk'); (b) the Ascension in the sanctuary ('Why stand ye gazing into heaven?')
40. The tenth-century church of St Pantaléïmon (Pantaleon), Boularií
41. Frescoes from St Pantaléïmon's, Boularií: (a) the Martyrs Nikítas and Pantaléïmon *orant* in the apses with the Madonna above; (b) the agonized St Pantaléïmon
42. The southward view from Koroyiánika over the isthmus of Cape Matapán with the Bays of Pórto Káyio to the left and Marmári to the right
43. Váthia: a forest of towers behind a hedge of prickly pear
44. Looking south-eastwards over the sixth-century basilica of St Peter at Kipárissos
45. The great carved *stelae* used as the jambs of the west door of St Peter's, Kipárissos, the near one honouring the Empress Julia Domna and still legible after nearly eighteen centuries
46. Irreverent donkeys at the church of Áyii Asómati at Ténaron, once the domain of Poseidon
47. A tower tapering in the older style at Láyia
48. The cliff-edge tower at Pírgi above Marmári Bay
49. Looking southwards to Flomochóri down the Sunward coast of the Mani peninsula
50. The Mavromicháles leading their Maniátes at Vérga in 1826

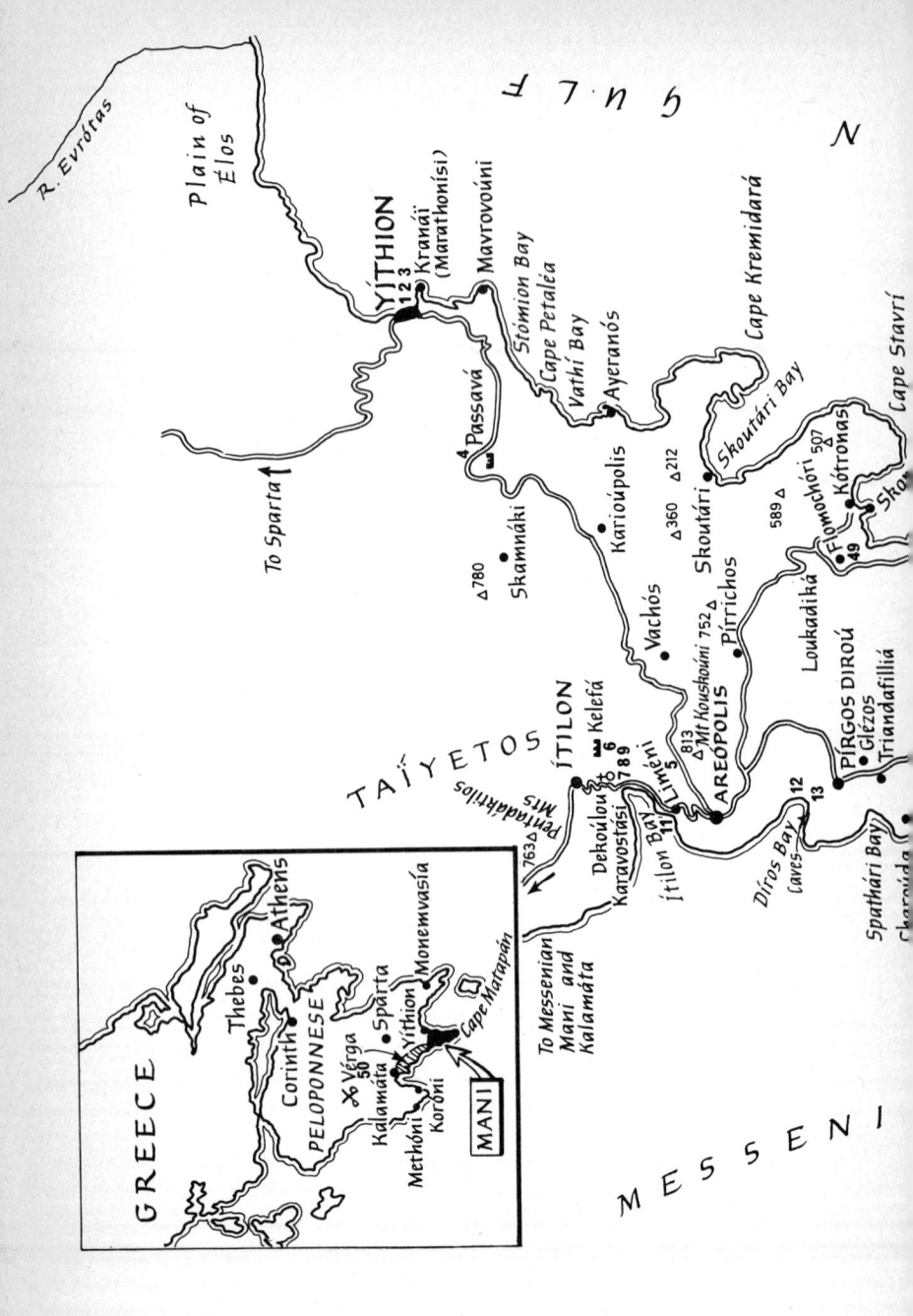

Laconian MANI
Bold numbers refer to the illustrations

Preface

My colleague Edward Eliópoulos first went to Mani in the War as a member of the Greek Resistance fleeing from a failed assassination attempt on a future Pope's brother, who was then at Yíthion as an Italian naval attaché. I first went after meeting Eddie ten years ago and seeing some of his eight thousand colour slides – the fruit of thirty years of exploration and study of what I soon agreed to be the most fascinating region of the Peloponnese, and possibly of the whole of Greece. You may have visited Mani on holiday, or perhaps had a literary introduction in Patrick Leigh Fermor's *Mani: Travels in the Southern Peloponnese*, a lovely book written over thirty years ago but happily still in print, and a pleasure not to be missed if you have not yet read it. But whether we are offering your first acquaintance with the region or not, we invite you to accompany us on this new exploration based on a journey deep into Mani in the early summer of 1980. We hope that you will not only enjoy our book in your armchair but also, when you go to Mani yourself, find it a practical guide to treasures that would be difficult to trace unaided even if you had known they were there.

Beginning with an introduction on the history and culture of the Maniátes from the Stone Age to the Second World War, we have tried to produce an agreeable mixture of Pausanian geography and Herodotean history – a blend of scholarly observation with vivid description, anecdote with history, exciting narrative with sensitive translations of the poetic lore in which the Deep Mani is unusually rich. The cultural heritage that we attempt to describe and illustrate is priceless, and if it is a forlorn hope that our efforts will succeed in retarding its rapid disappearance through neglect or ignorance, or worse, it will be something to have recorded what we can, and to have encouraged people to go and see for themselves before it is too late.

For the benefit of the prospective visitor perhaps some details about travel and accommodation may be helpful. The text simply refers to travelling by car, and undoubtedly a car is an advantage in exploring a remote region where local bus services are relatively limited. A self-drive car can certainly be hired at Sparta, less certainly at Yíthion and Areópolis, and as the roads have been greatly improved since 1980 it is no longer necessary to be so hesitant about taking one's own. But a car is not vital. There is a daily bus service from Athens via Sparta to Yíthion and thence to Areópolis and all the way down the peninsula to Yerolimín. There is also a daily service between Areópolis and Kalamáta, and this is a wonderful journey whether by car or bus – a spectacular drive round the head of the Gulf of Ítilon and through the pass into Messenia through which Mavromichális led the men of the Deep Mani to begin the Revolution of 1821. Indeed the motorist or bus-traveller who follows our route into Mani from Sparta via Yíthion ought to take this alternative way out through Messenian Mani to Kalamáta and thence back to Sparta over Mount Taïyetos by the pass that emerges at Mistrá, the Byzantine capital of the Peloponnese that held out against the Turks for seven years after the fall of Byzantium itself in 1453. As for reaching Mani from Athens, there is an air service to Sparta as well as the bus or a combination of train and bus; or for those who prefer a more leisurely journey by sea there is a coastal steamer that plies weekly if erratically from Piraeus to Yíthion. It is also worth remembering that a car-ferry service operates between Yíthion and the little Cretan port of Kastélli at least twice a week during the summer, and it would be difficult to imagine a more delightful holiday than one divided between Mani and Crete. As for local travel in the Deep Mani itself, visitors without cars will be able to hire a taxi (though not always immediately) at least at Yíthion, Areópolis, Yerolimín, Flomochóri and Kótronas; and even motorists may sometimes find it more convenient to let the village taxi leave them in one place and pick them up several hours later in another than to use their own car and have to return to the starting point of a long walk.

With regard to accommodation and what travel agents call 'tourist amenities', there are several hotels and attractive rooms to be rented in private houses in Yíthion, which is a very pleasant seaside town with a waterfront full of character and excellent tavernas. And while the harbour area is no place for bathing, there are splendid sandy beaches both to the north and south of the town, the best being to the south on the far side of the promontory of Mavrovoúni where they stretch for several kilometres and offer fine camping sites too. A glance at the map shows how the road from Yíthion to Areópolis then curves inland to Castle Passavá, but just beyond there (as described in chapter 1) you can take an untarred side-road to the left marked 'Belle Helène' that will bring you back to the exquisitely beautiful beaches in Vathí Bay, at the southern end of which are two more hotels, the Megaléxandros and the Belle Helène that was responsible for the road sign. For the region of Ítilon Bay, the Díros Caves and the northern end of the Deep Mani's western side there are small hotels and rooms for rent both at Areópolis and Pírgos Diroú, the latter now offering accommodation in a renovated tower; or for those preferring to stay right on the sea there is a new and comfortable-looking hotel on the beach at the head of Ítilon Bay below the monastery of Dekoúlou and the Castle of Kelefá. The only other hotels in the Deep Mani are two small but delightful ones at Yerolimín, which is a most alluring little harbour and the best centre for exploring the southern end of the peninsula described in chapters 3 to 6, though there are also rooms to rent at the old pirate-harbour of Mézapos, which is charming too and a good base for exploring the Cávo Grósso and Tigáni. And it is always worth asking at the kafeníon or village shop about accommodation in private houses in any other village that takes your fancy. Then on the eastern side it is possible to find rooms by the sea at least at Kiprianós in the south and the picturesque fishing village of Kótronas in the north in the shelter of Cape Stavrí, where the road has to bend inland again and recross the peninsula to Areópolis on the western side.

Finally a note about the transliteration and pronunciation of Greek names. The convention I have used for the names of places and people (e.g. Yíthion, Kranáï, Charoúda, Áyios Pantaleḯmon) is one that seemed to me to give a good guide to pronunciation and – most importantly – marks the stress accent, which is often on the syllable least expected even by those versed in classical Greek, whose rhythms depend on the length of a syllable rather than its accent (the classical accent presumably having been one of pitch rather than the modern stress that makes a modern Greek production of classical drama totally unmetrical). I hesitated only about rendering the Greek letter χ by the traditional 'ch' rather than simply 'h' and about leaving the Greek δ invariably as 'd'; but even though a road sign to Χαλκίς for example may be transliterated and pronounced more like 'Halkís' than with the hard 'ch' of 'Christmas' and though it is true that the Greek δ generally has a softer 'th' sound than the hard 'd' of 'dog' except where it is the first letter of a word like 'Díros', I have nevertheless kept to 'ch' for χ and 'd' for δ for ease of recognition of the roots of words that have passed into English from Greek. And perhaps perversely I have not even been wholly consistent in applying my convention to all words. I have not changed conventional English spellings of such well-known names as Sparta, Corinth, Athens and Thebes to Spárti, Kórinthos, Athíni and Thívi, nor have I changed the names of saints from the forms that are familiar to the English reader, except of course where the name of a church that may have to be asked for requires it: it is no use asking for St Michael's, for example, when the Greek knows him as Áyios Strátiyos. If scholarly linguists, who often have very fixed ideas about the transliteration of Greek, dislike my chosen convention or find themselves irritated by my inconsistencies, I can only beg them to be indulgent about my idiosyncracy, or at least to try not to find it so insupportable that they are put off going to Mani and seeing for themselves what is really important, so that they then may turn their anger on those who are responsible for the neglect and – not to put it too strongly – desecration of what cries out for preservation. And if I may advise prospective visitors with no knowledge of Greek, I do urge them to spend a few hours learning how to transliterate and pronounce Greek letters from a 'teach yourself' book or tape: it looks far more difficult than it really is, and I promise that once you have passed the psychological barrier of initial horror at so strange-looking an alphabet, you will be amazed how quickly you get the hang of reading road signs which, deep into Mani, are seldom given with the English transliterations that are common in the main tourist areas of Greece.

Peter Greenhalgh
London 1984

Introduction
The History of Mani

Of the three fingers that the Peloponnese thrusts southwards into the Mediterranean, the Mani peninsula in the middle is the longest, the boniest and the most significant. It is a continuation of the great Taíyetos mountain range which separates first the Messenian and Laconian plains, then the Messenian and Laconian Gulfs, before ending in the broken nail of Cape Matapán, the southernmost point of the Balkans. Between Kalamáta and the Bay of Ítilon on the Messenian Gulf – the so-called Outer or Messenian Mani – there is a long stretch of coast with a rich and fertile plain capable of supporting a considerable population; but southwards of the pass leading from Ítilon on the Messenian Gulf to Yíthion on the Laconian the landscape is very different. This is the Deep Mani, of which the western side is called Inner or Shadowy Mani, the eastern Lower or Sunward Mani. It is gaunt, barren and inhospitable, and, as is natural in more settled times when men can live freely and safely in more prosperous areas, it is severely depopulated. But such settled conditions are the exception rather than the rule of Greek history. While the very barrenness and remoteness of the Deep Mani attracted centuries of refugees from foreign invaders, its strategic position on the trade routes between Greece and North Africa and between Italy and the Levant also attracted men whose interests were neither agricultural nor peaceful. And the result, concentrated in an area far smaller than Corfu or the Isle of Man, is an idiosyncratic cultural heritage that is stranger, richer, more fascinating and less well known than almost any other in Greece.

Mani's history is a loose thread, interweaving itself with the multi-coloured strands from Sparta, Rome and Byzantium, the Franks, Venetians and Turks, but always creating a unique design of its own on the fringe of the main Greek pattern. It is a land of caves, churches and strange towers, of fortified villages on bare mountainsides, of Byzantine art and architecture of an extraordinary richness and importance, of feuds, fasting and lamentation. Until the present century it was almost a living fossil of the Middle Ages. It was a region of institutionalized civil war and chronic internal disorder, yet its ironic glory was to start the Revolution of 1821 which ended three and a half centuries of Turkish domination and created the unified nation-state in which Mani itself became an incongruity. Today the towers are mostly deserted, the long guns silent, and only a few old women still sing the funeral laments that are a dying relic of the feudal past. Byzantine churches of great beauty, often magnificently frescoed, are collapsing through neglect, and bells that even the Turks could never silence are rung only by winter gales. But though the visible pattern of Mani's long history is becoming sadly frayed, what remains is still fascinatingly intricate, extraordinary in its individuality and woven on a fabric of coasts and mountains whose natural beauty can never be destroyed.

The first thread of Mani's history, like that of Theseus in Crete, disappears underground into a labyrinth. Two thousand years ago the entrance to the Underworld was through a cave near the Temple of Poseidon at the southern tip of the Mani peninsula where Heracles had brought up Cerberus, but many thousands of years earlier the oldest Maniátes had known a better way down which was not rediscovered until the present century. It is in the north-western corner of the peninsula in Díros Bay, and though the Glifáda caves were first investigated by a local seaman about 1900, it was only in 1949 that systematic exploration was undertaken by a husband-and-wife team, John and Anna Petróchilos, of what has turned out to be one of the most spectacular and important cave systems in Europe. Nine years later the explorers followed up a local innkeeper's story of his dog which had gone down a foxhole and disappeared, returning after many days so thin and covered with dried mud that it looked like a 'walking tile'. They found not only many more vast caverns filled with magnificent stalagmites and stalactites but also signs of human habitation. The puzzling black dust which replaced the red of the outer caves turned out to be soot, and when the entrance was widened in 1961 to admit tourists, another huge hall was discovered containing human bones along with the bones, teeth and horns of many animals and many artefacts indicating human habitation in the Neolithic period. And in 1967 the first rock paintings were found, showing men, birds and animals and the female fertility symbol of which carved examples had already been discovered. The literally wonderful underground kingdom of these Stone Age Maniátes is described in chapter 2, and its availability to scientists and tourists today is almost entirely due to the courage and tenacity of Anna Petrochílou, who continued the work of exploration alone after her husband's death and so opened the first chapter of Mani's human history – a chapter that is still being written and expanded as new finds are made in these and in several newly discovered caves that are yet to be explored.

From the succeeding Bronze Age there is plenty of evidence of Early and Late Helladic occupation in the region of Yíthion, particularly the Mycenaean chamber tombs at Mavrovoúni, which were used as dug-outs by the Italians in the last war, but it is only in this Late Helladic period (1600–1100 BC) that there seems to have been any significant Bronze Age penetration deeper into Mani. Among several places with Late Helladic pottery the site near Láyia in the south-east of the peninsula is near the quarries of the purple *antico rosso* marble that was used to decorate the façade of the beehive tomb known as the Treasury of Atreus at Mycenae, and probably found its way to Crete. The Cyclopean masonry at Tigáni on the Shadowy coast suggests that Bronze Age Greeks had also occupied what became a great medieval fortress, and three of the towns listed by Homer as supplying contingents to Menelaus in the Trojan War are in Deep Mani – Las, Oetylus and Messe, of which the last two are still identifiable from their modern names of Ítilon and Mézapos, the two best harbours on the western coast. And it was on the little island of Kranáï in Yíthion Bay that Paris and Helen spent their first night of love after the abduction that took ten years and a thousand ships to avenge.

In the twelfth century BC the Bronze Age civilization of the Peloponnese was overwhelmed, and it may be that Mani provided at least a temporary refuge from the more primitive 'Dorian' Greeks who swept down from the north into the rich plain of Laconia as the Slavs were to do in the sixth century AD. But during the course of the Dark Ages which followed the collapse of Mycenae and all the other Bronze Age power centres, the Deep Mani was evidently Dorianized no less completely than the rest of Laconia; and in classical times its history is closely interwoven with that of Sparta, whose curiously masochistic militarism had given her hegemony of the Peloponnese by the end of the sixth century. Yíthion in particular grew important with the development of Sparta's international role, for Yíthion was Sparta's nearest port. And if it had not much mattered that the nearest port was nearly 50 kilometres away while Sparta had been purely a land power expanding territorially in the Peloponnese and frowning on commerce, it was a grave disadvantage when she became embroiled in a war with a power very different from her own, namely maritime Athens which had the Piraeus on her doorstep. But Sparta made the most of what she had. Yíthion became a hive of activity in the Peloponnesian Wars and a prime target of Athenian naval operations, as when Tolmides attacked the port in 455 BC with fifty warships and 4,000 men and set fire to the dockyards. Yet Sparta had defeated Athens by the end of the century, and another generation passed before she met her match in the rival land power of Thebes. The myth of her infantry's invincibility in pitched battle was destroyed at Leuctra in 371 BC, and in the aftermath she lost control of Messenia after an occupation of 230 years. She also temporarily lost control of Yíthion after a three-day siege, but she is said to have recovered her port after introducing 100 crack troops into the city on the pretext of sending athletes to compete in some games – a story which is worth repeating if only as a warning to those moderns who naively believe that the ancients kept sport sacrosanct from power politics.

Later in the fourth century the centre of gravity in the Greek world as a whole shifted northwards to Macedon, and in the Peloponnese to the so-called Achaean League based on Corinth and the cities of the north coast. With one or two short-lived revivals the story of Sparta is one of decline in the hellenistic period and Laconia was repeatedly invaded, though it was exceptional when Philip V of Macedon penetrated deep into Mani in 218 BC. But the Temple of Poseidon continued to thrive at the southern Cape, where its pilgrims were vastly outnumbered by mercenaries, often many thousands at a time, who waited there to be signed on for expeditions to Crete or Italy or the Levant. Then the second century saw Rome's increasing involvement in the eastern Mediterranean. In 196 BC Titus Flamininus proclaimed the 'liberation' of Greece after defeating Philip V, and in the following year his army crushed a recalcitrant Sparta while his fleet blockaded Yíthion, freed it from Spartan control and made it the head of a league of free cities that would counter-balance Sparta. This was the origin of the Union of Free Laconians, and when it was officially recognized by Augustus in 21 BC, the event signalled the beginning of a golden age for its member states, including Las (Passavá), Ítilon, Pírrichos, Teuthrone (Kótronas) and Kenípolis (Kipárissos), the last of which took over the official name and functions of the old city of Ténaron that had grown up around Poseidon's temple. The ancient travel writer Pausanias describes these places in his *Guide Bleu* for Roman tourists of the second century AD, and much still remains for us to see and describe in the following chapters, together with episodes from their histories and descriptions of other sites for which no history is known, not even their names.

The coins and inscriptions of member states attest the continuation of the Union of Free Laconians until well into the second half of the third century AD, and it probably continued until Diocletian's reform of provincial administration in AD 297; but already there were signs of turmoil in the Empire that would make Mani a haven for refugees in succeeding centuries. In AD 267–8 the southern Peloponnese was invaded by Goths and Herulians, and in the next century Alaric's Visigoths penetrated to Yíthion and destroyed what remained of the place after the earthquakes of AD 375. By then, of course, the Peloponnese was part of a nominally Christian empire ruled from Byzantium rather than Rome, and nearly another century later the name of a small harbour in Deep Mani became the toast of Constantinople for saving the Peloponnese from Genseric's Vandals. Having recently taken Carthage, the Vandal king was bent on extending his rival empire from North Africa into Europe and invaded the Peloponnese in AD 468, but when he threw his forces ashore at Kenípolis they were thrust back with such heavy losses that he 'sailed off to Zákinthos in a rage, took five hundred prisoners, hacked them to bits and scattered them over the waves on his way home to Carthage'. So it was fitting that Justinian's great general Belisarius put in there on his way to recover Carthage for the Empire in AD 533.

But Justinian's bloody reconquests of Italy from the Ostrogoths and North Africa from the Vandals in the sixth century were achieved at the cost of neglecting the other frontiers of the eastern Empire. While Huns overran the northern shores of the Black Sea and Persians penetrated Syria and Egypt and carried off the True Cross from Jerusalem, the Slavs and Avars were sweeping down into Greece. By AD 590 the Avars were in the Peloponnese, 'which they held for 218 years', according to the late eleventh-century Patriarch Nicholas the Grammarian; 'and so completely did they separate it from the Byzantine Empire that no Byzantine official dared to set foot in the country.' But these Slavic invaders evidently failed to penetrate deep in Mani, with the result observed by the scholarly emperor Constantine Porphyrogenitus in the political and geographical guide to the Empire, *De administrando imperio*, which he wrote for his son Romanus in about AD 950:

> Be it known that the inhabitants of Castle Maina are not from the race of the aforesaid Slavs but from the older Romaioi, who up to the present time are termed Hellenes by the local inhabitants on account of their being in olden times idolaters and worshippers of idols like the ancient Greeks, and who were baptized and became Christians in the reign of the glorious Basil. The place in which they live is waterless and inaccessible, but has olives from which they gain some consolation.

This is the first historical mention of 'Maina' from which the modern Mani derives, and there is much futile speculation about its etymology. What is clear is that there was a Byzantine power centre, 'Castle Maina', which gave its name to a wider olive-growing area over which it claimed control, and the likeliest candidate for the site is the fortified promontory of Tigáni with its possibly ninth-century basilica described in chapter 3. But was Christianity really as slow to take root in Mani as Constantine's statement suggests? Three earlier Christian basilicas, of the fifth and sixth centuries, have been discovered at Kipárissos in the south-west of the peninsula, and it is also possible that Tigáni's church is older than the ninth century. Moreover Constantine has been suspected of exaggerating the missionary triumphs of his grandfather, Basil I. But the early churches are all in seaside strongholds, and there is no reason to suppose that a mountainous interior that proved impervious to Byzantine officials and Slavic invaders was any more hospitable or attractive to missionaries. It is a remarkable indication of Mani's individuality that a place so close to the origins of Christianity should have resisted it until four hundred years after St Patrick converted Ireland. But in the ninth century the church was evidently sufficiently organized here for Mani to appear as a diocese under the authority of the Metropolitan of Corinth at the beginning of the tenth, and the extraordinarily rich concentration of Byzantine churches in Deep Mani from the eleventh to the fourteenth centuries is certainly appropriate to the zeal of a late convert making up for lost time.

The Peloponnese then remained under Greek control until the early thirteenth century, when it was conquered by the Franks in the wake of the Fourth Crusade. However genuine the spirit which had motivated the First Crusade in 1095 as a means of uniting Christendom against the Saracens, the Byzantine Empire had soon found its fellow Christians more dangerous than the infidels, and the principles that diverted the Fourth Crusade against Constantinople were no more elevated than base greed. Venice and the princes of Western Christendom divided the spoils among themselves, and Baldwin of Flanders became the first Latin Emperor. By 1205 the Pope was addressing a Baron from Champagne, William of Champlitte, as Prince of Achaea in recognition of his conquest of the western Peloponnese, and in 1213 his successor, Geoffrey of Villehardouin, carried his victorious arms over the eastern side too and gained control of the whole except for the Venetian bases of Koróni (Coron) and Methóni (Modon) in the south-west and Monemvasía in the south-east. Thus Mani became a southern extension of a Frankish principality whose ruler had turned Lacedaemon into La Crémonie and relied on his Hereditary Marshal, Baron Jean de Neuilly, to defend the Laconian plain from the Maniátes from his castle of Passavá which dominated the fertile plain south of Yíthion and the vital pass between Yíthion and Ítilon.

But the wild men of Mani were not so easily contained, nor

were they the only threats to Laconia. Just as Greeks had fled to Mani before the Slavic invaders, so dispossessed Slavs in their turn had fled to the mountains of Taïyetos further north; and while these 'Milengi' raided Laconia from the west and the Maniátes from the south, a third group of independent-minded mountaineers, the half-Greek, half-Slavic Tsákones, did the same from Parnón to the east. Just before 1250 William II, the fourth Prince of Achaea, decided to create or acquire new fortresses against all three. Against the Tsákones he acquired by siege the great rock of Monemvasía, the Aegean's Gibraltar, which had been a stronghold of pirates. Against the Milengi he built Mistrá to secure La Crémonie itself. And against the Maniátes he penetrated south of Passavá and built the castle of Great Maina 'at a fearful cliff with a high headland above'. Most probably this was again Tigáni, the site of the old Byzantine 'Castle Maina', a westward-facing Monemvasía magnificently fortified by nature and by art. A Latin bishop was even appointed for Mani, but the message of peace and goodwill was not well received from under a mitre, and after a few years of discomfort and terror the unhappy man was allowed to reside permanently in Italy. Even with a large castle there it is doubtful that Frankish control of the Deep Mani was very effective, and Great Maina itself did not long remain in their hands. In 1259 Prince William and his leading Barons were taken captive in the Battle of Pelagonia by the Emperor Michael Palaeológus of Nicaea, who went on to drive the Latin emperor from Constantinople and repossess his historic capital in 1261. As part of their ransom the emperor demanded the three great castles of Maina, Monemvasía and Mistrá together with hostages who included the Lady Margaret, daughter of Baron Jean II of Passavá. And from 1262 the Mani remained at least nominally under the Byzantine governor of the Peloponnese until 1460, when the Turkish advance engulfed Mistrá exactly seven years to the day after the fall of Constantinople in 1453.

For the next three and a half centuries Mani features as the Achilles' heel of the Turkish occupation of the Peloponnese, a source of repeated rebellions and repeated failures until 1821. The first came only three years after the fall of Mistrá, when Venice began the first of many wars with Turkey and found a ready ally in Korkódilos Kladás, the Greek lord of Élos at the head of the Laconian Gulf. The Sultan had granted him this estate in the hope that he would prove a loyal defender of Laconia from the Maniátes, but in 1463 Kladás donned the gold-embroidered cloak of St Mark and led a small army of mercenaries in anti-Turkish operations until 1479, when the Venetians made peace with Turkey and left the Greeks who had fought for them in the lurch. As part of the settlement terms they agreed to hand over 'Brazzo di Maina' to the Turks, and when Kladás refused to accept this, they put a price on his head and washed their hands of the problem. It was typical of the Venetian *Realpolitik* that was to characterize their relations with Mani in the succeeding centuries. Every time they came to blows with the Turks they tried to rouse the Maniátes, and every time the Maniátes responded they were left to face Turkish retribution alone. Kladás and his *stradioti*, now unpaid and unemployed, tried to maintain their independence in Mani, but though they defeated a first Turkish army near Ítilon, a second and more powerful force overwhelmed them, Mani was crushed, and Kladás fled to Naples with three of King Ferdinand's galleys which picked him up from Pórto Káyio – the beautiful Bay of Quails in the south-east corner of the peninsula that would be the scene of similar rescues from the German occupation in the Second World War.

The sixteenth century witnessed a tightening of the Turkish grip on the Peloponnese. In the wars of 1499–1503 and 1537–40 the Venetians lost their remaining possessions there, Koróni and Methóni in the first war, Náfplion and Monemvasía in the second, but Mani seems to have been spared any Turkish attempt to establish a permanent military presence until 1570, when Sultan Selim II, amiably nicknamed 'the Sot', decided to drive the Venetians out of Cyprus. In the context of this campaign the Mani peninsula became of great strategic importance on the Venetian lines of communication and reinforcement to their beleaguered island fortress, but as soon as the Turks began building forts to secure the bays of Ítilon and Pórto Káyio as permanent naval bases, the Maniátes alerted the Venetian admiral in Crete and helped his fleet to destroy them. Then in 1571, though Cyprus had fallen, the victory of the Christian fleet over the Turks at Lepanto raised hopes that Don John of Austria would champion the cause of Greek liberation, and the Bishop of Monemvasía raised the banner of revolution in the Peloponnese. But all in vain. The promised armies never came, and by 1572 the Bishop and his troops were driven back to Mani as the last bastion of a cause whose hopes finally expired when Venice made peace with the Sultan in 1573.

In the following decades Maniáte leaders sent streams of correspondence to prospective champions in the Christian West. In 1582 they begged Pope Gregory XIII to intercede on their behalf with Philip II of Spain. In 1603 they approached Pope Clement VIII who had taken the Cross, and when the prospect of a new Crusade died with him two years later, they centred their hopes on King Philip III of Spain, the Viceroy of Naples and the Grand Duke of Tuscany. And their approaches were not ignored. Naples, Venice, France, Spain, Genoa, Florence – all were interested in Mani and several exploratory missions were sent there, but little was actually done except for some Spanish raids of the sort which sacked Passavá in 1601. Then in 1612 Mani found a new champion in Charles Gonzaga of Mantua, who inherited the Duchy of Nevers from his French mother and claimed the throne of Constantinople through his paternal grandmother, the last member of the branch of the imperial line of the Palaeológi who had inherited the Marquisate of Montferrat. When Duke Charles sent secret envoys to Greece to sound out the likely support for his ambitions, the Bishop of Mani replied at once, addressing him as King Constantine Palaeológus and declaring that the Greeks awaited him as the Jews their Messiah. More letters followed and lists of fighting men were sent, but it was another false hope. Twelve years of plotting came to nothing, and in the meantime the Turks cracked down on Mani, which remained quiet until 1645 when Venice began her longest and bitterest struggle with Turkey, the war of 1645–69 which ended in her loss of Crete.

With the Turks preoccupied elsewhere, the Maniátes enjoyed virtual independence throughout this war. The Venetians egged them on to attack Turkish ships, and in 1667 they had become so daring that they sailed through the Turkish squadrons blockading Crete and fired and plundered several of the enemy ships. They also helped the Venetians on land, notably by assisting Morosini's capture and sack of Kalamáta in 1659, but in this, as in their maritime exploits, they were motivated more by profit than by piety, and Christians as well as Turks were victims of their depredations.

> For piracy is the most important business of the Maniátes [wrote a contemporary French traveller], and their chief commerce is of captives. Ítilon was called 'Great Algiers'. They take prisoners everywhere, selling the Christians to the Turks and the Turks to the Christians. They enjoy relating proudly their piratical raids, and they pointed out to me one of their most notorious pirates as a man who had reached the very pinnacle of quality.

When Crete had fallen and the victorious Grand Vizier Kuprili dispatched a fleet to subjugate the lawless peninsula, its conspicuous lack of success soon persuaded him to try the more subtle methods of diplomacy reinforced by a revival of the old scheme of putting permanent garrisons into the critical harbours. The popular will to resist was undermined by political and financial concessions – the right to ring church bells and put crosses on the top of belfries, the abolition of the hated child tax and a reduction of the normal tribute. Great castles were built to control Ítilon and Pórto Káyio, and the rivalries of local families were cleverly exploited on the principle of divide and rule. Indeed the treatment was almost homoeopathic. One of the most terrible of the Maniáte pirates who had been captured by the Turks was now freed and sent home to Ítilon to prosecute his family feuds. His name was Liberákis Yerakáris, and with the backing of the Turkish garrison he made life so miserable for his enemies, the Stefanópouli, that they and some other families, more than 700 people in all, sought asylum from Genoa, were granted lands in Corsica, and emigrated *en masse* in 1675, like the ancient Phocaeans who left Asia Minor in 560 BC for new homes in the West where they would be free of the Persian yoke. Their descendants are still there today. Nor were they the only emigrants from Ítilon. Their rivals the Iatráni – who used the Latinized form of their name, Medici, and claimed common descent with the great family of Florence – had already appealed to the Grand Duke Ferdinand II dei Medici and settled in Tuscany. And it was not long before Yerakáris himself fell foul of the Turks and was driven to rejoin the other Maniáte pirates whose activities, though curtailed, were still far from suppressed, as Bernard Randolph testified in his description of Mani's primary industry in the late 1670s:

> Yet do they continue to cruise about with their *Briganteens*. If they take any *Turks*, they sell them to the *Malteses* and *Legorneses*, as they do the *Christians* to the *Turks*. If any Ship come to Anchor on their Coast, many arm themselves and go to the place, over against where the Ship doth ride; some of them will be in Priests Habits, walking by the Sea side, with their Wallets, in which they will have some Wine and Bread. Their Companions lye hid behind the Bushes at some convenient Post. When any strangers come ashore, who do not understand their Language, the feigned Priests make signs to them, shewing them their Bread and Wine, which they offer to them for money, by which the strangers being enticed from the Sea side (and it may be to sit down and tast their Wine) the hidden *Manjotts* come and make their Prey. The Priests will seem to be sorry, and endeavour to make the strangers believe they were altogether ignorant of any such design. So a white Flagg is put out, and a Treaty held with the Ship for their Ransome.

In 1684 the future Doge Morosini took advantage of Turkey's preoccupation with Austria to take over the Turkish empire in the Peloponnese, and when the Maniátes were sure that he meant business, they rose again, destroyed the Turkish garrisons and earned specially favourable treatment from the new imperial power. Indeed, Mani was now more prosperous than any of the more naturally favoured parts of the Peloponnese, not only because she was so lightly taxed but also because she avoided the two horrors which desolated all the more naturally favoured areas: spoliation by the retreating Turks and depopulation by a plague that halved the numbers in the whole Peloponnese to a mere 100,000 souls. Moreover, the Maniátes were the only Greeks whom the Venetians found eager for military service, and it became even more vital to conciliate the warlike peninsula when the Turks appointed one of their Maniáte prisoners to help recover the Peloponnese for them. This was Liberákis Yerakáris again, the pirate who had been languishing in the Bagnio since his recapture in 1682 but now offered his services to the Porte on condition of being granted the Beydom of Mani to develop after the fashion of the internally autonomous Christian principality of Moldavia. But though His Highness the Ruler of Mani fought hard to give some substance to his empty title by several invasions of the Peloponnese, he too eventually defected to Venice in 1696, lost credibility with both sides and was removed from the scene altogether. His supposed subjects in the meantime continued to enjoy a greater degree of independence than ever before, but the main use they made of it was to develop the blood feuds and institutionalized civil war that were fed by overpopulation and freedom from control and became the dominant characteristics of Maniáte society in the eighteenth and nineteenth centuries. But the rest of the Peloponnesians enjoyed no similar freedoms. They found Venetian imperialism no less ruthless and much more efficient than that of the Turks, and the combination of heavy taxation with Roman proselytizing and the severance of tribute to the Orthodox Patriarch in Constantinople virtually extinguished any popular will to resist the reconquest of the Peloponnese by the Infidel in 1715.

It was 1770 before the Maniátes rebelled again, and this time their champion was not Venice but Orthodox Russia under Catherine the Great. A Russian agent had appeared at Ítilon as early as 1766 to try to persuade the Mavromichális clan to give the lead in a revolution that, it was hoped, would spread throughout Greece, but these wily lairds had been circumspect in their reply, warning of Mani's disunity when threatened by no common danger and refusing to commit themselves unless strong Russian forces appeared at their side. But when Russia was already at war with Turkey over Poland and Theodore Orlov, brother of the Empress's favourite lover, appeared in Ítilon Bay with five ships and a mere 500 troops, the Mavromichális and other Deep Maniáte clans were finally persuaded to act against their better judgement and became pawns to be sacrificed in a distant game of imperial chess. Orlov was no Morosini, his forces were small, and he was soon at loggerheads with the chief Mavromichális, 'John the Dog', who told him to his face that he seemed better at destroying the homes of Greeks than the castles of Turks. After that they operated separately, and by the end of the year the Russians had sailed away, the Turks were pouring Albanians into the Peloponnese to effect a reconquest, and the Maniátes were making their last bloody stand in Messenia before retreating from the Albanian terror to their mountain fastnesses. By 1777 they had had more than enough, and when the great Hassán Pashá was at Rhodes, he was visited by a laird of Messenian Mani, one Zanétos Koutífaris, who had been sent to seek an amnesty for Mani's part in the war, to assure him of their loyalty to the Sultan, and to claim his protection.

The result was a new system of government for Mani, or rather a modified revival of the system of indirect rule attempted in the appointment of Liberákis Yerakáris as Bey. Mani was again to be ruled by a Maniáte and Christian, but he would be responsible to the Capitán-Pashá for the collection of tribute and would depend on him to support his own supremacy over the rival lairds, whose jealous ambition might be relied upon to reinforce the taking of family hostages as guarantees of the Bey's allegiance to the Porte. It was an office that proved fatal to many of its incumbents over the next forty-five years. Zanétos Koutífaris was himself the first Bey, but he lasted only three years before being summoned to the Porte and put to death for trying to extend his beydom into the plain of Élos – an indiscretion that provided the Turks with an opportunity to confiscate his personal wealth to pay arrears of tribute. His successor was Michális Troupákis, but he too managed only three years before accusations of piracy, which he was not rich enough to counteract, caused him to be decoyed on board a Turkish ship and carried off to decapitation on the island of Mitilíni in 1782. The vacant beydom then passed from the Messenian Maniátes to the Grigorákis clan of Laconian Mani whose growing power in the Yíthion region had resisted the previous beys and alarmed the Turks. In 1780 the Pashá of Trípolis had tried to weaken this body by removing its head, but he had found himself with a minor rebellion on his hands after inviting the leading Grigorákis to his capital, fêting him like an honoured guest and then quietly hanging him. The clan reacted like the mythical hydra which could sprout new heads faster than Heracles could chop them off. They flew to arms, massacred the Turkish population in their vicinity, and so impressed the Porte that it seemed wisest to appoint the next Bey from what was evidently the most powerful clan and needed alienating from the rest. But Zanétos Grigorákis, the nephew of the murdered chief and leader in the vengeance, declined this dangerous privilege, and it was only after he too had been decoyed aboard a Turkish ship and threatened with decapitation that he was persuaded to agree.

Zanétbey lasted longer than his predecessors, and it was sixteen years before he came to grief after plotting revolution with the French. It was during his beydom that Europe was shaken by the French Revolution and Napoleon became the great hope of liberation movements everywhere. In 1797 he wrote to the Republic's General that he would gladly put the harbours of Mani at his disposal, and Napoleon responded by sending two of his fellow Corsicans, Dimo and Niccolo Stefanopoli, to Yíthion to begin conspiring for a general revolution throughout Greece. They were descendants of the Stefanópouli of Ítilon who had emigrated to Corsica more than a century before, and they were now claiming Byzantine ancestry from no less a personage than the last Emperor of Trebizond, David Comnenus Nicephorus: his son, they maintained, had fled to Ítilon and changed his name to Stefanópoulos. It was a fine conceit, and it would later extend to Napoleon himself for whom Ítilon was also claimed as a link between Byzantium and Corsica through a fictitious Kalómeros, a supposed ally of the Stefanopoli and a direct translation of Buonaparte into Greek. At any event Zanétbey's plottings with French agents, whether Byzantine or not, caused his deposition in 1798, though he continued to live as an outlaw in Mani and negotiated a shipment of French arms that led to a siege of his castles near Yíthion by the Capitán-Pashá in 1803 and a retreat further inland.

Zanét's replacement had been a certain Panayiótis Koumoundourákis, but when he proved incapable of suppressing his predecessor's revolutionary activities, the Turks got rid of him and restored the beydom to the now divided Grigorákis clan in the person of Antónbey, an ambitious but rather ineffectual cousin of the deposed Zanét with whom he was now expected to deal. And it was in Antón's beydom that the English Colonel Leake arrived in Mani on his tour of the Peloponnese in 1805. We shall be meeting Colonel Leake frequently on our own journey into Mani in the following pages, and we shall find him an interesting and entertaining companion, even if we do not share his military obsession with punctuality of which the following is a typical example:

> At 8.38 Mavrovoúni was a little on our left. Here some delay occurred, while the owner of a horse which I had hired fetched his musket from the village. We then descended into the plain of Pássava; at 8.52 lose fifteen minutes in searching for a fresh horse for one of the servants at a mandhra. At 9 cross a deep torrent-bed. . . .

When not looking at his watch he was a keen observer of the country, its society and customs, and a shrewd judge of character with a good ear for an anecdote. He was also no mean archaeologist, and if he seems to have had a blind spot for the wealth of Mani's Byzantine heritage, he went everywhere with a copy of Pausanias and scoured the country for classical remains with a thoroughness that would have done credit to any professional scholar.

As Antónbey proved unwilling or incapable of suppressing his more vigorous cousin, the Capitán-Pashá descended on Yíthion again in much greater force in 1807 and did much more damage to the Grigorákis houses and forts, but Antón himself remained Bey for another three years until he discreetly resigned in favour of his son-in-law, Konstantís Zervákos, who had gained the favour of the Pashá at Trípolis. But other Grigorákis captains and the chiefs of other clans did not share the Pashá's predilections, and when they had driven his protégé back to him, it occurred to the Porte that a good way of finding an acceptable Bey might be to let the Maniáte aristocracy choose its own. In 1810 the assembled chiefs at Yíthion elected another Grigorákis, Thodorós Zanetákis, nephew of the irrepressible Zanét, and Thodoróbey ruled until 1815 when he was deposed and replaced by the last and greatest Bey of Mani, Pétros Mavromichális.

This was the first time the beydom had been held by a laird of Inner Mani. Petróbey's castle was, and still is, at Liméni, the little harbour below Tsímova, now Areópolis, on the southern side of Ítilon Bay. He was the nephew of the Mavromichális, 'John the Dog', who had fought and died in the abortive Russian-inspired rebellion of 1770. In his youth he had himself

1. Yíthion harbour

2. Yíthion and Kranaï from Koúmaro

3. Kranáï at sunrise

4. Castle Passavá

5. Kouskoúni

6. Kelefá

7. The monastery of Dekoúlou

8. The Dekoúlou iconostasis

9. The Righteous Melchisedek

10. Petróbey Mavromichális

11. Liméni, Ítilon Bay and the Pentadáktilos

12. The explorer and discoverers of Alepótripa

13. In the Díros caves

14. Trissákia (14th century)

15. The Last Supper (14th century)

16. Miroloyístres

17. St Barbara's, Érimos (*c.* 1150)

looked to Napoleon as the potential liberator of Greece and served with the French forces in the Ionian Islands; and when he was suddenly appointed Bey in 1815 there were those who said that the Capitán-Pashá who so favoured him was in fact his cousin, a son of the canine John who had not after all been killed but captured as a small boy by the Turks in 1770, Islamized, and trained up for high office in the Turkish Empire. And it may even be true. But if so, it was certainly no service to the Turkish Empire that made this formidable character, who had so impressed Leake in 1805, the most powerful leader in Mani. By 1819 he was a member of the Filikí Etería, the secret international organization planning the Revolution, and on 17 March 1821 he raised Mani for the last time against the Turks. On 25 March Archbishop Germanós of Patrás proclaimed revolution throughout the Peloponnese from Kalávrita and this is the date now celebrated by Greece as its National Day, but by then the Maniátes had been in the field for a week, Kalamáta had fallen and Pétros Mavromichális was writing his famous proclamation to the courts of Europe from his camp in Free Messenia. It was the beginning of the end of more than three and a half centuries of Turkish domination.

Having launched the Revolution and sent her warriors north into almost all the theatres of war both in and beyond the Peloponnese, Mani herself saw little action until the dark days of 1826 when Ibrahím Pashá had swept back into the Peloponnese and the Maniátes were almost back to where they had started, making a stand in Messenian Mani at Vérga near Almiró, about 8 kilometres south of Kalamáta. It looked like 1770 all over again, and while his main forces besieged Vérga, Ibrahím struck deep into the heart of Inner Mani, now almost defenceless, with the landings in Díros Bay described in chapter 2. Miraculously he failed. His Egyptians were thrown back from Díros in 1826 like the Vandals from Kenípolis fourteen centuries earlier; Vérga proved impregnable; and the tide of Turkish reconquest was painfully rolled back until Navarino and the intervention of the Great Powers finally forced Ibrahím out of Greece altogether. The Peloponnese at last was free.

But this was not Mani's last rebellion by any means. By 1831 the majority of Greeks were wondering what sort of freedom they had been fighting for as their first presidency degenerated into autocracy presiding over anarchy, refusing all demands for liberal reforms and muzzling the press. John Capodistria was a Greek who had risen high in the service of Tsarist Russia, but his training was too much that of an official to make him sufficiently subtle as a politician. Mani in particular was up in arms over his persecution of the Mavromichális family, and when the great Petróbey himself was put under arrest, his brother John started raising the clans against the government in the confidence that there were sound pretexts to disguise less creditable motives of his own. Capodistria was so alarmed that he authorized George Mavromichális, a nephew of Petróbey, to go to Mani and bring John back to the capital for talks with the assurance that all differences between the government and the Mavromichális family could easily be resolved. But Capodistria's assurances were no more reliable than those of the Turks who had so often lured recalcitrant beys from their fastnesses with smooth words. The gullible John was simply arrested, and when Constantine, another brother, raised a second rebellion in the following year, he too was lured onto a ship and carried off to confinement in the capital. In vain public opinion condemned the President's high-handedness towards a distinguished family. The Russian Resident himself, Admiral Ricord, supported a petition for Petróbey's release, but Capodistria remained adamant, and it cost him his life. As he entered church for early-morning mass on 9 October 1831, he was approached by Constantine and George Mavromichális, who were allowed the freedom of the fortified city attended by guards. He thought they wanted to speak to him, but the time for words was past. Before their guards could move, the first President of Greece lay dead, his head blasted by a pistol ball, his chest slashed by a yataghan – the victim of Maniáte vengeance.

In the anarchy that ensued the Maniátes discovered that what they meant by Independence was less freedom from Turkish government than freedom from any government at all. They wanted to be left alone to go their own antisocial way without interference, to continue fighting and feuding and expanding their control over the more fertile plains of Messenia and Laconia which they now regarded as the prize of victory as the Great Powers clamped down on their piracy at sea. The very region which had seemed for so long the keystone of Greek independence was now threatening the stability of the nation-state that was supposed to embody what it had fought for; and when the Great Powers put the Bavarian prince Otho on the new Greek throne in 1833, his Council of Regency made the taming of Mani one of the top priorities and decided to destroy its towers. It was a decision that applied to the whole Peloponnese, not just to Mani, and in principle the idea of enforcing unity by destroying the bastions of individualism seemed not unreasonable. But in practice it was misguided. Even on the plains where it could be enforced it had a depressing effect on agricultural development by driving land-lords from fertile lands on which they were not prepared to live without the security of a fortified refuge. To the Maniátes it was an attack on the very foundations of their society. They were ready to fight to the death to preserve their deadly way of life, and when one of the new king's Bavarian regiments marched down into Mani to try to enforce obedience to the demolition orders, it was the Maniátes who did the compelling. They took up arms against these foreign invaders as enthusiastically as they had ever done against the Turks, and having surrounded an unwary detachment in a defile, they compelled them to surrender, stripped them naked, and ransomed them back to the king at an insultingly small price per head.

It was a disgrace that no government could afford to swallow, but vengeance against the Maniátes was more easily sworn than carried out. They fortified Petrovoúni, and when a much larger force of Bavarians came to dislodge them, they trounced them again and inflicted heavy losses. And a third expedition fared no better. This time 6,000 regular troops were forced back to Yíthion, and the result was a negotiated settlement that left the towers of Deep Mani intact. The Greek government was learning by painful experience what the Turks had discovered long ago, that in dealing with Mani the iron hand was often ineffective unless concealed in a velvet glove clutching a bag of silver. Just as Hassán Pashá had appointed Maniáte beys to control and divide the opposition, so now King Otho sent a diplomatic and well-funded officer, Max Feder, to secure the allegiance of the Maniáte lairds by enrolling them into his own forces with lucrative commissions in a special militia.

Feder's smooth-tongued corruption succeeded where force had proved powerless. The anti-Othonian coalition was gradually broken down, the new regiment proved invaluable in suppressing trouble elsewhere, and Mani became less of an embarrassment to the new nation she had done so much to bring into being. But even so it needed the regular army with artillery support to compel a cease-fire in a full-dress feudal war between two rival clans in Kítta as late as 1870, and it was not until the present century that Mani could really be said to have emerged very far from the Middle Ages.

It had been a strangely prolonged anachronism. Mani's social system in the nineteenth century had probably changed very little from the sixteenth. An aristocracy of the so-called Nikliáni was still feuding among itself and lording it over a subservient population, the *achamnómeri* or *faméyiï*, who helped them in their wars and subsidized them but shared few of their privileges and were kept in place by the Niklian towers. And there is much speculation about the origins of this system. Some derive the term Nikliáni from Níkli in Arcadia and suppose that dispossessed Franks fleeing from there in the thirteenth century carried the name with them into the Mani, which they proceeded to dominate. Others have gone still further back, connecting Níkli with Spartan Ámikle and even forcing a derivation for the social system out of the fairly superficial parallel with the ancient Spartans and their *perioikoi* and Helots. A more likely derivation for the term is the name Nicholas in the persons of Nicholas II and III of St Omer, great Frankish magnates of medieval Thebes who had close connections with Mani. Nicholas II's brother Jean married the Lady Margaret of Passavá, and when Nicholas II himself married the widow of the last Villehardouin Prince of Achaea, he built a castle in Mani as well as his great palace at Navarino. And Nicholas III became the most loved and feared of all the barons of Achaea. Their exploits loom large in the medieval Chronicle of the Moréa, and even without any blood connection it is possible that Nicholas provided an affected ancestry for the dominant families of Mani at a time when it was also both fashionable and useful to Latinize names like Iatráni to Medici.

But whatever the derivation the correspondence addressed to the Duke of Nevers early in the seventeenth century gives lists of aristocratic fighting men collectively known as Nikliáni, of which

Introduction

the largest contingent came from the Deep Maniáte town of Kítta, a name that may derive from the Frankish *cité* or *città* and could well have been the first as well as the greatest Niklian stronghold. The same correspondence also has two signatories surnamed Níklos among the Méditsi and Stefanópouli and other clan chieftains. If these Níkli and the Nikliáni are connected, there is an exact parallel for the name of an individual clan being shared by the whole aristocracy to which it belongs in the *Eupatridai* of ancient Athens. At any rate the Niklian aristocracy was definitely established before the end of the sixteenth century, and the strongest influences in its development were almost certainly the Veneto-Turkish wars which followed the Turkish conquest of the Peloponnese in the mid-fifteenth. With Maniátes and other Laconians forming the backbone of the *stradioti* and fighting under Italian officers in other mercenary armies of the Republic – then finding themselves regularly thrown on their own resources whenever the Venetians made peace – it is not surprising that Mani came to look as though San Gimignano had been transplanted from Tuscany and allowed to multiply throughout its mountain fastnesses. If agricultural possibilities were limited by soil and climate, there was piracy by sea or robbery on land to create prosperity even in Mani for those strong enough to control it while waiting for the next foreign enterprise that would seek their help against the Turks. And there was the basic attraction of freedom for turbulent and independent natures that cared nothing for peace and would not or could not kow-tow to the Turkish government or indeed to any government at all. To fight came as naturally as breathing, and as Mani became dangerously overpopulated in the eighteenth century, the fighting and feuding also multiplied to the point where Nikítas Nifákos could characterize Deep Mani in two lines:

One man holds his tower lest another man take it,
Neighbour hounds his neighbour, and another hounds him.

Many of the reasons for overpopulation in this relatively independent region are obvious, but one of the most important is usually ignored, namely that Mani was an extraordinarily healthy place. The gales and droughts which discouraged agriculture were evidently no less discouraging to disease than to the Turks, and the deeper into Mani you went, the safer you were from the plagues that repeatedly desolated the rich plains of the Peloponnese to the north. 'A boy even of fifteen has a wrinkled, weather-worn appearance,' wrote Leake in 1805, 'but diseases are rare, they live to a great age, and their chief evil is a population disproportioned to the natural resources of the country.' And if one wonders how a high population can coexist with permanent clan warfare, the answer is that breeding more 'guns' was part of the struggle for supremacy and that deaths were in fact less heavy than might be expected thanks to the highly formalized nature of the feuding. Wars were formally declared, whether between rival clans of different villages or of the same village. They would then take to their towers and blast away at each other with musket and cannon and showers of stones until the enemy tower was taken or surrendered or the differences were composed by the Council of Elders, the Gerontikí, which sometimes proved effective in resolving a stalemate. The wars or vendettas could go on for years – Leake mentions one in the village of Váthia that had been flourishing for forty years when he gave it a wide berth in 1805 – but there was a regular truce for sowing or harvesting, or occasional ones for the purpose of concerting action against the Turks. And Leake found it 'very amusing' to listen to his Turkish friend, Hassán Bey, describing them. 'Their own civil wars, Hassán says, are seldom very bloody, and months may pass without a single man being killed on either side.' It was, in effect, a training school for a more serious war, and when Mavromichális declared the general truce in 1821 that united Mani in the Revolution, the Turks were amused no longer.

But Greece had not done with foreign occupation even then, and when in 1941 her brave opposition to Mussolini's ambitions was finally crushed by the jackbooted heel of Hitler, Mani resumed her almost forgotten role as a centre of resistance and a haven of refugees. This time, however, the foreign threat did not unite her as the Turks had done. It was as though half a century of peace since the end of feuding had built up a tension that now released itself in an explosion of civil war between the forces of Left and Right; and with a natural extremism reinforced by ideology the struggle between the rival enemies of the occupying forces became virtually a war of extermination from which Mani has never recovered. Of those who were left at the end of it, the young went increasingly to the bright lights and industrial wages of Athens and America; and the decline of population and of what passed for prosperity in this remote and desolate peninsula continued to accelerate after the War until the last few years, which have seen the tentative growth of a new industry, tourism. And tourism, despite its dangers, gives the best hope of finding the money necessary to preserve the visible remains of a long history and rich cultural heritage of which this book will try to convey something of the wealth and importance and extraordinary fascination. But there is one characteristic of Maniáte culture that cannot be seen, is unlikely nowadays to be heard, and deserves a further postponement of our journey for a few more paragraphs of introduction – the *mirolóyi* or Song of Death.

Poetic funeral laments are not unique to Mani, of course, but nowhere in Greece have they been so highly developed, and there is even a fundamental difference between those of Outer Mani and of Deep Mani that almost seems to correspond to their different terrains. The *mirolóyia* of Messenian Mani with its more fertile coastal plain have a more lyrical quality in a fifteen-syllable line that is gentler and less robust than the Deep Mani's epic octosyllables, hard and austere as the rocks that echoed them. Like the epics of Homer they are of purely oral composition, thriving on memory-strengthening illiteracy and drawing on an inherited bank of formulaic phrases and similes which provided thinking-time for the creation of new material. But these modern Homers were women, *miroloyístres* or keeners, who gained high reputations for their expertise, were fiercely competitive among themselves, and were in great demand to perform – the word is accurate, not depreciative – with unbound hair, beaten breasts and nail-torn cheeks in the cathartic paroxysm of public grief that is so alien to the inhibited funerals of Anglo-Saxons. But it is very Greek, and it connects the Maniátes with their Spartan ancestors who made a similar exception to their habitual restraint at the royal funerals described by Herodotus in the fifth century BC: 'When a king of the Lacedaemonians dies . . . the women beat their brows vigorously and indulge in interminable lamentation, and say that the last king who had died was the best' (Herodotus 6.58).

The principle of *de mortuis nil nisi bonum* was observed by the Maniáte *miroloyístres* too. None better than the dead had ever lived, and the typical images by which the following young fighter was glorified have a local simplicity and an immediacy that are often very affecting:

> O John my noble *pallikar*,
> So young and brave, so tall and strong,
> Your footstep silent as the wolf,
> Your bearing lordly as the lion.
> O cypress-tree whose roots went deep,
> O draught of water cold and pure,
> O golden cross on lovely church,
> O stars and moon that lightened night,
> O sun that warmed my every day.
> O lovely eyes so blue and keen,
> O eyebrows dark and arched so proud,
> O curly hair so thick and strong
> Where nightingales could make their nests
> And sing your praises day and night.
> Your walk was like the fairest dance,
> Your standing like a silent song,
> And when you sat we seemed to see
> A golden eagle nestling down.
> O John, my crown, my marble prop,
> My little church with dome so fine
> That we shall never see complete:
> My chandelier of solid gold
> With trembling diamonds hanging down
> That made our nights as bright as day,
> You fell, and falling broke our hearts
> And plunged our home in deepest gloom.

In a society as belligerent and male-dominated as that of Mani it was naturally the fighting men for whom the *miroloyístres* produced their longest and most elaborate efforts, but women and children too were never buried without a *miróloyi*, and for a young woman in particular it could have a very delicate touch:

> Awake, awake, carnation lips
> With breast like cotton, soft and white,

> With neck of swanlike slenderness
> And sparkling partridge eyes.

But if the *mirolóyi* from which these lines are taken has a Sophoclean poignancy reminiscent of Antigone's lament for her untimely death before tasting the joys of love and marriage, there are others that are positively Aeschylean in their obsession with vengeance. Where a dead man had been killed in war or vendetta, the mourners would stand round the bier like the Chorus in the *Choephoroe*, listening like black-robed Furies while Orestes and Electra not only paid respects to their dead father but summoned up Agamemnon's spirit to help them avenge blood with more blood. Sometimes the *mirolóyi* served as a call to arms for immediate vengeance, sometimes as a reminder of vengeance to be taken at a more favourable time, a reminder that might be sung privately by the widow for years until her sons were old enough to avenge their father. And then the story of the vengeance would be added and preserved as a song of triumph to be sung by the mother and her daughters as they worked their handmills at night, and to be handed down from generation to generation as a cherished instalment in the family's poetic memory:

> On Easter Day in early morn
> When I came back from church,
> My heart was full of Nicholas
> Still unavenged for eighteen years
> Because our children then were small.
> But well did I look after them
> So they could quickly grow to men
> And take at last a sweet revenge
> For father's blood unjustly shed
> By our eternal enemies.
> And all this time I bore the shame
> In solitude, and kept apart
> From folk whose pitying looks I shunned.
> But now this Easter Day I laid
> The table with an extra plate,
> And when my children sat to eat
> And made their cross, they asked me why,
> And then I told them whose it was –

'It had its place but long ago,
For this was your dear father's plate,
Your father who died unavenged
Because you then were small and weak.
But now that you are grown to men
The time has come to take your guns
And hunt our enemies to death
And kill their leader, Koutalídes.
He rides quite often past our door,
So careless now that eighteen years
Have left him safe from our revenge
For what he boasts of having done:
Him must you kill, and if you fail
My blessings you shall never have,
But blackest curses born of shame.'
The children wept and thus replied –
'O best of mothers, come, sit down,
And eat the roasted lamb with us,
And bless us now with heart and soul
To prosper what we mean to do.
Before night falls this Easter Day
Our father's death shall be avenged,
For Koutalídes always comes
All dressed to kill on Easter Day
With fancy vest and golden belt
To greet our neighbour Koúbaris.'
The children scarce had spoken thus
When horses' hooves were heard outside
And Koutalídes came along
To greet his kinsman Koúbaris.
They took their guns and silently
They stood and waited by the road,
And when he came they called aloud,
'We pay our debts! Take what we owe!',
And quickly fired three shots at him,
And Koutalídes fell stone-dead.
His escort soon returned the fire
And all day long the battle raged
Till nightfall made them go away.
Then came the children home again

And when they reached the courtyard door
Their waiting mother wept with joy.
'Rejoice, dear mother, sweet revenge!
Our shame is washed away in blood!'
Their mother clasped them in her arms:
'Such joy, such glory now is mine,
I live again, I call myself
A mother now with noble sons.
No longer have I shame to bear
In solitude and keep apart
From folk whose pitying looks I shunned.
I walk today with head held high,
My loneliness is past!'

There is no clearer insight than through these *miolóyia* into the mentality of the blood feud and shame culture of which the forests of towers are the visible reminders, and we shall hear some others of special local or historical interest on our journey. We are now in Sparta, and having hired a sturdy car (carefully omitting to tell the lender our destination before negotiating the price) we are ready to retrace a journey deep into Mani in the early summer of 1980 and to recall in words and pictures some of the gleanings from over thirty years of exploration, study and photography which began when a member of the Resistance returned after the last War to the remote mountain refuges into which he had once fled for his life.

1

Yíthion, Passavá and the City of Ares

Starting from Sparta the modern visitor to Mani follows in the tracks of Paris and Helen as they fled southward to the port of Yíthion, which failed to impress the English Colonel Leake in 1805 but is now happily unrecognizable from his description of 'a hundred wretched houses in the midst of which stands a large church'. Today it is a pleasant seaside resort with comfortable hotels, a picturesque waterfront and a harbour that attracts a few cruise ships as well as the weekly ferries from Piraeus and Crete and the odd cargo boat. It looks out across the Laconian Gulf to the Maléa peninsula, a dark outline on the eastern horizon that shimmers in the midday haze and twinkles with the lights of its scattered villages at night. To the north the skyline is still dominated by the distant peaks of Taïyetos, snow-capped even in May, but the head of the Gulf is more gently crowned by the hot, flat, fertile plain of Élos that carries the icy waters of Evrótas into the sea. (See Plate 1.)

When Pausanias described Yíthion in the second century AD, it was evidently a town of some pretensions. It had been founded, so its citizens maintained, by Heracles and Apollo when they once decided to do something constructive after squabbling over a tripod. Pausanias records statues of these earthy divinities standing in the market square near one of Dionysus, and his list of sights worth seeing includes a Carneian Apollo, a sanctuary of Ammon, a bronze image of Asclepius in a roofless temple with a sacred spring, a temple of Demeter, a statue of Poseidon the Earth-embracer, a fine gate called the Gate of Castor, and a temple and image of Athene on the hill. What it fails to include is the one really impressive monument that is available for us to see *in situ* today, for while there are some lesser survivals from the Roman period in the small museum, the main part of the ancient town is now under the sea, and little of the rest has survived the ravages of nearly two millennia. But the theatre still exists near the northern end of the present town, a handsome structure some 80 metres in diameter with its tiers of stone seats still surprisingly intact in view of the amount of Roman remains Colonel Leake saw being carted off 'to build the Bey's new tower' in 1805. And the very fact that Pausanias evidently thought it too insignificant to mention gives a yardstick of Yíthion's prosperity as capital of the Union of Free Laconians in the first two centuries AD.

But Yíthion's most famous visitors came long before the Romans, and the temple to their patron goddess is certainly not ignored in Pausanias' ancient *Guide Bleu*. 'Before Yíthion lies the island of Kranáï,' he wrote, 'and on the mainland opposite the island is a sanctuary of Aphrodite Migonitis' – Aphrodite of the Lovers' Embrace – 'and the whole place was called Migonium.' And this was something no Roman tourist would have wanted to miss, for Kranáï is the island where Paris and Helen spent the first night of their illicit honeymoon – a night which the incorrigible lover recalled to Helen ten years later when she had reviled him for funking single combat with Menelaus before the walls of Troy:

So chide me not, my lady fair, rejoice instead in love!
For never have I known my heart so hopelessly enwrapped
With longing for thy love – not even when I snatched thee first
From lovely Lacedaemon's vale, put out to sea in hollow ships,
And on Kranáï lay with thee upon a couch of love – as now
Do I feel love for thee and suffer sweet desire. . . .
                                            (Homer, *Iliad* 3.441–6)

The modern name of Kranáï is Marathonísi, 'the Isle of Fennel', and there are spectacular aerial views of it to be had by climbing the high hill of Koúmaro, the ancient Laryssion, which rises steeply from the shore and carries the southern end of the town precariously with it through a maze of lovely old houses up hundreds of stone stairs. (See Plate 2.) In spring the whole hillside is ablaze with wild flowers, and over the patchwork of tiled roofs the little island seems almost to float in the bay, as though it would drift away but for the narrow causeway that now ties it to the mainland and makes a safe jetty for a little row of fishing boats bobbing up and down at their moorings. Some bigger vessels are usually beached for repairs near a little church that stands at the western end of the island near the causeway. A tall lighthouse challenges its gleaming whiteness from the opposite end, and in the centre stands a suitably romantic little fortress gradually crumbling into ruins. The whole place is enchanting, and never more so than when watching the sunrise from near where the boats are drawn up by the church. (See Plate 3.) The lighthouse, still flashing faintly, and the fort's sombre battlements are effortlessly transformed by the sun's alchemy into the *rose antique* of Mani's famous marble. The sea's dull lead becomes the imperial purple that Phoenicians and Greeks once manufactured here for Oriental kings and Roman emperors. The fishing boats are now gilded quinqueremes, the lovers are already aboard, and Menelaus will arrive too late to do anything but swear revenge as they disappear down the Gulf with ten thousand diamonds sparkling from their oars.

The little fortress on Kranaï was built to guard the harbour by Zanétbey Grigorákis, who was Bey of Mani between 1784 and 1798 under the Turkish policy of indirect rule of this indomitable peninsula. He also built what is now the southern end of Yíthion but was then the only town (the ancient site near the theatre having been long disused), and it took the name Marathonísi from the island opposite. His principal residence was some 2 kilometres to the south of Kranaï on the high promontory of Mavrovoúni, the Dark Mountain, from where he could also command the rich coastal plain of Passavá which stretches south-westwards from the promontory for over 3 kilometres. But wealth and power as a Turkish vassal did not prevent Zanétbey scheming revolution, plotting endlessly with other lairds and pirate-captains, and eventually negotiating the shipment of arms and ammunition from the French that brought him to grief. For Marathonísi was then besieged by the Capitán-Pashá and the Turkish fleet, the rebellion was nipped in the bud, and Zanétbey himself fled inland to preserve his freedom while a weaker and more amenable Greek was appointed in his place.

Zanét died in abject penury, but the glory which he won in the days of his power and prosperity were not forgotten, and his memory was particularly cherished by the recipients of an extraordinary generosity. Colonel Leake records being told how he used to 'ring a bell at supper-time and give food to all who came to him', and the Maniáte poet Nikítas Nifákos, admittedly not without an eye to patronage, had already eulogized this happy practice in verse:

> A bell rings out at supper-time,
>   'Come hither to my table!',
> And all who hear it enter in
>   And eat all they are able.
> He loves the poor and foreign guest,
>   He tends the homeless waif,
> But evil men he pounds like salt
>   To keep his province safe.

And the castle that had been the scene of all this hospitality, and of the revolutionary scheming that had brought it to an end, is still to be seen on Mavrovoúni, a rather melancholy reminder of one of the Mani's great eighteenth-century characters:

> For now gape wide his crumbling halls
> With silent mouths in broken walls
> That long to tell of Grigorákis
> Whose courage made him Capetanákis,
> The great Zanét who built Melíssi
> And here the lovely Marathonísi.

From Mavrovoúni a long, sandy beach stretches south-westwards for more than 5 kilometres to the next rocky promontory, Cape Petaléa, and the road at first runs parallel to it some 500 metres inland. It traverses a broad, flat, luxuriant plain with acres of orange groves on the seaward side and countless olive trees inland interspersed with figs and tall, dark cypresses. Beyond the bridge that carries the road over the ancient, slow-running Smínos, the plain opens out into richly cultivated fields for a considerable distance inland, and as the road curves further from the coast round the low hills that appear on the seaward side about 4 kilometres from Mavrovoúni, the olives give way to oaks while the distant peaks of Taḯyetos now corrugate the inland horizon, their snowy peaks revealing the source of the rivers that made this fertile region so coveted by Frankish and Turkish invaders. Another kilometre and the road plunges between two low hills with an interesting diversity of vegetation. The slopes on the left are thickly covered with the oaks whose acorns were a valuable export in the last century for the tanning of leather. Those on the right have orange groves, presided over by black cypresses standing to attention like Nubian sentinels in some Oriental palace-garden. But the road itself could be an English country lane, its hedgerows a tangle of blackberries and dogroses shaded by elegant birches shimmering and rustling in the gentlest breeze. Then suddenly, about 8 kilometres from Mavrovoúni, a bend in the road brings us below a conical hill crowned with the battlements of Castle Passavá. (See Plate 4.)

We are now among the range of hills that runs south-eastwards to form Cape Petaléa, and in order to pass the castle the road has to squeeze through a deep, narrow gorge directly below its walls. But while it is easy to see the advantage of the site for dominating this main road from Yíthion at the head of the Laconian Gulf to Ítilon at the head of the Messenian, and indeed the rich plain through which we have passed, we can only appreciate the superiority of this particular hill over the many others by climbing up it and seeing the view from the top. And there we find its massive stone ramparts, some 12 metres high, almost intact, so that it is possible to walk along the parapets almost all round this large castle, which is at least half the size of Mistrá.

The ground plan is almost triangular, with long walls on the eastern, southern and western sides but with the eastern and western converging to produce a very short northern side where two strong towers overhang the main road as it passes through the narrow defile. From the western ramparts the road to Ítilon can be seen snaking south and then south-west while an offshoot leads due west up an open valley to the village of Skamnáki and so into the heart of the distant mountains, whose black silhouette seems to come closer when the sun has just set behind them in a rosy haze. To the east the patrolling sentries had a fine coastal panorama divided by the hills of Petaléa, though they could not in fact see over this range from the eastern ramparts but only by looking across the whole castle from the much higher western walls. From there they had a marvellous view north-eastwards as far as Mavrovoúni, right up the long sandy Bay of Stómion and over the richly cultivated plain through which we drove from Yíthion. Or looking south-east they could see down a valley to the Bay of Vathí which Cape Petaléa separates from Stómion Bay: the towers of Ayeranós are clearly visible on the promontory that forms the southern side of Vathí Bay, and still further south the much greater Cape Kremidará with Skoutári Bay beyond. The view south and south-west is among the hills through which the road to Ítilon eventually disappears, but even so the hill-top village of Vachós can be seen over 7 kilometres away, and with the help of a few signalling posts on intervening heights very little would have escaped the attention of the lords of Passavá.

The great battlemented walls, and the ruined houses that rise between them with handsome arches among a tangle of oaks and some flowering exotics from once elegant gardens, are mainly Turkish from the eighteenth century, but the site had been inhabited intermittently for at least two thousand years before then. Vast blocks of Cyclopean masonry in the southern section of the eastern wall suggest a Bronze Age site, almost certainly the city of Las mentioned in Homer and visited more than a thousand years later by Pausanias, who saw ruins that were ancient in his own day and described a statue of Heracles in front of the walls and a trophy left by Philip V of Macedon when he invaded Laconia in 218 BC. When Leake visited the site in 1805 he found remains of classical pottery, and we found more on a recent visit when a hill fire had destroyed much of the vegetation on two sides. In Pausanias' time Las had been a member of the Union of Free Laconians and evidently a comfortable town with Roman baths and a gymnasium, but then it disappears from history until the Frankish conquest of the Peloponnese at the beginning of the thirteenth century.

The advantages of the site were as obvious to the Franks as to the ancients, and when this region was assigned to Baron Jean de Neuilly, he built his castle on this hill and called it Passavá, possibly from a family motto 'Pas Avant' or 'Passe Avant'. Although his barony was small with only four knight's-fees, his importance was recognized by the title Hereditary Marshal of Achaea, and clearly this castle was critical for the defence of Frankish Laconia from the Maniátes of the peninsula to the south, whose fierce independence and belligerence were to make it the Achilles' heel of occupying powers in the southern Peloponnese for the next six hundred years. But the Barony of Passavá was not destined to last more than half a century.

The last holder of the fief was Margaret, daughter of the second Baron Jean who rode with his liege lord William, Prince of Achaea, on the fateful field of Pelagonia in 1259. The battle that was to have extended Prince William's control over northern Greece ended in victory for Emperor Michael of Nicaea, who captured William and his barons and took them to witness his triumphant entry to Constantinople two years later. And when they eventually secured their release by accepting the suzerainty of Byzantium and ceding the castles of Mistrá, Monemvasía and Maína, Margaret of Passavá was among the noble hostages sent to the Emperor as sureties for the Franks' compliance.

Although Margaret was well treated at Constantinople and lived in circumstances befitting her rank, it was fifteen years before she was free to return, by which time her father had died and her castle had long since been overrun by the Maniátes. She found herself in the unenviable position of Baroness without a barony and Hereditary Marshal without an army, and though she had a claim to an even richer barony in Arcadia through her mother's uncle, it had now reverted under feudal law to Prince William himself, thanks to whom she had not been free to claim it within the statutory two years and two days after her great-uncle's death. Indeed it was only when she married the powerful Jean de St Omer, brother of the Baron of Thebes, in 1278 that Prince William could be prevailed upon to do the decent thing and give her at least part of her Arcadian barony; but by then of course control of Laconia had passed irrecoverably to the Greeks, and Passavá was no more than a name until its suitability as a power centre for an army of occupation was rediscovered by the Turks some two centuries later.

The importance of Passavá as a Turkish stronghold fluctuated with the ebb and flow of rebellion in Mani and the determination of the Turks to suppress it. The castle was strengthened after it had been surprised and sacked by a Spanish fleet which ravaged Mani in 1601, and in view of its strategic position between the ports of Yíthion and Ítilon it formed an important link in the chain of fortresses – Passavá, Kelefá, Zarnáta – by which Kuesy Ali Pashá was determined to fetter Mani against Venetian interference after the Venetians had been driven out of Crete in 1669. But fifteen years later the tide turned again, and when the Maniátes rebelled in support of the Venetians, Passavá surrendered and was destroyed. With the Maniátes as allies, the Venetians had no need of a fortress designed mainly to coerce the local inhabitants in the vicinity of an important pass. It was too far from the sea for the Venetians to hope to hold it against a Turkish reconquest, and it was too dangerous to leave the fortifications intact as a ready-made base for the enemy to reoccupy. They therefore carried off the cannons but destroyed the castle, and it probably remained destroyed until the Turks reconquered the Peloponnese in overwhelming force in 1715.

When the Maniátes next rebelled with the disastrous encouragement of Count Orlov and the Russians, the Turks had already evacuated Passavá by the time the insurgents reached it on their way to defeat at Trípolis by the savage Albanians whom the Turks now poured into the Peloponnese. For a while it continued as a centre of resistance, but it was eventually reoccupied and refortified by the Turks when the victorious Hassán Ghazi determined to subjugate Mani under a new system of indirect rule involving the appointment of a Greek as Bey of Mani. But in 1780 the arrest and execution of Éxarchos Grigorákis, uncle of the future Zanétbey and then head of the powerful Grigorákis clan of Skoutári and Ayeranós, roused his kinsmen to bloody reprisals on the nearest Turkish settlement, which was Passavá:

>So sadly tolled all Mani's bells,
>'For whom?' men asked each other,
>Then looking up they saw on high
>A hawk that screamed the evil news –
>'The Turks in Trípolis have killed
>By guile brave Éxarch Grigorákis.'
>Then everyone – man, woman, child –
>Converged upon the stricken house,
>The women's aprons amply filled
>With *xerotígana* and bread
>As gifts to pay their due respects

And mourn for Grigorákis.
The dead man's mother heard their cries,
And turned her heart to coldest stone:
'Ye men of Mani, women too,
If seeking vengeance for my son,
Stay not but go and weep no more.
Look there, my friends, at Passavá,
Up there behind those castle-walls
The faithless Turks who killed my son
Sit mocking us, and while they stay
The very air's not ours to breathe.'
Then hearkened all the Maniátes
And rushed at once to Passavá
And launched themselves upon the Turks
With flaming swords athirst for blood
And took their vengeance, right and wrong.
The castle fell, a thousand Turks
Were slain that day for one brave Greek,
And Turkey's yoke was thrust aside.

This simple but effective *mirolóyi*, chanted by generations of Maniáte women over their looms and handmills, is interesting not only historically and as an example of a typical Maniáte vengeance song but for its simple evocation of mourning customs that still apply in Greece – the taking of bread rings and the fried pastries (*xerotígana*) to the home of the deceased by those who come to pay respects – and for the remarkable honesty of its acceptance that the morality of revenge is not clear-cut – 'who took their vengeance, *right and wrong'*. The massacre was indiscriminate and effective. Men, women and children were put to the sword with equal enthusiasm, and of the seven hundred Turkish families that inhabited the area not many succeeded in escaping to the mountains of Vardoúnia. But the 'thrusting aside of the Turkish yoke' was still only local and temporary even here, despite, and ultimately because of, the efforts of Éxarch's nephew Zanét Grigorákis, who now assumed headship of the clan from his murdered uncle. For having organized the victory of Passavá, the energetic Zanét consolidated his independence and extended his personal power by building many castles and towers in the region; but after refusing Turkish offers to make him Bey of the whole Mani if he would accept vassalage, he was eventually enticed onto a Turkish ship for dinner four years later and carried off to be presented with an ultimatum. He chose to live, and for fifteen years the destroyer of Passavá ruled Mani as a Turkish Bey until his negotiations with the French in turn destroyed him. But neither Greeks nor Turks seem to have made further use of Passavá, which disappears from history in 1780 and was certainly in ruins when Colonel Leake visited it twenty-five years later.

From the gorge of Passavá where Turkish corpses rained down from the northern ramparts in the massacre of 1780, the road to Deep Mani continues south-westwards to the head of the Messenian Gulf, which is the only way (for wheeled vehicles at any rate) of circumventing the mountainous barrier to the peninsula proper; but with sufficient time to spare and a robust car it is worth making a detour to visit the Bay of Vathí and the Grigorákis strongholds of Ayeranós and Skoutári on the eastern coast. There is a turn left off the main road not far beyond Passavá signposted 'Belle Helène', and the long, sandy beach that it meets after two bumpy kilometres has many attractions besides its perfect bathing. A considerable river, formerly called Turkóvrisi, discharges its clear, cold waters into the Bay through a broad channel that it carves through the sand, and the reed-beds through which it emerges onto the beach are a paradise for bird-watchers in the spring. And though this area cannot have been very healthy in malarial times, there are considerable Roman remains to be seen and identified a little distance inland near the old village of Vathí. At the southern end of the bay there is an incongruous but happily unobtrusive new hotel which accounts for the signpost to 'Belle Helène', and beyond this point the road deteriorates still further as it climbs steeply through thick woods to the little village of Ayeranós with its two towers that could be seen from Passavá. They are both castles of the divided Grigorákis clan, and though the lower one has been crudely disfigured by the addition of a hideous concrete balcony to the main tower, its cliff-edge position on the wooded headland is superb, and the occupants of the balcony, who do not have to look at it, enjoy magnificent views over their crumbling battlements.

On the southern side of Ayeranós the road descends steeply to Kamáres Bay, from where it is necessary to struggle some distance inland and negotiate a spine-jarring maze of cart-tracks before meeting the road that climbs over the shoulder of Cape Kremidará to Skoutári. The village is on a high hill overlooking its bay, where refugees from the Skoutári district of Constantinople are said to have landed in 1453 and brought the name with them. The ruins of another Grigorákis tower still remain in the village square as a memorial to the efficiency of Hassán Pashá's artillery, and near them is the church of Áyios Ioánnis (St John Chrysostom), which has fine frescoes of the eighteenth-century style and an endearing inscription over the door with cleaning instructions to the verger. A steep road zig-zags down to the little bay with its church of Áyia Varvára and some Roman walls on the beach, while on the far side of the valley there is a pleasant walk up to a large deserted monastery of St George surrounded by once carefully cultivated gardens on the hillside terraces. But further advance southwards down the eastern coast of Mani is barred by the great range of mountains ending in Cape Stavrí, and though a road now runs south from the port of Kótronas only 4 kilometres as the crow flies due south of Skoutári, the crow has to fly over mountains 600 metres high to reach it, and a car has to make a detour of more than 30 kilometres through the western pass.

To get further south down the peninsula we must in fact drive almost due north for 5 kilometres and rejoin the main Yíthion–Ítilon road at Karioúpolis, which but for our long detour would have been little more than 3 kilometres beyond Passavá. And as might be expected at this important junction, there is a powerful castle on the hill that towers above it. It was the seat of the Kavallierákis family, whose founder, Thomas Fokás, then of Kelefá, adopted an equestrian surname when he became a Knight of St Mark in 1695 for services rendered to the Venetian Republic. His descendants still preserve his letter of appointment, signed and sealed in the ducal palace on 30 April in that year and listing many bloody proofs of his devotion to the Republic's cause in the Peloponnese. The family also like to connect this Thomas Fokás with the Byzantine Emperor Nicephórus Phokás, whose murder in 969 by the usurping John Tsimiskís caused a diaspora of the former imperial family; but though it is not impossible that a dispossessed Phokás fled for refuge to Mani, it is strange that the letter of knighthood makes no mention of such a connection among his other claims to nobility. And even without imperial blood in their veins the Kavallierákis family have fame enough in their record of resistance to the Turks, from their founder's exploits with the Venetians in the late seventeenth century to the Revolution of 1821 in which several of his descendants fought and died with great distinction.

Although it looks medieval, the Kavallierákis castle at Karioúpolis is not earlier than the late eighteenth century, and both the castle itself and its outbuildings are sufficiently well preserved to give a good impression of the life-style of these factious Maniáte lairds who were usually fighting each other when not united against the Turks. The main part of the castle is a long narrow building on two floors, about 22 metres long by 5 metres wide, and with a four-storey tower, 5 metres square, at the eastern end. The tower is windowless on the ground floor, the windows of its upper floors are few and very small though handsomely arched, and the corners are heavily buttressed. The family lived in the one long room on the first floor, which has a great fireplace at the western end. The ground floor was occupied by the garrison in time of danger and by storerooms and magazines which extend below ground-level in arched vaults. More storerooms have been built underground on the southern side, and there are many ruined outbuildings that were evidently the peacetime dwellings of retainers and animals. Nearby stands the little church of St Peter, which presumably served as the family's chapel and was probably built or rebuilt at the same time as the tower, whose tiny arched windows are identical. And the family crest is still to be seen above the gateway to a high-walled courtyard that lies between the church and castle – the two-headed eagle of Byzantium still proclaiming an imperial ancestry for the lords of a small and squalid fortress.

From Karioúpolis the main road first passes through an open valley with fields of corn and olives on either side before squeezing between more hills by a sunken river-bed that flows pink in spring and summer with the blossom of the oleanders that fill it. And when we emerge again into more open country we have our first glimpse of Kouskoúni, the grey, gaunt mountain that broods like a Spartan ephor over the entrance to Inner Mani. (See Plate 5.)

The change in the landscape is astonishingly abrupt as we approach Kouskoúni. Within a kilometre we say farewell to the fertile fields that stretch out to the prosperous hill-side village of Vachós and the oak- and olive-covered hills to which we have grown accustomed. Only the toughest and thorniest shrubs can survive on the foothills of Kouskoúni, and only goats can climb its scree-slopes with ease. And yet a tiny white speck on the very summit marks the Church of Profítis Ilías – the Prophet Elijah whose chariot of fire and a name sounding like Helios made him the natural patron saint of nearly all Greece's mountain-top churches where the Sun-god might have been worshipped in pagan times.

As the road curves west round this impenetrable barrier to the south we have our last glimpse back to the Laconian Gulf and our first of the Messenian, on which the port of Ítilon was once the west coast's counterpart to Yíthion on the east. Ítilon itself gleams white on the distant foothills to the west against the dramatic background of the Pentadáktilos – the five great peaks that look like the whitened knuckles of a clenched fist at the southern end of the Taïyetos range separating Laconia from Messenia. Ítilon in fact is the gateway between Inner and Outer Mani, which are connected only by the narrow road that rises in a series of hairpin bends from the port below to creep round the coastal mountainside into fertile Messenia. And since the control of this port and pass was obviously vital for an occupying power, it is not surprising to find another great monument to Turkish domination on the plateau that now lies between us and Ítilon and dominates the bay – the Castle of Kelefá. (See Plate 6.)

Its ruins are impressive. The large rectangular enclosure of some 15,000 square metres was capable of holding a garrison of at least five hundred men. The high curtain-walls and the three great curved bastions of the southern side are almost intact, and though the cannons that once threatened the bay have gradually disappeared in the last twenty years, the spectacular view from the gun platform is fortunately irremovable. The castle was built by Kuesy Ali Pasha in 1670, when the Grand Vizier Kuprili sent him to secure Mani against the Venetians after he had driven them from Crete, to control the lucrative trade that passed through the anchorage of Karavóstasi at the northern end of the bay, and to suppress the Maniáte piracy that had given Ítilon its nickname of 'Great Algiers'. And the troops and cannons of Kelefá were also used to support one group of Ítilon's feuding families against another in a policy of 'divide and rule', one effect of which was the emigration of the Iatráni to Italy in 1671 and of their rival Stefanópouli to Corsica a few years later. But even so Kelefá, like Passavá, remained only fifteen years in Turkish hands before falling to the Venetians and their Maniáte allies when Morosini began his Peloponnesian campaigns in 1685. The Maniátes already had the fortress under siege when Morosini's fleet appeared in the bay, whereupon the Turkish commander surrendered in exchange for a safe conduct for himself and his five hundred men to the island of Elafónisos off Cape Maléa. And though the Turks counter-attacked in the following year and nearly succeeded in breaching the walls, Morosini again arrived with reinforcements in the nick of time, and the banner of St Mark continued to flutter over Kelefá for the next twenty years.

The Venetian governors affected to consider Kelefá of relatively little importance – 'a fortress built rather to impress upon the sullen nature of the Maniátes the obedience due to High Dominion than to provide a post capable of strong resistance . . . or serve as a bulwark to assaults from overseas'. And to the extent that the sullen Maniátes were their allies, they certainly had less need of it than the Turks. All the same they did not destroy Kelefá as they did Passavá, and at least one *provveditore*, Francesco Grimani, realized how critical it would be for successful resistance to a serious counter-invasion by the Turks. But the Venetian Senate was ever more ready to receive money than spend it, and when Turkish armies swept back into the Peloponnese in 1715, Kelefá was in no state to defend itself, and surrendered without a fight.

Ítilon today is only a shadow of the 'Great Algiers' immortalized by Jules Verne, and though it remains the formal 'capital' of the region, it has long since yielded in importance and prosperity to Areópolis, which in the motorized age has also replaced it as the junction of the road from Yíthion and the pass from Messenian Mani that creeps round the Pentadáktilos and spirals down above Ítilon to the head of the bay. Indeed there is no road fit for cars across the gorge that separates Ítilon and Kelefá, and in order to reach one from the other on wheels – a distance of little more than a kilometre by foot or hoof – it is necessary to make a 10-kilometre detour to Areópolis, down to Liméni, and back along the coast through the fertile little plain that lies at the head of the bay under the guns of Kelefá. But even if you are not planning to follow the pass through to Messenian Mani, it is worth going to its foot to see the lovely monastery church of Dekoúlou, the benefice of a great local family. Its position is idyllic, nestling by a fountain among the trees on the seaward side of the valley below Ítilon and looking southward over the whole bay to where the road zig-zagged down from distant Areópolis. (See Plate 7.) And though the church is not old, at least by Mani's standards, its eighteenth-century iconostasis is exquisitely carved and painted (see Plate 8), and its many fine frescoes are beautifully preserved (though the Stygian darkness that has preserved their colours will mean a wasted visit without powerful torches to illuminate them). (See Plate 9.)

At the northern end of the bay only a few straggling houses mark the old harbour of Karavóstasi, literally 'ship-stop', which contributed so largely to Ítilon's prosperity in the days of sail; but there is much more to be seen at Liméni, the harbour of Areópolis, as might be expected of the ancestral seat of the great Mavromichális family. (See Plate 11.) Liméni is about 2 kilometres due south of Karavóstasi across the bay, and Petróbey's castle there has been so perfectly restored that, but for the smallness of the windows, it could be mistaken for a square-towered English country church. It was here that he received the beydom of Mani in 1815 after lavishly entertaining a representative of the Sublime Porte who had anchored his fleet in the harbour. And it was here that he conspired with the other great captains of Mani and with the Filikí Etería for the Revolution, which he proclaimed in the square of Areópolis on 17 March 1821.

That Pétros Mavromichális achieved great things will have been no surprise to Colonel Leake, who had been very impressed when he had met him ten years before he became

Bey – 'a smart-looking man of between thirty and forty, and the genteelest Maniáte I have yet seen'. (See Plate 10.) He was obviously a cut above the existing Bey, old Antón Grigorákis, 'an unhealthy-looking Greek, of weak character, easily made to change his purpose by those around him'. And when eventually the beydom passed from the Grigorákis clan of the Yíthion area to that of Mavromichális of Tsímova, Tsímova naturally grew in importance until in 1821 it began the War of Independence and earned its later change of name to Areópolis, 'City of Ares'.

About 2 kilometres of hairpin bends bring us up from Liméni harbour to Areópolis, a busy market town that sprawls untidily on its little plateau between the mountains and the sea. It has too many shoddy concrete buildings to have kept its charm unimpaired, but the atmosphere of old Tsímova still lingers on in the narrow cobbled streets of the old part of the town, and there is a fine church of the Archangel Michael – an appropriately warlike patron for the benefaction of the Mavromichális family in the City of Ares. But perhaps the most distinctive feature of Areópolis is the great white campanile that soars high above St Michael's and looks from a distance like a lighthouse warning the south-bound traveller of the dangers that lie ahead. For it was not without reason that the Maniátes could claim that their church bells were never silenced by the Turks: we have now entered what is politely called Inner Mani but rejoices in the more sinister names of Kakovoúnia and Kakovoúlia – the 'Bad Mountains' and 'Land of Evil Counsel' – that now lies between us and the southernmost point of the Balkans, Cape Matapán.

2

Caves, Churches and a City of Towers

When Colonel Leake and his heavily armed escort entered Kakovoúlia in 1805 he soon learned the origin of its evil name when the local chieftain commanding the escort confessed to his servant, 'If the Bey had not given such precise orders concerning you, how nicely we should have stripped you of all your baggage!' The Kakovouliótes were as notorious as robbers by land as pirates by sea, but the necessities of life in this remote and barren peninsula left little room for the niceties of civilization, and there was always Homer to provide a precedent for regarding piracy as an honourable profession. They would have understood perfectly how Prince Telemachus in the *Odyssey*, newly arrived at Nestor's palace, was regaled with dinner before being asked with great politeness whether he was on business or was a pirate 'travelling the watery ways and bringing evil to men'. What they would not have understood is how Telemachus could have reached Pylos safely by land in the first place, or, if he did, how he managed to leave in the same condition. For this is how Nikítas Nifákos characterized the Kakovoulióte conception of hospitality:

> They welcome strangers, 'Come and dine!'
>   They call them, 'Comrade, brother!'
> But when one seeks to take his leave
>   His protestations smother –
> 'Let us conduct you, be your guides,
>   But first take good advice:
> Remove your trousers, leave your cloak,
>   And waistcoat too (so nice!),
> Proceed in fact with nothing on
>   Our honour to retain,
> Lest others rob and strip you bare –
>   We could not bear that shame!'

Happily for the modern visitor times have changed and he need not fear being left to die of exposure on the slopes of Kouskoúni, but the Maniáte is still not the easiest person to get to know. Centuries of feuding, suspicion and isolation have eaten deep into the Maniáte character, and while the visitor is no longer likely to have his money taken from him by force, he will not find it easy to give of his own accord. A small child will decline a proferred sweet. A frail old man will be reluctant to accept a lift in your car until you pretend to need his help to find your way. And even a starving dog will cast a suspicious eye on a stranger's bone and wait until his benefactor is out of sight before devouring it. But as is often the case with people who are difficult to get to know, there is no better friend than a Maniáte when he is at last sure that your friendship is genuine and based on respect.

The corollary is also true, that there is no worse enemy than a Maniáte, and the forests of towers in the villages of Kakovoúlia bear grim testimony to Christianity's failure to moderate the implacable obsession with vengeance that they represent. For nowhere in Greece was there a greater concentration of churches nor a more devoted population, yet nowhere was the other cheek less likely to be turned. Indeed the priests themselves were often worse than their congregations, and the Maniátes' undoubted devotion was all to the ritual and nothing to the rationale of Christianity, as Leake observed for himself: 'No people are more rigorous in the observances of the Greek church than the Maniátes. A Kakovoulióte, who would make a merit of hiding himself behind the wall of a ruined chapel for the purpose of avenging the loss of a relative upon some member of the offending family, would think it a crime to pass the same ruin, be it ever so small a relict of the original building, without crossing himself seven, or at least three, times.'

But if such unsporting, let alone unChristian, methods of exacting unreasonable vengeance were unattractive to the English colonel, they were not only condoned but expected under the Maniáte code, and the Maniáte marksman who hid behind chapel walls to shoot another Maniáte in pursuance of a family feud was certainly no coward when it came to full-scale feudal warfare or to fighting hand-to-hand against the Turks. Nor indeed was his wife, and Leake gives several examples of brave women in Mani's endless civil wars at the turn of the eighteenth and nineteenth centuries: one who defended her tower by threatening to blow it up; or another whose battle scars and formidable reputation made him reluctant to set up his best hat for her target practice. But even Leake's Amazons are tame compared with the heroines of the Revolution who opposed Ibrahím Pashá's great attempt to crush Mani in 1826.

Having swept down through the Peloponnese like a hurricane after the fall of Mesolóngi, Ibrahím had now reached the south coast and was concerting a land and sea attack on the defiant Maniátes, who had concentrated their forces at Vérga, near Almiró, in Messenian Mani. It was one of the most critical confrontations of the whole war. The Maniátes were heavily outnumbered, but their fierce resistance under the leadership of Ilías and the other Mavromicháles (see Plate 50) decided Ibrahím to make a simultaneous attack on their home base in Inner Mani, which had been left almost defenceless. If he could secure the region around Areópolis, he would soon demoralize the defenders at Vérga, cut their lines of communication, and gain rapid control of the passes not only into Messenia but to Yíthion and so into Laconia.

His plan was excellent. His galleys achieved complete surprise when they appeared in Díros Bay, and fifteen hundred Egyptians were soon swarming up to the plateau above, where they set about devastating the country and taking possession of Areópolis about 2 kilometres to the north. But he had reckoned without the women who were out harvesting their crops. As the church-bells sounded the alarm, some three hundred women came together from the fields, soon to be joined by as many men from more distant villages. And though armed only with their harvesting tools, the women expressed their indignation in a manner worthy of their Spartan ancestors:

> O Turkish men, have you no shame
> To war with womenfolk?
> We are alone, our men are gone
> To fight at Almiró.
> But we with sickles in our hands
> Will lop your heads like corn!

The Pashá's troops fell back and fortified a position on the coast where they could be assisted by the fleet, but two days later so many more Maniátes had gathered, both women and men, that the Egyptians were driven into the sea, and only a third of them were rescued by Ibrahím's ships. In the meantime Kolokotrónis had arrived with reinforcements to threaten the rear of his land forces at Vérga, and when Ibrahím now rapidly returned, he saw no alternative but to abandon the whole offensive. And though he tried again two months later with a similar attack on the eastern coast of Mani, he suffered a similar repulse.

The heroism of the Amazons of Díros has an everlasting memorial in the history and mythology of the Revolution, but the bay is best known today for its wonderful caves, which attract thousands of tourists every year from all over Europe and are themselves a monument to female heroism and persistence. The story of Anna Petrochílou has already been told – how she explored and developed the caves, first with her husband and then by herself after his death. (See Plate 12.) But it is only by going there and seeing the vast size and complexity of these labyrinths that we can really appreciate her quiet courage. It feels adventurous even now to sail in the comfort of barges through the underground waterways of 'Glifáda' with their great halls and petrified forests of stalactites and stalagmites illuminated by electric light, but what was it like for a woman alone with only a Davy lamp and a dinghy? And while our photographs can show the beauty of individual formations (see Plate 13), it is impossible for them to convey either the vast size of some of the caverns or the great length of the waterways that stretch silently ahead with a depth of water that can vary suddenly between 2 and 20 metres.

The lighting of the caves is simple and effective, happily avoiding the psychedelic horrors of some of the world's other famous caverns that have been opened to tourists. The Díros caves have plain white lights that do not detract from the natural beauty of the formations, some of which have their own natural colours – the delicate orange for the 'carrots'; crimson in the 'dragon's lair'; chocolate in the 'gateau'; or a pearly white 'chandelier' formed of thousands of pencil-thin stalactites clustering on the ceiling of a large cavern. And if these names are corny and sensibilities may squirm at the flashing light that turns a particularly phallic stalagmite into a lighthouse, the formations *are* amazing and not easy to describe.

The boats take about forty-five minutes to negotiate the accessible parts of the Glifáda cave, and at one subterranean landing place they put their passengers ashore like Charon and leave them to explore Pluto's palace on foot. But unlike Charon they also return you to the light of day, which you can abandon again by entering the second great cave system, the dry Alepótripa or 'Foxhole', which was discovered only in 1958. And though Alepótripa lacks the constant reflection that makes Glifáda so enchanting, it is no less impressive and in some respects even more interesting.

Here the visit is entirely on foot through a succession of halls with amazing formations – the 'Olive Tree Hall' with tiny leaf-like stalactites providing the foliage for a great trunk of rock which rises in the centre; the 'Hall of Crystal Rain', whose ceiling shimmers with a petrified cloudburst of the same slim stalactites that formed Glifáda's 'chandelier'; the massively-columned 'Carved Staircase' leading up to the 'Secret Passage' where a skull was found with a pair of stalagmites growing through its right cheek; then the 'Balcony' from which the frozen curtains of rain are seen to their best advantage, and so through another passage to the 'Hall of Rocks', from where a staircase leads down to the 'Hall of Worship', which is the cavern richest in formations and smoke-blackened from the pine torches of prehistoric inhabitants. But the grandest sight of all is the last, the 'Great Hall', which is entered down a long ladder. It is truly palatial in size – some 100 metres long by 60 metres wide and 30 metres high – with a waterfall near the entrance and a great lake with huge stalagmites rising from its depths at the far end.

And the interest of the Alepótripa caves is not confined to their spectacular scale and the intricate beauty of their formations. They are doubly fascinating for the valuable archaeological material that they have yielded – many bones and skulls (of both the normal and low-forehead types), tools of stone, clay, copper and obsidian, arrow-heads and pottery, oystershell bracelets, silver earrings, marble idols and primitive rock-paintings. The prehistoric inhabitants evidently used the area nearest to the entrance for living and working and reserved the deeper regions for the greater mysteries – the intermediate halls for worship, and the 'Great Hall' for burial of their dead. And

18. St Theodore's, Vámvaka (1075)

19. Cloisonné decoration
(St Barbara's, Érimos)

20. Nikítas's marbles
(St Theodore's)

21. 'Kítta of the many towers'

22. Tourlotí (12th century)

23. Tigáni

24. Sassarians

25. Odiyítria (13th century)

26. The Archangel Michael (13th century)

27. Mezalímonas

28. Áyia Eleoússa

29. Episkopí (12th century)

30. The Nativity and a scene from the Last Judgement (12th century)

31. Vlachérna (12th century)

32. Our Saviour's, Gardenítsa (11th century)

33. St John's, Kéria (13th century)

34. Marbles embedded in the walls

their remains reveal that it was a very different Mani in which these early men hunted and fished – a land of great pine forests, not the dry, barren wilderness to which we emerge from the cool of the underworld to the heat and blinding glare of a summer afternoon.

Zig-zagging back up the road from Díros Bay we reach the village of Pírgos Diroú, which Leake had found unusually anti-British when he passed rapidly by it at seven minutes past nine on 12 April 1805 – 'on account of the capture at Díros not long ago by Capt. Donnelly of the navy, and the subsequent imprisonment at Constantinople, of twenty-five sailors of a pirate *tratta*, who were all natives of this village except the captain, a Cretan'. But today's visitor will find all nationalities equally welcome at the little taverns and cafés that have recently sprung up to refresh visitors to the caves below, and there is nothing for an Englishman to fear even from a restaurant specializing in 'Smashed Bowels in Roasted Spit': the dish was excellent, and had lost only in translation. But at least one relic of a less hospitable past remains uncompromisingly forbidding. The great square tower of the Sklavounákos family still stands to its full height of 25 metres, and for long after Leake's time its cannons continued to reinforce a medieval claim to familial supremacy and independence against the threats of rival clans or foreign powers.

Leaving Pírgos Diroú we can drive quickly southwards through the unassuming little plain that stretches more or less uncomfortably between the mountains and a series of rocky bays, but if we do, we shall be speeding past some of the first jewels in the extraordinarily rich treasury of Byzantine churches that lies in the 17 kilometres between Pírgos and Yerolimín. Few of these churches are very far from the main road, but they are not always easy to find all the same. Perhaps a tell-tale clump of cypress trees will betray a graveyard, but sometimes the most exquisite little church will be completely hidden among the olive groves or accessible only through a maze of donkey tracks leading inland to the mountains or seaward to the cliffs. And even when they are found, not all of the most interesting churches display their merits on the outside, for while some are immediately recognizable architectural gems, others are clumsy ruins whose external attractiveness is only to donkeys and sheep in search of shelter, and no one would guess that they contain beautifully frescoed walls or have exquisitely worked marbles lying filthy on their floors.

Within 3 kilometres of Pírgos there are three beautiful churches of the eleventh century – two dedicated to the Archangel Michael at Glézos and Charoúda, and the third to St Peter at Triandafilliá. Glézos is reached by driving up an unmarked dirt lane that turns left off the main road only 200 metres from Pírgos: the lane peters out after about 500 metres and St Michael's can be seen in the foothills among its graveyard cypresses five minutes' walk from that point. St Peter's is only a kilometre further south along the same contour line and opposite its little village of Triandafilliá, which is on the seaward side of the main road. And by going through Triandafilliá we can wind our way by car to St Michael's of Charoúda, which is still only 3 kilometres from Pírgos as the crow flies though $4\frac{1}{2}$ kilometres as the car jolts along the narrow lane that winds through groves of olive and fig down the little promontory separating the Bays of Spathári and Langadáki.

The ruined megalithic church of Our Saviour (Áyios Sotíras) which stands at a sharp corner in the road to Charoúda leaves us ill prepared for the soft elegance of St Michael's in its beautiful churchyard behind a high wall. Our Saviour's is a crude masterpiece of dry-stone walling whose huge, irregular blocks are stark and white, but St Michael's beautifully squared stones are a soft sandstone colour interspersed with slivers of brick in the same cloisonné style of its namesake at Glézos. Its east end has three apses, each with handsomely tiled roofs, and there are ceramic plates set into the masonry of the central one. The main part of the church is cruciform, surmounted by a beautifully restored octagonal dome, the arches of which are picked out with delicate cloisonné and separated by uprights of smooth, white marble. And though the campanile at the west end is modern, its handsome arches harmonize well enough with the rest, and there are many ancient marble blocks, several with inscriptions, incorporated in its fabric.

While the guardian of the keys (who has to be asked for in the neighbouring houses) is opening the west door, you suddenly realize that both lintel and step are marbles intricately carved with a skill that bears comparison with, for example, the famous monastery-church of Ósios Loukás near Delfí. And once inside, as your eyes grow accustomed to the gloom, you find yourself in a very different but no less colourful world. But whereas the colours of the graveyard were bold and harsh in the sun's glare – the bright red of geraniums rioting against the white marble tombs, the glossy black of the cypress trees against a sky of brilliant blue – the frescoes within are of delicate pastel shades, the walls and ceilings being covered by beautifully executed paintings, mainly of the eighteenth or nineteenth centuries but also with a few older ones belonging to a previous layer of decoration. And how delightful to see this ancient church so carefully restored and cherished, its chandeliers gleaming, its floors carpeted, its woodwork polished until it reflects the candlelight like glass! For this is sadly the exception rather than the rule for the ancient churches of Mani, of which there is so large a number but evidently little money or energy to preserve a priceless cultural heritage that is rapidly crumbling into oblivion.

A classic example of this unforgivable neglect is the extraordinary church called Trissákia near Tsópakas. This tiny village is just off the main road on the seaward side about 5 kilometres south of Pírgos, but not a place to visit in the dark for fear of driving into a vast chasm some 30 metres deep. The bottom is covered with shrubs and trees, but only one huge fig has managed to reach ground-level with its highest leaves, and the crater's sides are too precipitous to descend without ropes or ladders. What caused the earth to gape in this way is a mystery, but the luxuriant vegetation inside combines with a few stalactites under the overhanging edges of the eastern end to suggest undermining by water as being more likely, if more prosaic, than the meteoric or Olympian causes that would be more appropriate to the sinister atmosphere of the place.

But it was not the little white village church by the crater that we had come to see. Our destination could be reached only on foot or hoof, and after returning a little way towards the main road and parking at the first sharp left-hand bend, we followed a narrow mule track leading seawards across the fields between two stone walls. The path was a very rough one, first through open fields then between dense olive groves that crowded the track from either side; but after twenty minutes or so, just as we were convinced that we had gone wrong, we suddenly found ourselves on the edge of an oblong reservoir that was the home of many thousands of tadpoles. And immediately behind it, its three apses reflected in the reddish water, was Trissákia, which in the local dialect means 'Three Churches'. (See Plate 14.)

Trissákia is very different from the domed, cruciform churches of Glézos and Charoúda. It is a more primitive structure, with three single-cell, barrel-vaulted churches side by side – a large one constituting the main church in the centre with a smaller side-chapel to north and south. It has none of the grace and elegance of Charoúda or Glézos. Its masonry is of rough, odd stones overlaid with mortar, and it is in a sad state of dilapidation with great holes gaping in the apses where their roofs have fallen in over their altars. But when we struggled, bent double, through the west door and stood up again in the disproportionately large central church, the artistic treasures that greeted us in paint and marble reached the very limit of incongruity with their squalid surroundings.

The walls were once covered with frescoes, and though many have now crumbled to dust and the roof-fall in the apse has destroyed all but the hands of the great Madonna over the altar, there are still some wonderful fourteenth-century paintings on the side walls of the main church. And these are not the tiny scenes of the eighteenth- and nineteenth-century styles of Charoúda or Dekoúlou but large murals in the grand manner. In the first of four recessed arches, about 2 metres high and set into the southern wall, we are face to face with St Theodore Stratelates riding his great charger, his spangled cloak billowing behind him while the vanquished serpent writhes beneath flailing hooves. The composition is unusually full of life and movement, and the colours, though subtle, have been used to powerful effect. The midnight blue of the background throws the prancing horse and its gorgeous rider into dramatic relief – the horse in white, the saint with golden halo and breastplate, clothes of red and blue, and a star-spangled cloak that merges imperceptibly like the Milky Way into a night sky of infinite depth.

Originally there were similarly fine portraits in all eight of the blind arches of the north and south walls of the main church, but except for St Theodore only faint traces now remain of them, and even he has deteriorated rapidly in the last few years. But there are still some fine scenes from the life of Christ and of the Virgin in the higher decorative zone above the blind arches where the walls begin their inward curve to form the barrel-vault. Again they are better preserved on the southern wall, the best of all being a panel of three depicting Christ teaching in the Temple, the Last Supper and the Betrayal. In the Garden of Gethsemane it is interesting to find the soldiers dressed and armed like contemporary Crusaders, and when we look again at St Theodore below, we see him booted and spurred in the Western fashion, and realize that the whole fluidity of the scene is Western rather than Eastern in inspiration. And the faces too are unusually expressive, particularly in the Last Supper. (See Plate 15.) As Judas reaches across the table to take the fish which represents Christianity, his crude greed is almost pathetic in its simplicity, his crime more weakness and gullibility than satanic evil. Christ watches him with a look of sorrowful resignation, and the expressions of the other disciples range from puzzlement and worry to unobservant unconcern. They show between them a fair cross-section of human weakness.

The sunlight streaming through the broken roof of the sanctuary not only allows the frescoes to be seen in natural rather than torch light but illuminates the church's other minor masterpiece – the magnificent marble iconostasis or screen separating sanctuary from nave. There were some fine marble pieces lying among the rubble of the ruined side-chapel on the northern side, the largest of them featuring a great Cross of Lorraine, but they left us quite unprepared to find a complete marble iconostasis of this quality intact and *in situ* in the main church. The lintel is carved with groups of arches alternating with elaborate circles or protruding hemispheres with rosebud or floriate-cross designs. The jambs are tall, slender and elegant, and the great carved panels supporting the lost icons on either side have intricate patterns enclosing a central cross. And as with the frescoes, the quality of the artistry of these marbles contrasts unexpectedly with the rough fabric of the exterior, though the fact that the base-panels appear slightly too wide for this iconostasis suggests that they were not made for this church but for an earlier and perhaps finer one from which they were removed.

After seeing these lovely things the walk back to your car will be quicker than the walk down because you will be trying to work off your indignation at the criminal neglect of this church. Works of art that have survived here for six turbulent centuries are on the verge of wanton destruction in this supposedly enlightened age. The deterioration of the frescoes as witnessed by our photographs of twenty years ago and of today is as depressing as it is unnecessary, for even if there is no money to restore them, surely the roof of the church could be repaired and its doorways provided with doors whose keys could be entrusted to a local villager. Instead it is left open to the mercy of the weather, the admiration of the donkeys and sheep who shelter there, and the vandalism of the sacrilegious savages who have already destroyed some of the frescoes' heads in trying to remove them to sell in some sordid antique shop in the back streets of Athens. And it is not as if Trissákia is an isolated example of this neglect. Perhaps the authorities are blind to the importance of saving art for its own sake, but even the most philistine finance ministers must surely realize that the tourist potential of Mani can only be irrecoverably harmed unless immediate action is taken to do what any civilized society would have done long ago to protect such a heritage for future generations.

To investigate all the interesting churches in all the little villages that are strung out like two rows of beads on their ancient tracks to either side of the new main road between here and Kítta would require at least seven days to cover as many kilometres. On the seaward side you would want to see Kafíona, Kouloúmi and Érimos before you came to Mézapos, which is the first deep-water harbour south of Liméni and home of the famous – or infamous – Sássaris family business of piracy. At Kafíona you would find St Theodore's twelfth-century church whose frescoes, painted a century later, include a rendering of the doctrine of Transubstantiation and Re-embodiment which is unique in Byzantine art. At Kouloúmi you would find the Archangel Michael again, also a twelfth-century church though much restored in the nineteenth. Its frescoes have been whitewashed over in the benighted belief that this form of cleanliness was next to godliness, but the external fabric of the church contains a grave-inscription and several small, worked marble fragments that probably belonged to the sill-course of an ancient shrine. And only a few minutes' walk to the south of the church is another great crater like the one at Tsópakas, perhaps 50 metres across and 30 metres deep, which was evidently the site of some ancient cult since a crude rock-cut relief of Heracles, a frequent visitor to the Underworld, was found on its northwestern lip. But if time was pressing and you could see only one of these three villages, it must be Érimos, whose St Barbara's is one of the finest Byzantine churches in Greece.

Áyia Varvára is reached by turning seaward off the main road at Lákkos, a village where some years ago a little boy was tragically killed playing with a wartime hand grenade that he had found among the rocks. It was harrowing to see all the family kissing the pathetic remains that had been collected and placed with the disinterred bones of an elder brother. The dead boy's schoolfellows stood biting back the tears like true Spartans, but the mother and grandmother were beside themselves with grief, and the *miroloyístra* tried to comfort them with the useless thought that their suffering was not unique:

> Lament and yet endure your loss,
> In grieving you are not alone,
> For hearts there are that burn inside
> And yet give out no smoke to show
> The searing pain that once let loose
> Would blacken all the sky.

But the grandmother, herself a *miroloyístra*, replied at once that the grief of a mother is boundless (see Plate 16):

> A mother once a serpent bore
> And cast it deep into the woods
> Yet when the woods caught fire she screamed
> And begged to know with anxious heart –
> 'The snakes, are they all burnt to death?'

The official *miroloyístra* then held back no longer but gave vent to a passionate outpouring of grief that rose and fell like waves in the sea, sometimes indescribably gentle in its eulogy of the dead boy, sometimes rough and wild in condemnation of his cruel fate, and at its peaks almost incomprehensible as the frenzy of the *miroloyístra*'s possession communicated itself to the other women and they wailed together, tearing their hair and bruising their breasts in a great crescendo of lamentation that really did seem to sear the sky.

From Lákkos a little side-road will take a car a few hundred metres through olive groves as far as a ruined megalithic church from where St Barbara's dome and belfry can be seen over the trees. A car can go no further, but an ancient carriage-road leads down to the harbour of Mézapos past several more crude churches now in ruins. But St Barbara's is neither crude nor ruined, though in urgent need of restoration. It is a most beautifully proportioned cruciform church with narthex, and its masonry is worthy of its architecture. (See Plate 17.) Its large grey squared stones, carefully interspersed with marble blocks in the lower part of the walls, are relieved by thin slivers of brick in the very finest cloisonné style. Higher up there is a handsome frieze of lozenge-shaped plaques set diagonally, and the separate architectural features are further emphasized by dentil-course bands. The windows are faced with carved marble panels, their arches most intricately decorated with brick. (See Plate 19.) And though, incredibly, this superb Byzantine church has been left untiled with naked roofs and dome, it is still exquisitely beautiful, particularly when dawn is getting her first rosy finger-hold on the mountains to the east and gently warming its grey stones and marbles with a soft, pink light.

Returning to the main road the first village we see on the mountainside opposite is Mína, a thicket of white towers and dark cypresses. From there starts one of the few passable tracks through the mountain chain to the Sunward coast, not passable for cars of course – there is no way that even a Land Rover can cross the 20 kilometres between the Areópolis–Kótronas road in the north and the Álika–Láyia pass in the south – but possible for a caravan of donkeys laden with contraband from Mézapos. Even so it is a gruelling journey. To attempt it in the heat of a summer's day would be almost suicidal, and only a very early start makes it possible to reach the delicious shade and cool fountains of the monastery of the Dormition of the Virgin on the other side before the sun is at its fiercest.

Mína itself is remarkable for its many fine towers, but the more northerly mountainside villages that we neglected while looking at the seaward ones are equally remarkable for fine churches, and two at least should not be missed – Bríki and Vámvaka. Bríki indeed, once a monastic community with a large number of monks, had no less than four important Byzantine churches: St Leo, St George, Holy Trinity and St Nicholas. Leo and George are in ruins, the former a very early church of the tenth century and therefore a great loss, the latter still preserving among its rubble a most beautiful carved marble lintel to reward the visitor who bothers to stop at this sad roadside ruin and look inside. And the lintel still bears the craftsman's inscription: 'Nikítas the Marbler, Servant of Christ'. Holy Trinity is the present monastery church and modernized almost beyond recognition, but St Nicholas is still unspoilt and contains fine fourteenth-century frescoes crying out for preservation.

Vámvaka is about a kilometre north of Bríki along the upper, older road which runs parallel to the main one, and suddenly St Theodore's appears round a corner past a small forest of prickly pear. (See Plate 18.) A large threshing-floor has been built nearby in the shade of some trees, and it gives a wonderful view westwards and south-westwards to the sea, past the villages of Kouloúmi, Angiadáki and Koutréla with their churches and towers to the distant promontory of Tigáni beyond Mézapos, and to the northern end of the Cávo Grósso beyond that. The site is a perfect one for a beautiful church, and St Theodore's is worthy of it – a lovely example of the domed, cruciform distyle type, not quite as perfectly proportioned as St Barbara's at Érimos but nearly a century earlier, being dated exactly to 1075 by an inscription on the west tie-beam of the nave. Its masonry is also cloisonné, and though it lacks the elaborate architectural features and decorative refinements of St Barbara's, there are in fact more bricks used in producing the cloisonné effect here than in any other of Mani's churches. It also has the earliest grouped window of any Mani church (another feature greatly refined by the era of St Barbara's), and though most of its frescoes have been whitewashed over as at Kouloúmi, its carved marbles are second to none.

The eleventh-century craftsman who carved them was rightly proud of his work and recorded his own name, together with that of the church's benefactor who paid for them: 'Remember, O Lord, Thy servant Leo and his wife and children. His great devotion having provided these adornments, let those who sing here pray for him. Amen. They were accomplished by the hand of Nikítas the Marbler, August 6583.' It is obviously the same craftsman who carved the fallen lintel that we found in the ruined church of St George at Bríki, and suddenly the eleventh century seems less remote now that we know the name of one of the creators of its usually anonymous works of art.

Even finer than his inscribed tie-beam in the nave are the lintels over the iconostasis and the west door, both of which include animal motifs alongside the intricate patterns of the marbler's usual repertoire. (See Plate 20.) On the interior lintel there are griffins, those fabulous eagle-lion hybrids that also feature on the marbles of Áyii Asómati high in the mountains behind Kítta. But for the west door Nikítas chose peacocks carrying bunches of grapes in their mouths and flanking an elaborate cross, below which runs a second beam of purely geometric designs. And nearby we find names even older than that of Nikítas, for set in the wall to the right of the door is a marble block that was evidently spotted as useful building material when the church was constructed – an ancient upside-down tombstone with the laconic valediction 'Farewell Diophantes, Farewell Dawn, Farewell Fortuna'.

Saying farewell to St Theodore's and wondering how long it will be before it joins the other beautiful churches that have crumbled through neglect we can drive slowly down through Vámvaka village with its towers and handsome half-ruined arches to meet the main road and turn south again to Kítta. And this time we are determined to do what most tourists do and speed down the peninsula disregarding the Byzantine treasures that lurk in the tiny villages to either side. The rough tracks to Koutréla, Kouloúmi and Érimos flash past on the right, to Vríki and Mína on the left, and in our eagerness to see the City of Towers we even ignore the sign to Mézapos, though mentally reserving it for another expedition. Then suddenly we are much further from the sea. The coastline has fallen away westwards, and the narrow coastal plain down which we have been travelling now widens to some 4 kilometres or more in a great western cape known simply as the Cávo Grósso. For the next 5 kilometres the mountains are separated from the sea-cliffs by the largest cultivable area of Deep Mani, and a glance at the map suffices to explain the development of Kítta as its centre. But just as we are skirting the base of the great conical mass of Mt Áyia Pelayía on our left, we are pulled up short by the sight of an exquisite little church in the foothills about 300 metres from the road: its patron saints are Sergius and Bacchus, and once spotted from the road it is impossible to pass.

Its local name is Tourlotí, 'the Domed One', and it was the orange tiles of its carefully restored dome that caught our eye. (See Plate 22.) While lacking a narthex and neither as large nor as elegantly proportioned as St Barbara's, its nearby contemporary of the twelfth century at Érimos, the church of SS Sergius and Bacchus has some of the most carefully executed masonry in Mani, and we rejoice to see how carefully it has been restored – an exception to the rule of neglect and dilapidation which is thus even more sickening in contrast. Like St Barbara's its fabric is cloisonné, with a similar use of panels of diagonally-set lozenges, dentil-courses and composite windows comprising arches and semi-arches. In the lower parts of the walls the marble blocks are so arranged as to form a pattern of T-type crosses, which is highly effective from a distance and prevented from appearing clumsy close up by the distraction of the elaborate decorative brickwork above.

Inside there are fine marble tie-beams and sculptured capitals to the four columns that support the dome. And though only a few of the frescoes are preserved, there is an intriguing Last Supper in which St John is sitting upright instead of leaning forward over Christ – an archaic iconographical feature preserved by an idiosyncratic painter in a remote area long after it had been given up in the Byzantine canon, but also perhaps connected with the eastern origins of the founder whose inscription is still preserved over the west door: 'O Lord, help Thy servant George the Marasiate, who built this most holy Church of the Sacred Martyrs Sergius and Bacchus and of St George with much devotion and labour.'

Now Sergius and Bacchus were soldier-saints and to that extent not inappropriate for a church in belligerent Mani, but they are far from home here. Their cult was in Resafa in Syria, and their patronage of a Maniáte church is puzzling until we learn from this inscription that its founder came from the ancient city of Marash, some 150 kilometres north of Aleppo.

But why did he come to Mani? Was he a refugee escaping persecution, or a malefactor escaping punishment? Only one thing is certain – that he brought enough money with him to build a beautiful church to dedicate to his favourite Syrian saints and to the universal George.

From Tourlotí it is less than a kilometre to this chapter's goal – 'Kítta of the many towers and Nómia the same'. Kítta's position is a dramatic one. (See Plate 21.) It nestles in the deep cleavage of the two stark conical mountains of Áyia Pelayía and Áyii Asómati, and the visitor who is game for a stiff climb up the latter to about 800 metres above sea-level should certainly go and see the little church that houses its incorporeal patrons so near to heaven. The starting-point is the village of Kallonί, which is a tiny cluster of towers just above and inland of Kítta. From where a car can go no further a rough track leads steeply up the left side of the ravine between the two mountains through a harsh and arid landscape that seems incapable of supporting life even for the half-wild highland cattle that pasture there. But Mani is ever surprising, and when after about half an hour you reach the head of the gorge and can turn right (southwards) across it, you suddenly see, half-way up the saddle that confronts you, an oasis of green even in September – a ruined maze of dry-stone walls and ruined farm buildings overgrown by a profusion of fig trees, chestnuts, apples and blackberries, all thriving luxuriantly on a spring that rises inexplicably at this great height. Climb up to it, and as you emerge on the higher side you will see against the skyline, close to the mountain's peak, the ruined dome of the early tenth-century church of Áyii Asómati – 'All Saints'.

The church is early cruciform in style, with three apses and an octagonal dome of a primitive but unique construction when seen from the inside where diametrically placed stone beams form a cross in a circle whose four segments are filled with dry stonework. Indeed the fabric of the whole church, made from purely local stone, is fairly crude, but for a building to survive for a millennium on so exposed a site requires more solidity than elegance; and what it lacks in elegance is more than made up for by its position, for the views are magnificent – northwards across the neck of the ravine up which you climbed to the vast cone of Mt Áyia Pelayía, or south to Cape Matapán across a broad mountain saddle whose far rim is crenellated with the towers of Moundanístika, one of the highest villages in Mani. Nor is elegance altogether lacking inside the church: there are still some fine green-tinged marbles to be seen, long beams delicately carved with arches, intricate rosettes, ornamental crosses and splendid griffins like the ones favoured by Nikítas at Vámvaka some 7 kilometres to the north.

Even for very energetic hikers at least three hours are necessary for this walk, and the cool of the early morning is safer for a first visit than leaving it to the early evening and risking being stranded on so desolate a mountain, for the descent would be impossibly dangerous after sunset. But sunset is a good time to visit Kítta itself, when the clustering towers loom larger and more sinister in silhouette. When Colonel Leake arrived here in 1805 he was staggered by the twenty-two towers sported by Kítta alone, and observed that its then population of between eighty and a hundred families made it by far the biggest village through which he had passed. And while many of the towers that Leake saw and others built later in that century are now more or less in ruins, there is still the impression of wandering through a petrified medieval forest, and a considerable credibility gap between the appearance of these strongholds and the nineteenth-century dates that some of them bear. While the Industrial Revolution was in full swing and the cotton-kings of Lancashire were vying with each other in the height of their factory chimneys, the local magnates of Kítta and Nómia were still competing with medieval towers and feuding with musket and cannon over family honour and bits of stony ground. And it is staggering to think that as late as 1870 Kítta was staging a full-scale feudal war between two rival clans, the Kaouriáni and Kourikiáni, who blasted away at each other night and day from their rival towers and required the intervention of the Greek regular army and artillery to compel a cease-fire. But this was one of the last flings for a glorious anachronism, and only the broken towers remain as monuments to a dogged medievalism that endured into the age of the transatlantic telegraph.

3

Mézapos, Tigáni and Cávo Grósso

Cávo Grósso, 'the Great Cape', radiates from Kítta like an erratic semi-circle some 10 kilometres in circumference. Kítta itself stands on a ridge at the base of the mountains forming its diameter, and the view from there is a commanding one: northwards up the coast to beyond Areópolis; southwards almost to Álika; and westwards for about 5 kilometres across a plateau that rises in several steps to a high bank before plunging into the sea in precipitous cliffs. This plateau contains some of the best – or least poor – land in Inner Mani, and it is not easily accessible by sea at any point on its circumference between the harbours of Mézapos at its northern end and Yerolimín at the southern, for reasons that an attempted circumnavigation on any but the very calmest day can make terrifyingly apparent. And even then there is something forbidding about these towering cliffs pockmarked by the caves that made the ancients call it Cape Thyrídes, 'the Windows'. You are uncomfortably conscious of an enormous depth of sea beneath you, and the caves are like windows to the underworld in which the water turns black and a gentle swell pulsates with the dull, rhythmic echo of a subterranean heartbeat. It is a place where the monstrous world of Greek mythology must come alive for even the most prosaic imagination. The Scylla's six pairs of eyes could be leering hungrily from any of the caverns above your head, while the sea birds scream like ghostly echoes from the centuries of shipwrecks that have given this cape a reputation even more evil than that of Matapán:

'From Matapán stay forty miles,
Twice that from Cávo Grósso!'

Nor were they only natural perils that inspired this laconic couplet. The calmest sea could be as deadly as the worst tempest if an approaching sail turned out to be a Maniáte pirate ship from

Mézapos, which is the best harbour on the western coast south of Liméni. For this was, and still is, the home of the Sássaris clan, whose ancestors were the scourge of the Turks during the occupation: they were prominent among the Maniátes who marched to Kalamáta after Petróbey's proclamation of the Revolution on 17 March 1821, and they saw no reason to alter their way of life after Independence. Piracy was their hereditary profession, and if its main motivation was nothing more elevated than a fairly indiscriminate greed, it continued to enjoy at least a veneer of respectability as an anti-Turkish crusade as long as other areas of 'Greece' remained 'unliberated', even though Turks were by no means its only victims.

Of the scores of songs and stories celebrating the exploits of the Sassárians one of the best is the *mirolóyi* for a certain Nicholas Sássaris, a romantic swashbuckler who had lost an eye and a hand on the Barbary coast. His bloody career has usually been assigned to the seventeenth century, but Mani is such a place for anachronism that there is no reason to discount the evidence which points to the nineteenth, probably the 1830s when the Turks and Egyptians had been driven from the Peloponnese. The *mirolóyi* is sung by the widow, and it is remarkable not only for its simple but vivid evocation of a way of life but for its complete lack of humbug about the squalid reality of piracy. Although devoted to her dead husband and enjoying the wealth and status that his activities brought her, she nevertheless acknowledged that he was no crusading altruist, plundering the rich infidel to sustain the Christian poor. These pirates fell on defenceless coastal villages, killed or enslaved the men and women, plundered their meagre possessions, left orphans destitute. Having known poverty herself, she had sympathy for her husband's poor victims, and her implicit acknowledgement that his fate contained an element of nemesis gives an Aeschylean echo to these simple and unaffected verses:

> Though Koúkos crowed upon the heights
> And others ruled the villages,
> The seas belonged to Nicholas.
> Four brothers lived but owned no fields
> Yet I possessed a piece of land

And sowed and reaped and harvested
And I was really someone here.
I took some piastres in my hand
And visited the village store
And bought a blouse, a gown and shawl,
And wearing them I watched the seas
To wait for Nicholas to come.
For he had gone for piracy
Though I had begged him on my knees,
'O dearest Captain Nicholas,
Sail not again to Turkish lands
To strip the poor, take goods and slaves
And leave poor orphans destitute,'
But never would he hear my pleas.
He called his sailors, manned his ship
And boldly sailed to Turkish lands
And set about his pirate raids.
And then one day, one Sunday morn,
A holy day, a Christian feast,
I changed my clothes, put on my best
And wore my lovely *vláchiko*,
My sweeping dress agleam with gold.
I went to church and made my cross
And when the priest had finished prayers
And all the congregation left,
I sat outside to be admired
And felt the stares of jealous eyes
That took me in from head to toe.
And then I started up for home,
And sat upon my window-seat
And had my little girl with me
And washed and combed her pretty hair,
And then I took the telescope
And looked ahead far out to sea
And suddenly I saw a sail
Just rounding Cape Mavróspelio
And thought it looked like one of ours.
But as it neared the land I saw
The oars were black, and black the sails,
No flag was raised, no cannon boomed,

But silently the ship came in
And anchored by the shore below.
At once I feared for Nicholas,
I pushed aside my little girl
And down I ran to where I found
A crowd of men beside the quay,
Some wounded, missing eyes or legs,
But nowhere saw I Nicholas.
I greeted them, and they replied
'We greet you, Madame Nicholas.'
'But where is *he*?' I cried aloud,
'Where is your Captain Nicholas?'
They all looked down except for one,
My husband's brother, who replied
'We found a ship, a Turkish ship,
A bigger boat than ours by far
With mighty guns that blasted us.
The infidels, the filthy dogs,
They blasted him right overboard,
And day turned black for Nicholas.'
'O Nicholas,' I cried in grief,
'You were to blame, my one-eyed lord.
I begged, implored, with all my heart,
I begged you not to go again
To ravage homes and rob the poor,
For I was poor once too, you know,
Until God willed I should become
A Captain's wife, a Sássaris,
First lady here in Mézapos.
But consolation must I find –
My husband's brother's still alive,
To sit upon the golden stool
And take the keys of Nicholas
And hold now all the honours here.
And still I have my little girl
Who now, poor soul, is all alone,
And I am still a housewife fair
Among the Sássaris estates.'
Then answered straight my brother-in-law,
'What can I say, my little bride,

> I wish these honours were not mine,
> These honours and this great regret.
> There's nought I want but Nicholas,
> The first of brothers, and the best,
> Now lost to us for evermore.'

Mézapos today has the melancholy air of a mistress grown old, neglected now and poor but full of memories of a glittering, exciting and rather wicked past. Not long ago two steamers put in every week from Piraeus to take on board the local produce and unload everything from Yardley's soaps to pruning-hooks for the three big stores that served the whole area, but with the opening of a motor-road down the peninsula Mézapos has suffered even greater depopulation than the rest of Inner Mani. The steamers call no longer, the deep-water harbour shelters only a few fishing boats or the occasional yacht, and the village is too far off the beaten track to have responded rapidly to the new industry of tourism. But reminders of the past are everywhere, and not only in the form of material remains.

María Sássaris keeps the tiny café at the top of the steep little street that leads down to the quay. As usual in Mani most of the young generation have left to seek their fortunes in Athens or America; and if you ask old María about the many photographs on her walls, she will tell you proudly of her eight children, the boys now doing famously as doctors, businessmen or officers in the forces, the girls well married with affluent families. Nor is it surprising that the Maniátes are bright and go-ahead. Generations of struggling to snatch an independent living from Mani's barren land and dangerous seas have sharpened their wits to a degree that makes these people very different from the dull agriculturalists of the richer farming areas where life and thought are slow and unimaginative.

Mani's relative independence attracted men of independent spirit, and the law of the survival of the fittest developed brain as well as brawn. War too is in their blood, and a disproportionately large number of officers in the Greek Air Force are in fact Maniátes – typically attracted to the fastest and most exciting craft of modern warfare just as their seafaring ancestors delighted in the danger and speed of their rakish *trattas*. Or if they go into business, these Maniáte Captains of Industry have the same cut-throat ambition and aggression of the pirate captains whose genes they have inherited.

A typical ancestor, besides Nicholas, was Michael Sássaris, another famous head of the clan whose cracked tower still stands at Mézapos in silent witness of his determination to defend his local independence and, indirectly, of the difficulties of incorporating the feudal society of Mani into a modern nation-state after independence. Yermanós Mavromichális of the great family of Liméni, being well in with the royal government, was trying to get control of other harbours of Deep Mani by constructing forts near them, but when he sent his men to build one near Mézapos, they found that the Government's writ carried little weight with Michael Sássaris and his followers:

> 'What need we tell you, Sássaris?
> We've all been sent by Yermanós
> To whom permission granted is
> By Government Authority
> To build a tower here at Kabí.'
> 'Just tell this much to Yermanós
> That while Michális lives and breathes
> He cannot build his precious tower!
> Take crow-bars now and ply your picks
> And smash this work to smithereens,
> For while Michális lives and breathes,
> He'll not set foot at Mézapos!'

Mavromichális' men did their best to carry out their orders but eventually they had to report to Liméni that every time they completed the foundations, the Sassárians emerged at night and destroyed them. Old Petróbey Mavromichális was furious, and when an armed cutter happened to tie up in Liméni harbour, he approached its Captain Tsikákos and offered him 250 gold pounds to go and coerce Sássaris by destroying the family tower. Tsikákos agreed, sailed down to Mézapos and opened fire, but though he scored a direct hit on the Sássaris tower and cracked its walls, he failed to silence its cannons. Tsikákos had his ship blown from under his feet, and with it sank Mavromichális' hopes of gaining control of Mézapos.

The battered tower is easily recognizable above some disused salt-pans by the sea to the north of the harbour, and when we last visited it we met a little old lady in black who emerged from one of the tiny houses nearby and turned out to be another Sássaris. Her name was Zacharoúla, 'Little Sweetie', and pointing up the stony valley behind she told us proudly that her husband, George Sássaris, was buried there. At first we could not understand where she meant, but as so often in Mani what looked from a distance like a rough shepherd's hut turned out to be a church, this time St Basil's and the Sássaris family chapel. The sick old man had been taken to hospital in Athens, but when he knew he was dying he begged to be laid to rest among the bones of his ancestors in this little frescoed church which overlooks Michael's tower, the great bay, and the long, thin peninsula of Tigáni that forms its western edge.

From Mézapos harbour it is possible to get a young Sássaris to take you the 2 kilometres across to Tigáni in his fishing boat. (See Plate 24.) The negotiation will be brisk and laconic. If he likes you, he will take you. If he doesn't, he won't, and vast largess will be regarded more with contempt than favour. Our Sássaris was a strong and fine-featured man of about thirty-five, with a look of almost aristocratic cruelty about his mouth and a mahogany skin betokening the African blood that runs in so many Maniáte veins. And his extremely beautiful wife was even more African in appearance. Besides the dark complexion she had full lips, a flattened nose and a totally un-Greek elegance of movement that were inherited perhaps from one of Ibrahím Pashá's Sudanese troops in the War of Independence, or from a pretty captive saved from the seraglio by one of the Sássaris pirate ancestors.

The handle of the 'frying-pan', which is the meaning of Tigáni, stretches nearly a kilometre out to sea before expanding into a great crag crowned with ancient and medieval fortifications. And whether or not you can persuade a Sássaris to take you across the bay in a boat to the base of the crag, the gruelling journey overland should not be missed by those fit enough to undertake it. The starting point is the little acropolis of Áyia Kiriakí, a deserted hamlet perched high on a conical hill like a Puy inland of where Tigáni joins the mainland – the hand that holds the frying-pan. A stiff walk for 2 kilometres along the cliffs will take you there from Mézapos, but it is easier to go by car by driving back from Mézapos to the main road, going a little further south towards Kítta, then turning west again on the side-road to Psíon and then Stavrí, a semi-circular journey of some 5 kilometres. From Stavrí a cart-track leads northwards for about 750 metres to Áyia Kiriakí and a most splendid panorama from the little white church at the top.

Inland the towers of Kítta and lesser villages gleam white across the cultivated plateau against the background of Mani's mountainous spine and the two saintly peaks of Áyia Pelayía and Áyii Asómati. Almost due east lies Mézapos, the little town nestling at the corner of its bay where the coast turns northward and gradually disappears in the haze, except on a few unusually clear days when the snow-capped peaks of the Pentadáktilos are visible behind Ítilon some 20 kilometres away. Tigáni juts out into the sea to the north-west, but the coastline below it falls back south-westward to the Lion's Head, the great crag that guards the northern end of Cávo Grósso and rises to nearly 300 metres above sea-level. In every direction the views are magnificent, and whatever powers held the castle at the end of Tigáni will not have failed to post sentinels and signallers on Áyia Kiriakí.

Our 2 kilometre hike to the castle begins at the south-western foot of Áyia Kiriakí. With the steep slopes of the little acropolis rising on our right in a tangle of prickly pear we walk north-west for about twenty minutes through rough stony fields until we meet an ancient carriage-road some 2 metres wide, its white stones overgrown with tiny shrubs almost like moss. In spring the whole area is heavy with the scent of herbs, and even as late as June there are clumps of colour among the rocks – tiny pincushions of pink or the taller yellow-flowering sages with their beautiful silver leaves. As we walk on, the coastline to our left falls away behind us to the south-west in cliffs some 150 metres high with a narrow step breaking their near verticality. We are now approaching the western edge of the peninsula's shoulder, and when we reach a ruined dry-stone chapel on the cliff-edge, Tigáni lies before us like a long arm ending in a great, clenched fist. (See Plate 23.) The arm is flat and white, its bleached rocks rising only 5 to 10 metres above sea-level, and it narrows to about 150 metres before the great crag at its extremity. The path descends steeply now, and once down at sea-level we have to pick our way across a surface of such sharp and jagged rocks that some giant fakir might have used it for a bed of mortification: they will slash any but the toughest boots to ribbons, and the carriage-road that led to the castle has been eroded long since. And yet bare-footed salt-gatherers worked here until recently, sleeping rough in a big cave down the coast and collecting salt from the square rock-cut pans that are now disused and rapidly weathering into fantastic shapes.

Some 500 metres ahead the fortified crag looms dark and forbidding in the evening light, its natural defences reinforced by ramparts and two great towers on the landward side. The entrance is by the cliff-edge at the south-east corner, dominated by the best preserved of the towers and leading up to the summit by a steep staircase carved from the rock. The Sassárians told us to look for a hoof-print on one of the steps, and it is still there to show where a defeated princess leapt on horseback into the sea to escape capture by the conqueror of her castle. But when we emerge at the top, we find it hard to see how this great fortress could ever have been conquered. Some two-thirds of its circumference are protected by virtually unscalable cliffs plunging almost sheer more than 30 metres into the sea, and even so they are reinforced by walls and turrets, some actually built out of the cliff-face itself and visible only from the sea. And though the cliffs are not so high on the landward side, they are more heavily fortified with medieval walls. Indeed its only weakness, as with the similarly situated castle of Monemvasía, is the lack of fresh water, but the enclosed area is similarly honeycombed with cisterns to collect rain-water, and it would have needed a very long siege in the heat of summer to compel surrender even on that score.

To visit this remote crag and remain unexcited would be possible only for the dullest and most unimaginative of men. Even if there had been no human occupation, the scenery is dramatic – the narrow white promontory leading back to Áyia Kiriakí, the bay of Mézapos on the south-eastern side, and the Lion's Head of Cávo Grósso to the south-west. As it is, there are the ruins of a great medieval power centre, not only the walls, ramparts, towers and turrets of the 750 metre perimeter but also ruined barracks and houses within, crumbling arches, great cisterns, and in the very centre the remains of a large Byzantine church, which is one of the largest and possibly earliest churches in Mani.

This church was recently excavated by Professor Drandákis of Athens University, and its main body is now clearly revealed as a rectangle some 22 metres east-west by 15 metres north-south, the east-end terminating in three apses which are semi-circular on the inside but semi-hexagonal on the outside: the central apse has an internal diameter of about 5 metres, the others of 2 metres. But the walls are not particularly thick for so large a church, and its roof, or the greater part of it, is more likely to have been of wood than stone. Many column bases remain along with some broken columns, some fine fragments of sculptured marble, and even some frescoed plaster on the waist-high sections of walls that have been uncovered at the western end. And many more pieces of marble have been carried away for use in more recent churches: identical column bases form the altars of the church on the quay at Mézapos and of St Nicholas' at Stavrí, which also has a piece of Tigáni's marble screen in its walls. Some of the designs suggest work of the eighth or ninth centuries, but other features are not earlier than the thirteenth, and it is hard to give a date for the original foundation since the three-apsed basilica of this type is known in Bulgaria as early as the sixth century and in Sparta as late as the tenth. The most that can be said with confidence about its date is that it was in existence at least as early as the ninth century, and to judge from its impressive proportions it could well have been the cathedral for the Byzantine bishopric of Mani recorded for the time of Emperor Leo the Wise (AD 886–912) in the list composed for him by Patriarch Nicholas the Mystic.

But Tigáni's history goes back much further than the Christian era. A cross-wall some 2 metres thick at the south-western corner is typical 'Cyclopean' masonry of the Greek Bronze Age and could well belong to the thirteenth century BC, as could some of the great blocks in the base of the medieval rampart's central tower. Admittedly no pottery has yet been found to confirm this dating, but there is no room for doubt that there was Bronze Age occupation on this coast or that the Mézapos area contained a power centre: Late Bronze Age pottery has been found at ancient Hippola on the ridge of Cávo Grósso, and Mézapos derives from 'dove-haunted Messe' which Homer lists among the towns contributing to Menelaus' contingent in the Trojan War. And if it is possible that Tigáni was the citadel of

Bronze Age Messe, it could also have been one of the last bastions of the Achaean Greeks against the Dorian invaders who swept down into the Peloponnese and destroyed the 'Mycenaean' civilization in the twelfth century BC.

Whether Tigáni was continuously occupied, or occupied at all, in the two millennia that separated the Cyclopean walls and the Christian basilica is unknown. Pausanias recorded 'the town and harbour of Messa' in the second century AD, but we cannot be sure that this was on Tigáni itself. On the other hand the existence of a virtually impregnable crag alongside a bay with a deep, safe harbour creates a westward-facing Monemvasía that has obvious attractions to a power whose base is overseas. When therefore Procopius tells us that the Emperor Justinian inaugurated a crash programme of fortification of the Peloponnese in the sixth century, it is possible that Tigáni was one of his castles, even though we cannot yet be sure that the great church dates back before the ninth century.

But what of the medieval fortifications that still cover the site and reinforce the natural defences with walls and towers? Are they Frankish or Venetian? Or both? Is Tigáni the site of the Castle of Maina built by William of Villehardouin, Prince of Achaea, and ceded to Byzantium along with Mistrá and Monemvasía in 1261? It seems very likely that it was, despite the rival claims of Kástro tís Oriás which we have yet to visit on the ridge of Cávo Grósso. But whether William's great castle was here or not, it is likely that the two-headed eagle of the house of Palaeológus fluttered over Tigáni and its great church in the thirteenth century, and when the last great era of Byzantium had passed and the Peloponnese became a battleground for Turks and Venetians, it is no less likely that the Lion of St Mark claimed this Maniáte Monemvasía for the Republic more than once in the fifteenth century.

If Tigáni is ever to reveal its secrets, much more digging will have to be done both on the site itself and in the medieval records of many libraries. At present it remains a tantalizing mystery, though what it lacks in hard fact is more than made up for by a great encrustation of folk-lore and legends of which the ballad of Mavroeidís and Cháros is a good example. Cháros is Death, the ancient ferryman of the Styx metamorphosed into a great Black Knight in medieval legend. Greek popular ballads are full of his battles with Mavroeidís, the 'Dark-formed' – an epithet of Digenís Akrítas whose name is still a byword for patriotic heroism today among those who have no more knowledge of his origins than of the lives of most of their saints. Indeed many a Cypriot asked to identify Digenís will say 'General Grivas' without realizing that the name goes back a thousand years to the eastern frontiers of the Byzantine Empire. Digenís Akrítas, meaning literally 'He of double birth on the frontier', was the son of a Saracenic emir of Syria and a daughter of the Doúkas family whose castle he had stormed. This hybrid product of a Moslem father and Christian mother became a great hero of the frontier, and though the original Digenís epic is lost, the tale as told in the sixteenth century was revealed by a manuscript discovered at Trebizond in the latter part of the last century. It is an almost Arthurian romance, and among its stories of chivalry and great exploits against the wild beasts and brigands of the frontier there is a description of the great palace and garden that the hero built for himself and his bride on the banks of the River Euphrates. But the Maniátes know better than to believe this. It was on Tigáni that Digenís built the castle for his princess – do they not have her horse's hoof-print to prove it? – and it was here that he fought Cháros for her life:

> My God, but what became of them,
>   The castle's heroes brave,
> Whose names adorn no wedding-song,
>   Nor share in death's sad dirge,
> The men who went to rob and spoil
>   The castle of a king,
> Whose daughter, ever beautiful,
>   Had dark and lustrous eyes?
> The girl enthralled Mavroeidís
>   Who wished her for his bride,
> And so they sailed and captured her
>   And carried her aboard,
> And casting off they sailed away
>   To far-off Mani's shores.
> And finding there an arm of rock
>   Extending far to sea,
> With wave-lashed cliffs and gloomy caves

And water black as pitch,
They built upon Tigáni's crown
　　A castle of their own.
They brought from France both iron and steel,
　　From Venice glass and pearls,
And marble from Byzantium,
　　And sacred fish of gold,
And raised aloft a tower of glass
　　To keep the girl apart,
And set a guard by night and day
　　To keep their princess safe.
And when their castle stood complete
　　They locked and barred the gates,
But Cháros came, that dreaded lord,
　　The blackest knight of all,
In fatal search to find the girl
　　And take her for his own.
He hailed them first from far away,
　　He hailed them twice from near:
'My greetings, all,' he cried aloud,
　　'Success be yours in war!'
And they returned his fair address—
　　'Your lordship's welcome here.
Come sit with us and drink and dine
　　And rest yourself awhile,
And tell us, Cháros, whence you came
　　And whither you are bound.'
'I came not here for food and drink
　　Nor yet to rest awhile,
I came but for the fair princess
　　To take her for my own.'
'The girl is in her tower of glass,
　　She loves Mavroeidís,
And never shall we give her up
　　Nor shall she captured be,
While stand these mighty castle-walls
　　And men both strong and brave.'
Then Cháros, hearing this, grew hot
　　And shouted loud and clear—
'A sword of steel, a belt of iron,

A chest of marble strong,
Who has these things and courage bold
   To beat me all alone?'
Mavroeidís this challenge heard
   From high upon the tower,
And waxing wroth at such offence
   He put the girl aside,
And running down with angry heart
   He gave his bold reply –
'A sword of steel, a belt of iron,
   A chest of marble strong,
These things I have and courage bold
   To beat you all alone.
Come, Cháros, if you have the strength,
   If you are really brave,
Come, let us fight and show our worth
   Upon my threshing-floor,
This floor whose base is solid iron
   Whose walls are steel all round.'
With seven blows Mavroeidís
   Beat Cháros as they fought,
And seven times great Cháros reeled,
   But then, in anger roused,
He summoned all his mighty strength
   And smashed the young man's sword,
And seizing then his flowing locks
   He flung him helpless down.
'Enough, great Cháros, *pax* I pray,'
   Cried bold Mavroeidís,
'I bravely fought but now disarmed
   I taste the vanquished's gall,
And wish no more to spend my life
   In this the upper world.
So show me now your own dark road
   And I shall bring the girl.'
Then Cháros mocked him cruelly
   And taunted him with scorn –
'Your sword of steel, your belt of iron,
   Your chest of marble strong,
They lie, it seems, with all your boasts

Upon your threshing-floor.
But bring the girl, and quickly now,
   And you shall follow me
Along my dark and seaward path
   And never look behind.
Upon yon mountain fix your eyes
   And on the cape below,
Whose cliffs and caves the stormy seas
   Will never cease to flay,
And when you reach the rocky edge
   And start the steep descent,
You'll find my cave, grim Hades' gate,
   The door to worlds below,
And when you see its gaping hole,
   You'll soon regret your haste
To feel the dark and icy halls,
   The curtains spiders spin,
The walls of bones, the roof all hung
   With maidens' tresses shorn.'

Without wishing to follow Cháros' directions too exactly it is worth trying to persuade a Sássaris to take you right round to Yerolimín, which is only 6 kilometres due south of Mézapos in a straight line but 12 kilometres by sea round the great cape. It would probably mean starting at first light, for even on calm days the wind often gets up in the afternoon and the Sássaris will not want to be marooned at Yerolimín overnight. Rounding Tigáni under almost sheer cliffs crowned with fortifications some 30 metres above your head reveals the natural impregnability of its seaward side, but even so there is one turret sticking like a limpet to the cliff-face about 5 metres from the top. Then after creeping southwards along the western side of the panhandle we are under the cliffs of the coastline which recedes south-west, and with a last look over our left shoulder to Áyia Kiriakí we are heading for the Lion's Head. The cliffs now rise to about 100 metres, with a natural step running horizontally about half way up, along which a tiny track creeps from below Áyia Kiriakí to a white blob that turns out to be a church perched fantastically on the ledge – the Church of Odiyítria, 'Our Lady Who Shows the Way'. (See Plate 25.) We could have reached it on foot from the same starting point as for our walk down to Tigáni, and once seen from the sea it demands and rewards the difficult walk to investigate it, for the faith that built such a church in such a place is not far removed from that which moves mountains. It is not, as one would expect, the rough shelter of some eccentric hermit, but a fine thirteenth-century cruciform church with dome and narthex, with an elegant marble arch over the entrance to the sanctuary, handsome column-capitals and the remains of beautiful frescoes of two periods. There is an eighteenth-century Virgin Glikofiloúsa, the Mother kissing the Christ-child with a natural tenderness that is unusually affecting. And there are several much earlier ones, possibly of the same century as the church itself, including Christ carrying his cross and the Ascension. But most striking of all is the Archangel Michael wearing the magnificent imperial robes of Byzantium. (See Plate 26.) There are more elegant St Michaels of similarly early date in other churches in the area, but what this one lacks in elegance of feature he more than makes up for in the lively expressiveness of his wide face with its bent nose and big eyes. For this is no heavenly bureaucrat or armchair general but a real leader of the Host who has fought manfully against the powers of evil in a harsh world.

Beyond Odiyítria the cliffs are as full of holes as a ripe Gruyère, and as we sail close in under them we can see that many have been walled up despite their inaccessibility to any but a skilled rock-climber. These are the treasuries of Sássaris' pirate ancestors, and they are so stained with the miasma of ancient blood and crime that the local people will not go near them even today. What is in them we cannot say, and it remains for more agile foreigners with ropes and better heads for heights to explore their secrets and risk pollution from the blood of ill-gotten wealth.

As we approach the Lion's Head with its massive wall of rock that we shall have to round before going south, the cliffs on our left have less verticality before sloping upwards at a more gentle angle that allows vegetation to grow on them, but there is no external indication that the corner holds a tiny natural harbour from which a steep donkey track leads up a valley to the plateau above. Even when Sássaris steers for it, the entrance to Mezalímonas is so well concealed that we seem bent on destruction until we suddenly find ourselves in it and looking up at the ancient wooden cranes that can lift a boat out of the water and moor it safely in mid-air. (See Plate 27.) They can also lift heavy cargoes, and it would be tactless to inquire too closely what manner of catches are landed here on moonless nights while a string of panniered donkeys waits patiently above.

Leaving Mezalímonas and creeping round the base of Lion's Head is a rather sinister experience. The cliff wall is over 250 metres high, and there is the uncomfortable sensation of an equal depth of water below. The ledges in the cliff-face seem scarcely wide enough to carry the few tufts of vegetation and sea-birds' nests that cling to them, yet here too, at dizzy heights, natural holes have been walled up by pirates in positions that could be reached only by ropes from the top. And once round the point another architectural surprise awaits us about a kilometre down the precipitous west-facing coastline that now runs due south for about 6 kilometres. About 150 metres up the red cliff-face, and perhaps 70 metres from the top, a small black aperture with a white surround stares blindly across the Messenian Gulf like an icon's gouged-out eye. Through binoculars the pupil is revealed as a square doorway in the mouth of a walled-up cave, but this is a priest's, not a pirate's, lair. An embrasure above the door is in the shape of a cross. A wooden cross protrudes from a rock nearby, and a small bell still hangs from the branch of a solitary tree clinging precariously to the cliff-face. This is the Church of the Virgin Eleoússa, 'Our Lady of Compassion'. (See Plate 28.) In terms of inaccessibility it rivals the aerial monasteries of the Metéora, yet a solitary monk not only built a church here but made it his home and lived here almost like a stylite, except that what he needed to sustain life could be lowered down from above as well as drawn up from below.

To climb down from the cliff-top without ropes needed more nerve and skill than we possessed, but on a calm day a Sássaris took us to the foot of the cliffs in a small boat and we managed the longer but less difficult climb up from there, though the return was less comfortable when we had to look down. By the time we reached the cave our waiting boat had telescoped to the size of a cork bobbing gently on the swell, and we were glad to get inside the church, which turned out to be surprisingly large and little changed from when the hermit had been alive. As his home as well as church it contained a rather melancholy mixture of things sacred and utilitarian. Several icons still hung from the smoke-blackened iconostasis among lamps and censers and the graffiti of some Communist guerillas who hid there in the 1940s. And his simple possessions still littered the floor – a small table and stool, a worm-eaten chest containing bible and breviary, and a few clumsy storage jars, pots and pans. There was no water supply except rain, but he had contrived to dig cisterns out of the rock outside and the storms filled his jars. For food he relied on baskets lowered to him by local villagers from the cliffs above, or the odd loaf and a few fishes thrown on the rocks below by a passing fisherman. Thus he lived and prayed, for many more years than anyone could remember; and when he felt his time had come, he lay down in the grave he had already excavated for himself from the rocks and died as he had lived, quite alone. He was buried, so it is said, by the red earth washed down by the winter storms, and no hand was needed to toll the bell that hung from the gale-lashed tree. His grave is still there with its crumbling wooden cross and the bell still hangs from the tree, but the tree died with him and only its leafless skeleton remains.

From Áyia Eleoússa the coastline runs due south for another 5 kilometres before rounding the southern point of Cávo Grósso and turning north-east to form the bay and harbour of Yerolimín. For the greater part of that distance its cliffs are supporting a high, narrow plateau fluctuating between 200 metres and 300 metres above sea-level and with a similar width, the widest and highest section being at the southern end. The landward cliffs are between 40 metres and 70 metres above the lower plateau, and they are climbable by several steep paths, particularly from behind the villages of Kipoúla at the northern end, Koúnos in the middle and Drí in the south. In spring there is enough vegetation on the top for flocks and bullocks to be driven up to eat it, but by the end of May its rock-covered surface has been burnt bare of anything more nourishing than the wire-netting spurges. There are no sources of fresh water, and walking is about as comfortable as on Tigáni's jagged promontory. And yet there are not only seven churches lining the eastern ridge but evidence of an extraordinary amount of building in both ancient and medieval times, including several deep cisterns, as on Tigáni, to collect and store the precious rainwater.

The best place to start is behind Kipoúla, where a winding track eventually reaches the top of the ridge up a flight of broad stairs carved out of the cliffs between high rock walls. It emerges near the two most northerly of the line of churches, which are the only two not in total ruin: St George's and St Theodore's. They are both disused except by the animals who take shelter in them, but St Theodore's has some fine carved marbles, the remains of several layers of frescoes, and two elegantly fluted marble columns flanking the doorway through the screen into the sanctuary. These could well have come from the temple of Athena Hippolaitis which Pausanias mentioned at the town of Hippola in the second century AD, for there is little room for doubt that this is the site of ancient Hippola. The name is preserved in that of the modern village of Kipoúla below, and much ancient pottery has been found here, not only from classical times but from the Bronze Age too. And though Hippola was evidently deserted by Pausanias' time, the piles of stones from medieval and more recent structures indicate that it was sooner or later reoccupied.

But why was so inhospitable a place ever inhabited at all – a place bitterly cold in the winter, baked by the summer sun, lashed by gales all year round, and devoid of fresh water? Admittedly the views from up here are magnificent and its height brings temples and churches nearer heaven, but we can hardly populate a whole settlement with ascetic aesthetes. The answer can only be security. The inhabitants of Hippola will have owned and tilled the land below, but the only safety for themselves and their possessions was on the ridge above, where they built not only houses and places of worship but deep cisterns to provide themselves with water. And with their panoramic view both inland and over the Messenian Gulf they will have run little danger of being taken unawares by land- or sea-borne enemies and having no time to take their flocks as well as themselves to the safety of their cliff-top defences.

This ridge is also one of Tigáni's rival claimants to the site of the medieval castle of Great Maina, either here at ancient Hippola or on the highest part of the ridge near its southern

35. St Nicholas's, Ochiá (12th century)

36. Towards Matapán from Cávo Grósso

37. The Mantoúvalos tower, Boularií

38. St Michael's, Boularií (11th century)

39. The Healing of a paralytic and the Ascension (12th century)

40. St Pantaleïmon's, Boularií (10th century)

41. The east end and St Pantaleïmon

42. Cape Matapán from Koroyiánika

43. Váthia

44. St Peter's, Kipárissos

45. Stele honouring Julia Domna

46. Áyii Asómati, Ténaron

47. Láyia

48. Pírgi

49. Flomochóri and the Sunward Coast

50. The Mavromicháles at Vérga

end, due west of the village of Drí, where it rises to a height of 309 metres above sea-level in two conical hills joined by a narrow saddle. The northern one, which has a triangulation point, shows no sign of human occupation, but the southern has a ruined, single-cell church built of big, rough-hewn stones with a large marble slab forming the lintel of its low door (which is in the south wall) and inside the base and feet of what was evidently a large ancient statue, though the inscription on the base is unfortunately illegible. A few other remains there could also be medieval and the area rejoices in the name of 'Kástro tís Oriás', though the 'Beautiful One' whose castle is supposed to have been there was not Prince William of Achaea but the ubiquitous Helen of Sparta and subsequently of Troy. But there are no remains comparable to Tigáni's great fortifications, and while it is true that the Franks as a land-based power might not have been as concerned with the maritime importance of Tigáni as the Byzantines, the latter remains the most likely candidate for the main power centre of both in this region, though probably the Franks at least installed a garrison on this ridge too.

To walk the full 5 kilometres along the ridge you need about four hours, strong boots and a sharp eye for sherds and snakes, and even if the surface had been barren of archaeological interest the hike would be worthwhile for the splendid views. The landward view is as good as an aerial photograph for pinpointing some of the more southerly villages, almost all of them with at least one Byzantine church worth visiting, but it is one thing to pinpoint them from above and quite another actually to find them through the maze of little roads and unmarked cart-tracks. All the same, there are a few that are not to be missed and are well worth getting lost for before leaving the Cávo Grósso.

Beginning at the northern end the first and quintessential is Episkopí, a beautiful twelfth-century church in a spectacular position overlooking Mézapos Bay. It can be walked to in about half an hour from Mézapos village along the steep mule track that climbs along the cliffs towards Áyia Kiriakí (from where we first spotted the church); but it is more easily reached by driving back to the main road to Kítta, turning right towards Stavrí about 2 kilometres before Kítta (as on our visit to Áyia Kiriakí

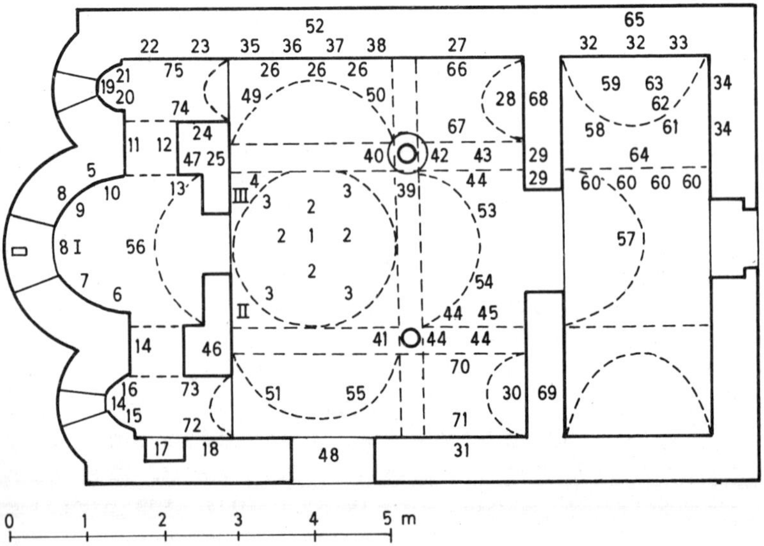

52
65
22 23 35 36 37 38 27 32 32 33
75 26 26 26 66
21 19 20 74 49 50 28 68 59 63 62 34
24 67 58 61 34
11 12 47 25 40 42 43 29 64
5 13 4 44 29 60 60 60 60
8 10 III 3 2 3 39 53
9
8 I 56 2 1 2 57
2 54
7 6 3 3
II 44 45
14 46 41 44 44
70
16 73 51 55 30 69
14 15 72 71
17 18 48 31
0 1 2 3 4 5 m

The wall-paintings of the Church of Episkopí

(The arabic numerals refer to the paintings of the twelfth century,
the roman to those of the eighteenth century.)

1. Christ Pantocrator
2. Angels
3. Prophets
4. St Matthew
5. St Leo the Great
6. St Gregory
7. St John Chrysostom
8. Hierarch
9. St Basil
10. St Nicholas
11. St Euplus
12. St Eleutherius (?)
13. St Luke of Stiria
14. Saint
15. St Gregory of Nyssa
16. Hierarch
17. St Blaise (?)
18. St Clement of Ancyra
19. St Theodosius
20. St Polycarp
21. Hierarch
22. St Gregory of Agrigentum
23. St John the Almsgiver
24. St Romanus the Melodist
25. Christ the Mediator
26. Military saints
27. The Archangel Gabriel
28. St Procopius
29. SS Cosmas and Damian
30. Saint
31. The Archangel Michael
32. Hierarchs
33. St Alexander
34. Female saints
35. Saint
36. St Gurias
37. Saint
38. St Abibus
39. St Mennas
40. St Simeon
41. St Simeon Stylites
42. St Cyrus of Alexandria
43. St John of Alexandria
44. Saints
45. St Victor
46. The Holy Mandilion
47. The Holy Tile

Narrative scenes from the life of
Christ and the Dodekáorton
48. The Annunciation
49. The Nativity
50. The Presentation in the Temple
51. The Transfiguration
52. The Healing of a blind man
53. The Entry into Jerusalem
54. The Deposition from the Cross
55. The Descent into Hell (Resurrection)
56. The Ascension

Scenes from the Last Judgement
57. The Second Coming
58. Simon the Apostle
59. Philip the Apostle
60. Apostles
61. The Unsleeping Worm
62. The Unquenchable Fire
63. Gnashing of teeth
64. Fishes giving up corpses
65. Hades presiding over torments

Narrative scenes from the cycle of St George
66. The distribution of his wealth
67. Teaching in prison
68. The raising of the ox
69. The raising of a dead man
70. Before the Governor (Dacianus)
71. The destruction of the idols
72. The martyrdom of the stone
73. The beheading
74. St George appearing to Theopistus in a dream
75. The feast of Theopistus

I The Virgin Mary
II The Virgin and Child
III Christ

and Tigáni), but turning right again after about 1½ kilometres to Áyios Yeóryios and continuing through that tiny hamlet until the road peters out by two tall, deserted towers known locally as the Kolóspita. A stony path passes between them and begins to descend the slope between two stone walls overhung with prickly pears. The bay stretches out to the right with Áyia Kiriakí straight ahead in the distance and the long arm of Tigáni projecting from its side. Where the path diverges we keep left, and suddenly round a corner, only about 100 metres from where we left the car, we almost stand on the orange-tiled dome of Episkopí nestling in its hollow in the hillside. (See Plate 29.)

The track descends steeply by the seaward side, bringing us to eye-level first with the dome, then the roof, then the north door. The church is cruciform with narthex, about 9 metres long by 6 metres wide, and though its exterior lacks the elaborate cloisonné masonry of St Barbara's or Tourlotí, it has elegant marble pieces between the arches of the octagonal dome, lion's-head gutters, and beautifully tiled roofs which show the care lavished on it by the Committee of Byzantine Antiquities of Mistrá – a happy contrast, as is Tourlotí, with the appalling dilapidation of so many other deserving churches. It is all the more surprising therefore to find the west door fastened by a bit of string tied to a rusty nail. Has the Committee of Byzantine Antiquities lost interest now that Episkopí's beautiful frescoes have been published in the learned journals? Is it really too much to expect that all their labours should not be wasted? Or must these frescoes too be vandalized by antique-grabbers until the church is again fit only for sheltering donkeys and sheep?

Perhaps the terrifying Last Judgement on the ceiling of the narthex is expected to act as a deterrent to any evilly intentioned visitor entering the west door. Saints and hierarchs line the lower part of the walls, but above them on the eastern wall of the south side the apostles Simon and Philip sit enthroned in judgement, their expressive faces watching with horrified compassion the scenes of damnation opposite – women of easy virtue being devoured by serpents among the flames, great gnashings of teeth and the Unsleeping Worm. (See Plate 30b.) But Hades has no compassion: he presides grim-faced and remorseless over the false kings and bishops who writhe in a sea of unquenchable fire on the southern wall while he rides his dragon triumphantly over them.

The cruciform nave is distyle, its two columns having fine Ionic capitals, its marble cross-beams nicely carved. The iconostasis is modern with frescoes of the eighteenth century – a Virgin and Child to the left of the entrance to the sanctuary, Christ enthroned to the right – but its fine marble architrave is old and extremely unusual, a feature of early Christian churches that had largely disappeared by the Byzantine period. The Virgin Platytéra and the Christ child who look down from the apse above the altar are also of the eighteenth century, but almost all the other paintings, both in the cross of the nave and in the northern and southern apses, are of twelfth century date like those of the narthex.

Our first glance towards the east end is arrested by three portraits of Christ above the screen – Christ the Mediator and His sacred face imprinted on the Holy Tile and the Mandílion or Holy Handkerchief, the physical repudiations of iconoclasm. Then entering the sanctuary and looking up we can still see much of the Ascension, the disciples clustering in amazement on each side as the angels above them support the risen Christ. In the chambers of the cross we find scenes from the Dodekáorton, notably a fine Nativity (see Plate 30a), the Presentation of Christ in the Temple, the Transfiguration, the Descent into Hell and the Entry into Jerusalem. And on the southern wall we are face to face with a magnificent Gabriel, his clothes depicting the gorgeous opulence of the Byzantine court. But perhaps the most interesting of all are the series of narrative scenes from the Life of St George, which we find divided between the nave and the northern and southern alcoves – the distribution of his wealth, his teaching in prison, his destruction of the idols, his martyrdom by the stone, and the curious feast of Theopistus, the last of which has a very special interest to the historian of Byzantine iconography and hagiology.

Theopistus was a farmer in Cappadocia in the time of Theodosius the Great. One day he lost two oxen while ploughing and begged St George to help him find them, with the promise that he would then slay one of them in gratitude and invite the saint to dinner. But when the oxen were found,

Theopistus regretted his rash promise and slew a kid instead. The saint then appeared to him in a dream and reproached him for his inconstancy, but still Theopistus could not bring himself to slay an ox, and hoped to satisfy the martyr first with a sheep and then a lamb. But the saint was not to be mollified, and after several similar occurrences he became really tough and ordered Theopistus to slaughter all his cattle at once on pain of finding himself, his family and all his property consumed by fire. This time Theopistus obeyed, and calling in paupers and priests to share the feast, he sat chanting through the night as he waited for his martyred guest of honour. Eventually St George appeared in the form of a nobleman with a great train of attendants, and when the feast was over and all the animals had been consumed, he ordered all their bones to be collected together, and blessed them. Immediately the animals were miraculously restored and their number multiplied threefold, whereupon the saint disappeared.

Now depictions of this strange story are by no means unusual, but what makes this one particularly interesting is that it antedates the earliest written source, the Ambrosian codex of the fourteenth century, by well over a century. Until the discovery of these frescoes the earliest representation of the posthumous miracles of St George had been held to be a fifteenth-century icon from the Rogozskij cemetery in Moscow. Episkopí now makes it clear that manuscripts illustrating these traditions must have existed at least as early as the twelfth century.

In the neighbourhood of Episkopí there are two very different churches to be visited on foot, one for the scholar, the other for the poet. The scholar's church can be seen from Episkopí's west door about 500 metres away at an angle of about 30 degrees south of Áyia Kiriakí. To reach it means walking downhill and climbing again in the direction of Stavrí, and it is only as you get near it that a ruined heap of stones resolves itself into the simple single-celled church of St Procopius. But inside there are traces of decoration to electrify the Byzantinologist who has walked there following the gaze of the Sacred Face on the Holy Handkerchief of Episkopí, the relic sent by Christ himself to Abgarus, Prince of Edessa, and carried off to Constantinople by the triumphant John Curcuas in 942. For this justification of iconolatry is staring straight at one of the four known examples of iconoclastic church painting. The ruined church of St Procopius retains traces of its simple decoration with cross motifs and is datable to the first half of the ninth century, the very last period of Iconoclasm.

The poet's church, known as Vlachérna, is almost directly below where we parked the car, midway between the two towers and the sea. The steep descent on disused donkey tracks takes about fifteen minutes to where Vlachérna stands in as melancholy a state as Episkopí before its restoration. Though slightly larger, Vlachérna is of similar date and style to Episkopí, but has no comparable frescoes (at least revealed) and is dreadfully dilapidated. The huge blocks of which it is built make for solidity rather than elegance, and though the arches of its dome are tall and graceful, the tiles have long since come off the top and left a pathetically ridiculous impression, as if Elizabeth I, when old and bald, had appeared at court in a perfect ruff without her wig. And yet the very desolation and melancholy of this neglected church in so beautiful a setting would have stimulated Byron or Shelley to write verses that Burne-Jones would have loved to illustrate. It stands in a glorious wilderness of evergreen oaks and wild flowers rioting all over its graveyard. Nearby is a ruined tower, only two storeys still remaining but with its great vaulted storeroom still intact. And nothing can destroy its magnificent view, which is over the whole bay from Mézapos in the east to Tigáni in the west. (See Plate 31.)

But this trio of churches near Mézapos represents only a tiny fraction of Cávo Grósso's Byzantine churches. To visit all of them even cursorily would take many days, and to describe them adequately would require a whole book in itself. But it is impossible to go down to Yerolimín without seeing at least three more, the first of which is not far from Episkopí at Gardenítsa. The little village is just off the main road to Kítta between the turns to Mézapos and Áyios Yeóryios, and its church of Our Saviour (Áyios Sotíras) dates from the early eleventh century and exemplifies important innovations in church building. It is one of the earliest examples in Mani of the development of the early cruciform plan into the simple distyle. It shows brick in use for the first time, and with it the embedded pattern and cloisonné techniques of which we have already seen developed examples at St Barbara's, Érimos, and at Tourlotí. It has large hewn stones from some ancient building incorporated in its walls, and the 'τ' patterns in which some of them are set are the earliest examples of Kufic letters as a feature of exterior decoration in Mani. It is also one of the only two churches in Mani with a domed porch, a handsomely arched structure that was probably added to the west end in the twelfth century. Indeed the whole church is aesthetically very attractive, particularly when seen from the west against the background of Mt Áyia Pelayía's great barren cone, and it will reward a visit even by those with little interest in the subtleties of Byzantine church architecture. (See Plate 32.)

Our other two churches were ones that we pinpointed from our southern walk down the high coastal ridge of Cávo Grósso – St John's at Kéria and St Nicholas' at Ochiá. Kéria is a tiny hamlet between Ochiá and Koúnos, and not easy to find on the unmarked dirt roads. When you enter a village with a huge cannon barrel lying at the roadside you have entered Drí by almost inevitable mistake, and should ask again. But Kéria, when found, is fascinating. (See Plate 33.) It is a nice example of the complex tetrastyle cruciform type of the thirteenth century, but what makes it exceptional is not so much its architectural plan as the bizarre appearance of its walls, which incorporate an amazing number of ancient marbles and sculptured reliefs in their construction. (See Plate 34.) For while we have seen this phenomenon already, for example the Diophantes inscription in the west wall of St Theodore's at Vámvaka, that was nothing in comparison with St John's, which has over a dozen pieces, some very large, set into its south and west walls. They are both ancient and Byzantine, the former providing a physical parallel to Christianity's adaptable incorporation of pagan cults in its hagiology. There are exquisitely carved panels with scrolls or floral cross motifs, obviously from the iconostases of earlier churches. There is a tiny plaque of a man with his dog in the top right corner of the west wall; a similar one of a horseman to the left of the door; and to the right a huge horizontally placed tombstone featuring two men and two women clasping hands. (See Plate 34.) But curiously, though the church itself is nicely proportioned, little thought was given to achieving a symmetrical arrangement of these miscellaneous marbles. They seem to have been regarded simply as useful building materials, and incorporated more or less willy-nilly as they came to hand.

Ochiá is only about a kilometre south of Kéria, and St Nicholas' is immediately recognizable standing by itself in open country in the shadow of a great campanile that rivals St Michael's at Areópolis – a square tower three storeys high with a pyramidal roof. The church itself was built in the twelfth century, the campanile only in 1861, but their stylistic incongruity seems only to enhance them both. In design and masonic technique St Nicholas' is very similar to Our Saviour's at Gardenítsa, and though there are one or two interesting peculiarities like the Gothic gargoyles that form the waterspouts on its dome, it is the overall effect and setting that make it so dramatic when seen from the east. Its background is the huge step to the westernmost ridge of the Cávo Grósso, the nearly vertical cliffs dwarfing the tall towers of the village where evening falls early in their shadow. (See Plate 35.)

At Ochiá we are in the south-western corner of the great cape, and by driving as far as possible due south and continuing on foot we reach the south-facing cliffs about a kilometre from the church. Indeed the cliffs are facing almost south-east here because we are just round the point where the coastline turns abruptly north-east to Yerolimín before continuing south-east down to Cape Matapán. And all this coastline is visible from here to the great bulge of Matapán shimmering in the haze some 7 kilometres ahead. The view is superb, the drop vertiginous, and when we last went to that point and found three young girls kneeling in black on the very edge of the cliffs, we were surprised and alarmed. (See Plate 36.) All sorts of crazy ideas flashed through our minds. It was at a time when the newspapers had been full of mass suicide pacts in America, and while we were anxious not to disturb private devotions it was a great relief when the girls eventually stood up, threw something from their baskets over the cliffs, and turned round to walk home. We apologized rather clumsily for intruding on their privacy, but they were neither embarrassed nor annoyed to be seen with tear-stained faces. It was the anniversary of their father's death, they explained. His fishing boat had been smashed to pieces against these cliffs three years ago, and they had since come up here every year from Yerolimín to remember him and cast their offerings into the sea.

4

Yerolimín, Boularií and the Unhappy Bride

The little fishing village of Yerolomín, the 'Sacred Harbour', is the best centre from which to explore the southern part of Mani. It has two comfortable and unpretentious hotels (the only ones south of Pírgos), and these together with its three or four shops, post office, police station and a couple of cafés make it quite a metropolis in Deep Mani terms. But it is happily unspoilt by the tourism that is slowly restoring some of the prosperity lost through Mani's accelerated depopulation after the last war. A rack of coloured postcards outside one of the grocers and a sign advertising Kodak film are a far cry from the commercialized horrors of Míkonos, and there is nothing to detract from the unaffected beauty of the little harbour with its couple of fishing boats tied up against the quay, their nets laid out every day to dry in the sun, and the dramatic natural backdrop of the wall of rock rising sheer from the far end of the little beach.

Today it seems entirely natural that Yerolimín should have developed as a port serving the southern end of the Cávo Grósso region just as Mézapos served the northern, but in fact it is not nearly so safe a harbour as Mézapos, and its commercial development was entirely due to the wealth and energy of one man late in the last century. Mézapos had been a port, at least intermittently, for nearly three thousand years by the time a rich merchant from Síros made Yerolimín its rival in the 1870s, and even then he chose Yerolimín only as second best after the Grigorakákis family had driven him from Pórto Káyio, which had been his first choice. In 1870 there was nothing here but a scattering of houses and a pebbly beach on which boats could be drawn out of the sea, but by 1880 the new jetties were attracting all the coastal steamers plying between Piraeus and Kalamáta, and they were still calling in the 1950s when this local *sátira* was written, though it now seems like a faded vignette of much longer ago:

On Saturdays the steamer comes and down come all the girls,
Dressed up in all their finery, their hair in tightest curls,
From all the mountain villages to brave Yerolimín
Where Saturday's the greatest day to see and to be seen.
Among the blushing newly-weds are maids who long to marry,
And widows too and divorcees who're always glad to tarry,
They crowd upon the motor-boats that take them to the steamer,
Return with frilly petticoats and purses ever leaner,
And then they stroll and talk and flirt – the harbour wall's so nice! –
While in cafés the older folk debate the marriage-price.
'Look here,' we cry in anger fierce, 'the dowry's not been paid,
No marriage now, no bridal feast, your daughter stays a maid!'
For handsome men are few, you know, and girls without much money
May never know a man's embrace or mix the milk with honey,
But go back home to lonely beds to toss and turn and dream
Of what they never could afford at brave Yerolimín.

The entrepreneur responsible for Yerolimín's development was a certain Michael Katsimantís, a native of nearby Kipoúla, and though it was only one of many of this tycoon's commercial enterprises, it must have been unusually satisfying for him to flex his commercial muscles so close to his birthplace from which he had been driven in poverty as a young man. Why he was driven out is not recorded, but he was an *achamnómeros* rather than a Níklian, and Mani's still feudal society afforded little encouragement for a career open to the talents that this young man evidently possessed. At any rate it was the best thing that could have happened to him. Setting off to make his fortune in the best rags-to-riches fashion he sailed to the island of Síros, which was then the commercial centre of the Aegean. He got a job with a European firm of dye merchants, and by his unusual combination of intelligence, diligence and honesty he worked his way up from there to amass a considerable personal fortune and become the biggest colourman in the Levant. He had a large and gracious establishment in Ermoúpolis, the island's capital and port, and when one of his former enemies was forced into the harbour by a storm, his revenge took a painlessly pleasing form. He invited the man to stay at his house, regaled him with conspicuous extravagance, and only when his guest was departing after many days did Katsimantís refer to his banishment. 'So what did you Kipoúla people get out of driving me away?' he asked. 'All you did was make me great and rich! My Good Friday is better than your Easter Day!' It made the point with a phrase that was well designed to be repeated and remembered back in Mani, and it is a pity that the departing guest could not accept it with better grace. But success is hard to forgive, and the only thanks Katsimantís received for his hospitality was a surly insult that shows the less attractive side of Maniáte pride and arrogance: 'My midden in Kipoúla is worth more than the whole of your precious Síros.'

Katsimantís' original warehouses with their fine arches can still be seen and two of the jetties still bear his name, but despite his services to the community the name that dominates Yerolimín and the whole vicinity is that of Mantoúvalos, the lairds of the nearby village of Upper Boularií in the foothills of Mt Elijah (Oxovoúni) about 2 kilometres north-east of the little port. Yerolimín's tiny square is named after Major Panayiótis Mantoúvalos, whose heroism in the hideous Albanian War of 1941 is recalled by a bust and an inscription: he was a worthy descendant of his ancestors who fought in the War of Independence over a hundred years before. But of the origins of this lordly family very little is known. Little reliance can be placed on the Byzantine antecedents affected by this as by many other Maniáte families, and the first certain mention of their supremacy in this area seems to be Pouqueville's record of an incident in 1786 when a French ship, the *Jesus of the Sacred Heart*, was wrecked at Yerolimín. 'The captain and his crew were conducted to Boularií, which belonged to Ilías Mantoúvalis,' writes the French traveller, and adds a succinct testimony to the locals' efficiency in activities best known to English readers from *Jamaica Inn*. For that was evidently the last the good captain saw of his cargo or indeed his ship. 'The vessel itself, the cables, the rigging and the very masts were all cut up into pieces, divided by lot, and loaded onto the backs of the womenfolk who carted it off to the store-chests in their homes.' No army of red ants could have been more thorough: the *Jesus of the Sacred Heart* could not have disappeared more completely if it had gone to the bottom of the Atlantic.

At this time, and indeed for most of the nineteenth century too, the local harbour was about 2 kilometres south of Yerolimín, where the little coastal plain shelves gently down to an inlet called simply Yiáli, 'The Beach'. It is quite deserted today, but it is readily recognized from the couple of ruined windmills, a little stone church and the foundations of a tower from which the Mantoúvali controlled the moorings and exacted harbour dues from any who put in there. And this was the setting for an incident that led to war between the Mantoúvali and the great Mavromichális clan. The Mantoúvali were as fiercely possessive of Yiáli as the Sassárians were of Mézapos, and when Katsákos Mavromichális and his nephew Voïdís anchored their schooner there one day and refused to pay up, there was trouble. 'You cannot demand harbour dues from me,' cried the proud Mavromichális. 'I am Katsákos.' But the guardians of the tower were soon swarming over the schooner's sides in overwhelming force and the furious Katsákos was powerless to stop them helping themselves to his cargo, though – according to their own version at any rate – they were scrupulous about taking only enough to cover the dues.

Of course it was unthinkable that Katsákos would swallow this insult, and it was not long before he was bringing some of his followers and a large cannon overland from Tsímova to make war on the Mantoúvalos stronghold at Boularií. The three Mantoúvali brothers promptly barricaded themselves in their tower. The besiegers stationed themselves at the little church of the Panagítsa just opposite, and Katsákos called upon them to surrender and pay restitution for the goods they had taken from his schooner. His answer was a shower of insults and a musket ball which took off his fez. Then the battle began.

Although the Mantoúvalos tower was strong and well defended, the Mavromichális contingent had been reinforced by the defenders' local enemies both from inside and outside the clan, and the three brothers were hard pressed. But they were in no danger of running out of supplies. Their womenfolk were forever running backwards and forwards from the tower with ammunition and refreshments, and under the code of war such unarmed female assistants ran no risk of being deliberately fired upon. For this type of warfare was simply the most dangerous form of sport. It had its own rules, and the rough aristocrats of Mani were as punctilious in observing them as any medieval knight or duelling Junker. They were also as susceptible, and when Voïdís Mavromichális saw the beautiful Helen Mantouválou struggling heroically through the clouds of smoke with fresh supplies of powder for her beleaguered brothers, his heart was pierced by a shaft less deadly than a musket ball but no less irresistible.

'My lady,' he cried out to her, 'you please me much. Do you permit me to see and speak to your brothers?' And evidently the admiration was reciprocal. 'Certainly,' she called back. 'My brothers are not afraid of you. If you care to advance unarmed, come to the tower.' She then called up to her brothers to receive him. One was so full of fight that he wanted to hang Voïdís from the roof, but the other two were more reasonable, and after a short parley Voïdís emerged intact to call off the attack and mollify his uncle, who found it hard to leave the hole in his fez unavenged. The betrothal was celebrated at once, and having stopped fighting as impetuously as they had begun, the two families now competed in gargantuan excess in a feast lasting many days, during the course of which the marriage was duly solemnized and Voïdís returned to Tsímova as brother-in-law of the men he had come to kill.

Such, at any rate, is the story as recalled and embroidered by a great-grandfather of the present Montoúvalos generation, and however fanciful some of its details may be, there are other sources to confirm the essentials – the quarrel between the Mantoúvalos and Mavromichális families over the harbour dues, the declaration of war and the happy reconciliation based on a marriage alliance. And the tower still stands in the middle of the village, where it is easy to find and unmistakable when you see it. The little road that branches sharp left off the main road just before you enter Yerolimín from the north will bring you straight to it in about 2 kilometres. The little church of the Panagítsa is still there on the left, and on the right looms the tower, which was reputedly restored after its battering at the bridegroom's expense as part of the marriage contract. (See Plate 37.) And the present Mantoúvalos family are to be warmly congratulated on maintaining so fine an example of the late eighteenth and early nineteenth century type – a massively solid and square tower about 18 metres tall, impressively buttressed at the corners below the flat roof, and still carrying the plaque recording the date of the repair in 1811.

About 30 metres beyond this tower is another, much older one, the Anemodourá tower which, though not 'medieval' as is commonly claimed, may well go back to about 1600 and is the earliest surviving prototype in Mani. Its pattern is basically the same – the tall tower at one end of a long, narrow two-storey 'living' building – but it is constructed of huge, dry stones, the tower tapers towards the top, and it has only the most minute of embrasures. It takes us back to the time when the great Nikliáni of Mani were pledging their services to Charles, Duc de Nevers, their would-be champion against the Turks and restorer of the lost glories of Byzantium. This little village was evidently a great place then, and in the lists of forces which were sent to the new Palaeologue to encourage his attempt, its promised contingent is as much as half as numerous as great Kítta's and much more numerous than most others. But these two towers, exciting as they are, are only the most immediately visible of the buildings that make Upper Boularií one of the most rewarding villages in Mani. Upper and Lower Boularií have between them no less than twenty-one churches ranging from the tenth to the eighteenth century, and though most of them are more or less dilapidated, there are two of outstanding interest and importance – Áyios Strátiyos and Áyios Pantaleímon.

Passing the two towers the narrow road climbs steeply to the modern church of the Dormition, turns left over a little bridge, then climbs again sharp right towards the hills until it ends by a ruined medieval church and one or two old houses perched on the hillside above it in a tangle of geraniums and prickly pear. The seaward view from up here is magnificent, down over the towers of the two villages to the harbour of Yerolimín and the southern cliffs of the Cávo Grósso; and while we were contemplating it, we were ourselves being contemplated by two elderly ladies in black from their wild garden just above us. They reassured us that we had come to the right place to see Áyios Strátiyos, but they explained that the church was locked and there was no one in the village with a key. We should have to apply to the police station in Yerolimín.

It was a nuisance to have to return to Yerolimín for the key, but it was good news that the church was locked because it contains the fullest programme of medieval frescoes of any Maniáte church. But we could at least see the outside now, and after being pressed to a glass of fiery fluid and some lupin seeds by the hospitable old ladies, who were most curious to compare the prices of grapes and olives in Yerolimín and London, we followed their directions down the little path that led past the ruined church to emerge after about 100 metres in a little mountain valley among high, bare peaks. Incredibly there are towered houses on the very top of one of these peaks, but the church itself is nestling comfortably near the valley bottom, where a little stream runs riot in winter storms and there is sufficient water underground to support a few olives and a fragrant wilderness of camomile and sage among the tombstones. (See Plate 38.) And as soon as we saw it, we recognized Áyios Strátiyos as a contemporary of Our Saviour's at Gardenítsa, which it so closely resembles. It is similarly one of the earliest experiments in the domed, cruciform, simple-distyle type that dates from the early eleventh century. In both churches the nave and narthex are included under a continuous vault in the old basilican tradition, and St Michael's single-light windows with their arched lintels have the same derivation. And there are other primitive features here in the level eaves of the ill-lit dome and in the three apses of the east end whose external contour is of the semicircular rather than the pentagonal type that we found even at Our Saviour's. In both churches we see the first experiments with brick and the introduction of the cloisonné technique, which was soon found to require a much more accurate squaring of the stones than was easy with the hard local marbles and limestones and thus led to the importation of more tractable materials; though where the local materials were still used, as here, there is compensation for the irregularity of the masonry in the pleasing polychrome effect of layers of rich, purple limestone set in horizontal bands. And if St Michael's brickwork patterns are rather coarse and there is no attempt at the Kufic lettering that enhances the fabric of Our Saviour's, the basic plans of the two churches remain almost identical, even to the addition of domed porches (the only examples in Mani) in the twelfth century. (Compare Plate 32.)

Having seen the exterior we were eager to get hold of the keys, but this proved easier said than done. Repeated application at Yerolimín's tiny police station at different times of the next day found the officers either just going to bed or getting up, invariably trouserless but apparently full of good intentions to find the keys if we would only return later. Presumably they hoped that we would give up, but when we persisted they eventually confessed to having lost their set, or pretended to have done so to save themselves the trouble of accompanying us. They referred us instead to the priest of a remote village in the centre of the Cávo Grósso, and when we eventually found it, the good man had gone to take a funeral at Mézapos and would not be back that day. But we left a message, and as so often happens in Greece when an apparently simple quest is beset by Byzantine difficulties, there is an overwhelming compensation at the end. When we eventually made contact with the priest of Eliá the next day, we blessed the police for their unhelpfulness that led us to the kindest and most delightful of men. For though he was a very busy man, having the whole of the Cávo Grósso and Cape Matapán area for his parish and a different church for almost every day of the year if he wanted it, he immediately offered to take us to Áyios Strátiyos; and thus we looked at its frescoes through eyes that saw them as something more than beautiful works of art.

But the first problem was to see anything at all, for though the narthex gained some illumination from the open door, almost no light at all percolated into the nave or the three apses of the east end. Until we brought our powerful torches from the car we could only feel the hundreds of eyes watching us in the gloom, but when we flooded the church with artificial light all the walls and ceilings suddenly sprang to life in a blaze of twelfth-century colour that was truly breathtaking. Walking round the nave was like inspecting the noble army of martyrs and military saints on parade. We were eye to eye with the full-length saints of the lower register, and the busts of a second rank looked down on us from over their heads. At the western end of the nave we found a contingent of female martyrs, Polychronia, Parasceva, Anastasia and the great Thecla, the first-century maid of Iconium who heard St Paul preaching from her window and became his disciple, 'protomartyr among women and equal with the Apostles'. Nearby stood the physician Pantaleḯmon (Pantaleon) facing his mentor Hermolaus, and with them those two other '*anárgyroi*', SS Cosmas and Damian. They also treated their patients without pay and lost their lives under Diocletian's

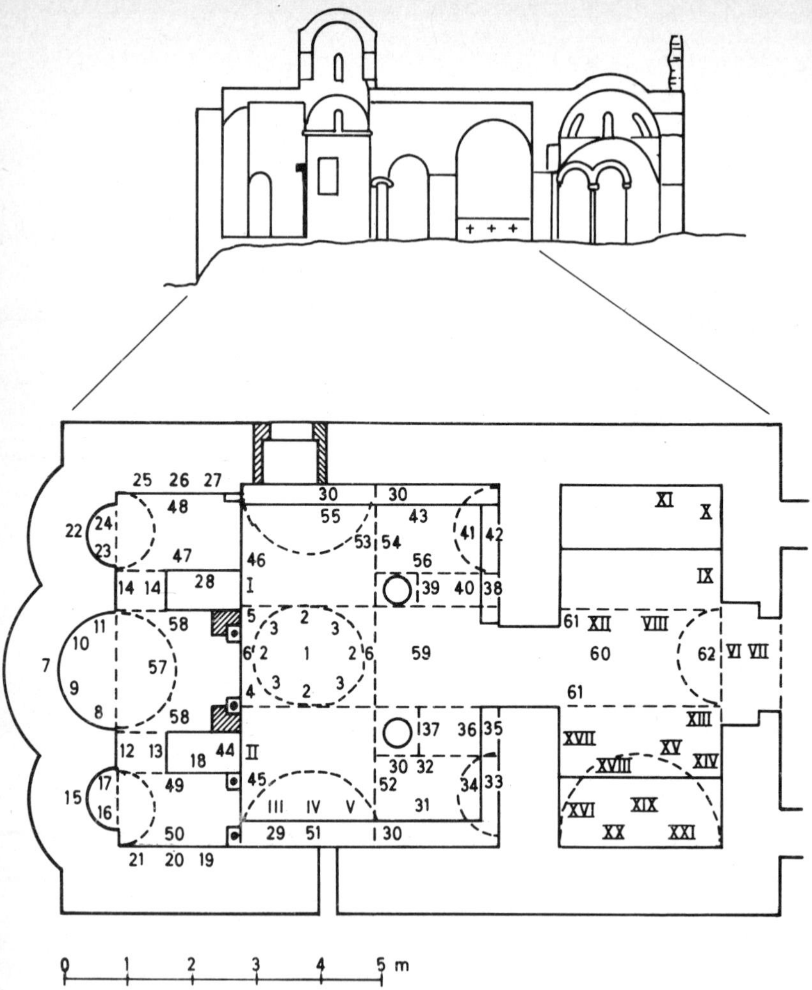

25 26 27 30 30
22 24 48 55 43 41 42 XI X
23 47 53 54 56
14 14 28 46 I 39 40 38 IX
11 58 5 2 3 3 61 XII VIII
7 10 57 6 2 1 2 6 59 60 62 VI VII
9 3 3
8 58 4 2 61
XIII
12 13 18 44 II 37 36 35 XVII XV
30 32 XVIII XIV
15 17 49 45 52 34 33
16 III IV V 31 XVI XIX
50 29 51 30 XX XXI
21 20 19
0 1 2 3 4 5 m

*The wall-paintings of the Church of Áyios Strátiyos
(the Archangel Michael) at Boularií*

(The arabic numerals refer to the earlier layer of paintings of the twelfth century, the roman numerals to the later layer of the thirteenth and fourteenth centuries.)

1. Christ Pantocrator
2. Seraphim
3. Prophets
4. St Matthew
5. St John
6. Head of angel
7. The Virgin Mary
8. St Nicholas
9. St Basil
10. St John Chrysostom
11. St Polycarp
12. St Gregory the Great
13. St Gregory of Armenia
14. Hierarchs
15. St Theodosius the Cenobiarch
16. St Tarasius
17. St Blaise
18. St Eleutherius
19. St Epiphanius
20. St Athenogenes
21. Hierarch
22. St George
23. St Leo of Catania
24. St Leo the Great
25. St Proclus
26. St Gregory the Theologian
27. St Therapon
28. St Agathangelus
29. SS Anempodistus, Aphthonius and Elpidephorus
30. Full-length military saints
31. SS Eustratius, Auxentius and Mardarius
32. SS Orestes and Eugenius
33. St Pachomius
34. St Thecla, Protomartyr
35. St Anastasia of Rome
36. St Hermolaus
37. St Pantaleon (Pantaleímon)
38. St Parasceva
39. St Cosmas
40. St Damian
41. St Polychronia
42. Female saint
43. SS Gurias, Abibus and Samonas

Narrative scenes from the life of Christ and the Dodekáorton
44. Angel of the Annunciation
45. The Nativity
46. The Presentation in the Temple
47. The Healing of a paralytic
48. The Healing of a paralytic
49. The Healing of a crooked woman
50. The Healing of a blind man
51. The Raising of Lazarus
52. The Entry into Jerusalem
53. Washing the Disciples' feet
54. The Last Supper
55. The Crucifixion
56. The Descent into Hell (Resurrection)
57. The Ascension
58. The Apostles watching the Ascension
59. Pentecost
60. The Last Judgement
61. Intercession with angels (Déïsis)
62. Apostles

I Christ
II The Virgin and Child
III The Archangel Michael
IV St Babylas
V St George
VI Inscription
VII Female head
VIII The Last Judgement
IX St Thecla
X St Nicholas
XI Angel
XII Intercession (Déïsis)
XIII St Cyriaca
XIV St Nicon
XV Christ
XVI Hierarch
XVII Archangel
XVIII Christ before Pilate
XIX The Betrayal
XX The Prophet Elijah
XXI The slaying of a dragon

persecutions, but their miraculous cures did not end with their deaths: they were still able to heal Justinian I over two centuries later, and that grateful emperor paid appropriate honours to the town where their relics lay. Pachomius was there too, the Egyptian monk who founded cenobitic monasticism. On the northern and southern walls the roll-call reverted to martyrs, the great military saints interspersed with more of Diocletian's victims – Eustratius, Auxentius and Mardarius from Armenia; Gurias, Samonas and Abibus from Syria; and to remind us that persecution was not a Roman monopoly, we saw the Persian martyrs Aphthonius, Elpidephorus and Anempodistus who suffered under Shapur II, the enemy of Rome.

The apsed chambers of the east end were populated with churchmen of even higher rank, patriarchs, hierarchs and the founders of liturgy. In the northern apse we found Theodosius the Cenobiarch flanked by the patriarch Tarasius of Constantinople and Bishop Blasius of Sebaste, better known in the western church as St Blaise. In the southern apse was St George with the two Leos: one being 'il Maraviglioso', bishop of Catania, the other the Roman pope. And in a less prominent position we discovered Athenogenes of Pontus, the aged theologian who had faced martyrdom singing the great hymn of joy that became the beautiful *Phos hilaron* of the Byzantine vespers. But in pride of place in the sanctuary, accompanying the Mother of God in the central apse, were the four great hierarchs: Nicholas, Basil, the eloquent Chrysostom, and the martyr Polycarp who had been converted by John the Evangelist himself.

'Eighty and six years have I served Him and He hath done me no wrong,' said a voice behind us. 'How then can I speak evil of my King who saved me?' It was the voice of the priest quoting Polycarp's words to the proconsul who begged him to save his life by reviling Christ. Then we noticed St Gregory between the northern and central apses. 'An unusually sensible and saintly pope,' observed the priest. 'He did much to promote the painting of churches and icons. It was he who said, "Painting can do for the illiterate what writing does for those who can read". All these paintings are of course part of the liturgy too, but their greater value is as a medium of education, a vast illustrated bible-cum-patrology without text, or at least with only a few words inscribed here and there.' And as the whole iconographic programme was gradually explained to us, we gained a remarkable insight into a medieval equivalent of confirmation classes that must have had far more impact on the pupils than the more sterile lessons of our literate age. For besides the pageant of saints and martyrs from which to learn the stirring tales that go with their faces, this church has the most complete series of narrative scenes from the Bible, including most of the feasts of the Dodekáorton and many of Christ's miracles and other details from His life, death and resurrection. And the closer the subject matter of the scenes to the fountainhead of Christianity, the nearer they are placed to heaven in the church itself, until we come to Christ the Ruler of All in the highest position of all, on the ceiling of the central dome.

'From Heaven did the Lord behold the earth,' said the priest as we shone our torches up into the dome: 'To hear the groaning of the prisoner; To loose those that are appointed to death; To declare the name of the Lord in Zion, And his promise in Jerusalem, When the people are gathered together, And the kingdoms to serve the Lord.' These verses from Psalm 102, the prayer of the afflicted, evidently encircled the Pantocrator, who was also surrounded by his now faded apostles. Underneath stood prophets alternating with seraphim on the vertical sides of the dome, and below them, in the squinches, the four Evangelists, though only Matthew is well preserved. And just as the All-ruling Christ dominates the whole of the church from the dome, so the Infant Christ in the arms of the All-holy Virgin dominates the apse above the sanctuary where they are flanked by two exquisitely painted angels bowing low with gifts. On either side of the iconostasis are another Virgin and Child (left) and Christ (right), facing into the nave and therefore visible to the congregation (though these are later than the twelfth-century frescoes). And from here we are ready to follow the narrative cycle which begins on the west-facing panel of the wall separating the sanctuary from the northern apse.

Only the Archangel Gabriel remains intact from the Annunciation scene, but the Nativity is preserved in full as at Episkopí, though with considerable differences in the arrangement and representation of the figures. Joseph is bottom left here, bottom right at Episkopí. The bathing of the Holy Infant, depicted below Mary at Episkopí, is here on the top right, where Episkopí had a little shepherd boy playing a recorder. The area below and left is here reserved for the three Magi, one of whose horses is turning back. And Mary herself is not sitting up by the manger as at Episkopí but reclining in an extraordinary relaxed and natural position, her chin propped up on her left arm, her right arm stretched out along her side with the hand resting on her slightly bent knees.

On the equivalent panel on the right of the sanctuary is the Presentation of Christ in the Temple, and though the Baptism has not survived, the life story is elaborated by several of the miracles in the northern and southern apses. In the northern we found the Healings of the Crooked Woman (Luke 13. 11–14) and of the Blind Man, the latter being told 'Go, wash in the pool of Siloam' (John 9. 7) as his eyes are anointed with the clay. In the southern apse are two Healings of Paralytics (Matthew 9. 1–8; Mark 2. 1–12; John 5. 5–9), and in all these scenes Christ is attended by the bearded Peter and the beardless John, both elegantly draped in robes of the most exquisite rose-red and pale blue while Christ stands out in clothes of a similar but darker red, almost merging into mauve. In one of the scenes the paralytic is depicted lying on a litter almost covered by a white sheet: 'Arise and walk', says the inscription, and the building behind is labelled 'The Porch of Solomon'. In the other the paralytic has already risen: he rests the litter against his shoulder, and the inscription reads 'Take up thy bed and walk'. (See Plate 39a.) The priest pondered these for a long time, looking again and again from one to the other and muttering uncertainly under his breath, but it was only later that he would tell us what was puzzling him.

From the miracles of healing in the apses we returned to the nave to find the Raising of Lazarus on the north wall above the standing figures of SS George, Babylas and Michael which, though very fine, are of later date. It is a beautiful, balanced composition, skilfully grouped round the little window. Christ, accompanied by Thomas, extends his hand over the top of the window to the cave on the right where the shrouded Lazarus rises stinking from his open tomb. They are totally intent on what they are doing, and the concentrated gaze of Thomas and

Christ as they stare at the tomb has the effect of pulling you into the scene and making you share the awe and amazement of the original onlookers. Then crossing to the two columns with their Ionic capitals we found three scenes that brought us closer to the end of Christ's life – His entry into Jerusalem, washing His disciples' feet and the Last Supper – and we are thus prepared for the Crucifixion on the southern wall opposite the Raising of Lazarus. And though the lower part of this scene is almost obliterated, Christ himself is still visible on the Cross in an attitude of unspeakable suffering, his head drooping on his chest, his naked body sagging with exhaustion, his brows hideously contorted in the agony of pain and grief.

'He descended into Hell,' said the priest, pointing to this depiction of the Resurrection by the more southerly of the two columns. Holding aloft a great Cross of Lorraine, Christ was trampling Hades under his feet and reaching out for the hand of Adam, who was struggling to rise from his shattered tomb. Death had been conquered, and we returned to the sanctuary itself for the Ascension, where Christ occupied the centre of the ceiling supported by angels and watched by his wondering disciples from either side. 'Why stand ye gazing into heaven?' said the inscription (Acts 1. 11). (See Plate 39b.) The disciples had work to do, and the granting of the power to found the Church is the equivalent scene of the barrel vault of the nave to the west of the dome. 'And they were all filled with the Holy Ghost, and began to speak with other tongues as the Spirit gave them utterance' (Acts 2. 4). The disciples here at Pentecost are similarly divided into two groups on either side as in the Ascension scene, but they are seated this time, with cloven tongues of fire radiating down upon them from the central orb in which the ascended Christ is replaced by the 'Throne of Preparation', represented by a cross and with the dove flying between the sponge and spear.

With a shock we all suddenly realized that we had been in the church for three hours and the priest had promised to be home over an hour ago, but we had seen all the best of the frescoes. There were only traces of the twelfth-century Last Judgement in the narthex, and though there were many more fine saints and martyrs there, they are of later date and less interesting than those of the nave and the east end. Only the marbles remained to be examined, and a quick scrutiny was enough to identify the work of an old friend, for though they are not inscribed they are almost certainly by the hand of Nikítas the Marbler who had autographed his work at St George's, Bríki, and St Theodore's, Vámvaka. But as we drove quickly back to the priest's own village, we remembered his puzzled scrutiny of the Healings of the Paralytic and asked him again about it. 'I am getting old,' he replied evasively. 'Wait till we get home.' And back at the vicarage he disappeared into his study for a few minutes before emerging triumphant with his fingers separating two passages of the New Testament. 'I thought so,' he announced. 'The words "Arise and walk" belong to the healings of Capernaum described by Matthew and Mark, but in the church they were written against the scene that had the Porch of Solomon, which was of course at Jerusalem. And in the Jerusalem healing, which was by the pool of Bethseda as described by John, the words are "Take up thy bed and walk", but these were the words given on the other panel.' It was a display of erudition that would have done credit to the Metropolitan in Athens let alone a parish priest born and bred in remotest Mani, and we wondered how many of his scattered and dwindling flock realized what a remarkably learned shepherd they had.

Having thanked the priest for his kindness – and our best thanks were hopelessly inadequate – we returned alone to Boularií to see St Pantaleímon's, and for this we needed no key because it had no door and even less roof than poor Trissákia. We parked this time near the modern church of the Dormition, crossed the little bridge on foot and followed a narrow mule track that the priest had pointed out to us on our way down from Áyios Strátiyos. It led north-westwards along the contour of the hillside, through neglected olive groves and past several disused threshing floors and a ruined tower in a field on the left. A megalithic church on the right contained only bats hanging from the single dilapidated apse, but some distance further on, about 500 metres from the car, we found St Pantaleímon's almost overgrown by olives in a field on the left. (See Plate 40.) From the outside it looked just like a one-room cottage, its walls a jumble of miscellaneous stones with huge slates covering what little remained of its roof. But when we had struggled through the low door under the overhanging olives and thorns, we found the east end astonishingly intact and two of the Great Martyrs gazing wide-eyed at us from the two shallow apses. (See Plate 41a.)

However many times you experience it, you never cease to be amazed by entering an apparent hovel and finding priceless works of art miraculously preserved for centuries; in this case for nearly ten centuries as these paintings were dated by an inscription to 991. That made them more than two centuries earlier than the paintings of Áyios Strátiyos, and they were strikingly different both in style and arrangement – much more primitive but no less important and, to our eyes at least, more dramatic. What we had found turned out to be the earliest two-apsed basilica in Mani. The apses are adjacent, and the Virgin who occupies the great central apse of Áyios Strátiyos and the later churches is here squeezed into a sort of squinch between the two arcs. And the martyrs *orant* who dominate the two apses belong to a much earlier iconographic tradition going back to the catacombs of the fourth and fifth centuries and to such early churches as Ravenna's lovely St Apollinaris in Classe of the mid-sixth. Here we have the beardless Pantaleïmon in the southern apse and the bearded Nicetas in the northern, and though they lack the refinement of the Áyios Strátiyos artistry, it is easier to believe in the reality of their suffering from these distraught and tortured faces than from the graceful tranquillity of the later representations. (See Plate 41b.)

Pantaleïmon, the 'All Compassionate', was a native of Nicomedia who became physician to the court of Galerius, whom Diocletian had appointed Caesar of the East in 293. He had been brought up a Christian by his mother, and though he had drifted back to his father's paganism under the influence of the imperial court, he was recalled to the faith by a certain Hermolaus, the saint who was depicted opposite him in Áyios Strátiyos, in time for the outbreak of persecution at Nicomedia in 303. Pantaleïmon showed his compassion for the victims not only by healing the sick without payment but by distributing his wealth among the poor Christian population, and this gave his jealous rivals the opportunity to denounce him to Galerius, who was genuinely fond of him and admiring of his skill. But the future Emperor begged him in vain to apostatize. Pantaleïmon justified his refusal by a miraculous healing of a paralytic, and when torture failed to compel compliance with the imperial will, he was sentenced to death. But the sentence was more easily passed than carried out. The increasingly exasperated authorities tried a succession of burning, liquid lead, drowning, wild beasts, the wheel and the sword, but only when he had made his point by refusing to succumb to any of these methods did Pantaleímon finally allow himself to be beheaded, whereupon his veins poured out milk instead of blood and the olive tree to which he was tied suddenly burst into fruit. And to this day the relics of his blood which are preserved in Constantinople, Madrid and Ravello are said to liquefy on his feast day, exactly as that of St Januarius does at Naples.

St Nicetas passed to glory about seventy years after Pantaleímon and beyond the imperial frontiers, for he is one of the two greatest martyrs among the Goths. He was born near the Danube, was converted and ordained by the great missionary Ulfilas who was an early believer in vernacular Bibles, and died in the persecutions of Athanaric, the Gothic Diocletian, who ordered an idol to be paraded through the Christian villages and decreed death for all who failed to worship it. And however much or little one may be disposed to accept of the agglomeration of details surrounding these two martyrs, there need be no doubt that the two men existed or that they suffered a hideous death whose horrors the painter of this little tenth-century church at Boularií has captured in their faces. Their eyes and mouths are wide in terrified awe and prayer, their huge hands outstretched in simultaneous supplication and blessing. They seem at once to be blessing the congregation and praying to their Risen Lord, whose Ascension is depicted on the ceiling of the sanctuary with his disciples gazing up at him from either side. But this is not the tranquil Christ of Áyios Strátiyos or the stern Pantocrator of Dáfni's terrifying mosaic. This is Christ the Compassionate, who is no less haggard-looking and horrified than the martyrs upon whom he looks down and gives his blessing. He has overcome the world, triumphed over Death and gone to prepare a place for his followers where he might wipe away their tears, but he has not forgotten his own bodily existence: he understands the weakness of the flesh, however willing the spirit, and his heart is clearly bleeding for the sufferings of Pantaleímon and Nicetas and for the endless cruelty and blindness of their persecutors.

On the side walls just before the sanctuary we found the remains of two narrative scenes from the Life of Christ – the Bathing of the Holy Infant from a Nativity scene on the north wall and the Baptism on the south. They are of the same early date and primitive, though highly effective, style. The heads and hands of the figures are disproportionately large, and they clearly derive their inspiration from the Eastern influence that is seen for example at St Apollo's at Bawit in Egypt. There are also seven full-length, though rather faded, saints occupying the lower register of the east end, and on the north wall a much later portrait of St Cyriaca (Kiriakí) in quite different style and colours. But how long will any of them last with the greater part of the church unroofed? Repetition of the same complaint is tiresome, but the repeated neglect of such important and beautiful works of art in so many Maniáte churches is criminal. A prefabricated roof and a locked door are surely not too much to ask, or that a responsible local villager should be entrusted with the key and granted a small pension to show these churches to visitors as well as to keep them safe. For it is just as wrong that the genuinely interested public should be denied access to them as that they should be left to natural decay or desecration by pilferers and vandals.

After returning to Yerolimín we set off southward the next day, leaving the southern cliffs of Cávo Grósso behind us and heading for the other great cape of Mani, Cape Ténaron or Matapán. Our road turned sharply inland as we left the village before continuing parallel to the coast midway between sea and mountains along a stony, shelving plain about a kilometre wide. To our left loomed the great crag of Mt Elijah above Boularií, stark in the morning light but exquisitely beautiful when we had seen it the previous evening in the full glow of sunset. The bare cliffs had then turned exactly the same soft colour as the robes of Christ and his disciples in the healing scenes of Áyios Strátiyos, an indescribably rich yet delicate shade somewhere between rose-pink and mauve that lasted about five minutes before the sun disappeared into the Messenian Gulf. To the right we saw the little inlet of Yiáli where the Mantoúvali boarded the Mavromichális schooner. Then about 4 kilometres from Yerolimín we reached the village of Álika, where the mountains come closer to the sea before the coastal plain opens out again. And here the road divides, for Álika is at the western end of the first motorable pass across the central spine of the peninsula since the Areópolis–Kótronas gap more then 20 kilometres to the north. The left turn in the village leads across to Láyia, from where it is possible to drive all the way back to Kótronas along the east coast of the peninsula. The road ahead continues along the west coast and creeps round the mountains to the narrow isthmus that joins Cape Ténaron to the rest of the peninsula, but though this was our destination and there is no other way onto it except by boat, we first drove to the top of the pass in order to take a little road that runs due south from there along the mountain ridge to where it suddenly breaks off in steep cliffs and gives a bird's-eye view of the whole configuration of the Cape spread out below. (See Plate 42.)

The road to the pass zig-zagged steeply up the side of a barren valley for about 4 kilometres before levelling out just before the village of Tsikaliá and running southwards again along the mountainside. From the little roadside chapel of St Charalámbos we had superb views, not only down to the coast below where the other road from Álika takes its lower course towards Ténaron through Kipárissos but also back to Álika and far beyond to the southern cliffs of Cávo Grósso above Yerolimín and its stepped plateau climbing in stages to the high west-facing ridge of Kástro tís Oriás. Another kilometre brought us in sight of Váthia, a spectacularly spiky village on a more seaward hill to which the coast road to Ténaron has to climb before continuing southwards to the isthmus. At this point we were almost at eye-level with Váthia, but after dropping slightly our road started climbing again over the head of the valley until we were looking down on Váthia's cluster of towers and having our last view of the west coast. For this was the pass proper. The road turned sharply east, and as we climbed to the watershed and our first glimpse of the eastern sea since crossing from Passavá to Kelefá, we very nearly missed the red earth track that turns sharp right to the viewpoint. It looks like the sort of cul-de-sac where a road-mender would park his bulldozer and it is hard to believe that it can lead very far at this altitude, but in fact it continues southwards more or less in a straight line for 3 kilometres through a high narrow plateau between parallel lines of conical hills. And though today only a few sheep and hardy bullocks are left to graze the rough pasture among the boulders, this whole, bleak plateau was once intensively cultivated, and the remains of elaborate terraces spiral incredibly almost to the tops of the hills. But there is no sign of human habitation until the road ends at a cemetery, a cliff edge, and a cluster of towers set back on the side of an even higher peak – the village of Korogoniánika, or Koroyiánika for short.

'Standing like an unhappy bride' was Nifákos' simile for it in his poetic catalogue of Maniáte towns, and whatever it was like in the eighteenth century, Koroyiánika is certainly forlorn today. Only three aged inhabitants cling on to this bleak and desolate place where even in summer the wind screams like a banshee through the crumbling towers. In a summer storm they operate like lightning conductors, and in winter they provide only a cold and draughty protection from the blasts of horizontal rain and hail against which it is often impossible to force open the doors. Only the gravest perils of living near the sea and a great pressure of overpopulation could ever have driven people to live up here, but three still do, and of their several churches the one they still use is perhaps the most beautifully maintained of any we have seen. It is not very old but it is very lovely, its walls minutely frescoed in the eighteenth-century manner, its brasses gleaming, its woodwork like mirrors and its floors so spotless that we found ourselves tip-toeing as though on carpets of imperial purple. And while we were admiring it and following the pageant of scenes from the life of Christ and of innumerable saints and martyrs, we heard the sound of footsteps stumbling up the cobbled track outside and went out to see the agent of this cleanliness approaching from where we had left the car. Or rather we could see no one at first but only two moving haystacks propelled by legs: one by four legs, the other by two and a stick. An old woman dressed and hooded in black was struggling painfully up to her house, bent double under a mountain of hay tied to her back and leading a donkey who was similarly loaded and almost invisible. At first she was suspicious that strangers were messing about in her church and fearful that we were up to no good, especially as she could not straighten up to see what was happening. But when we had helped her off with her load, she was mellowed by our sincere compliments about the church, though conversation was not easy. And this difficulty was only partly due to the strength of her dialect and her toothlessness, which together made us about as comprehensible to each other as Londoners and Geordies or Highlanders from Caithness. The real embarrassment was not language but anachronism. With our cameras and binoculars festooned around us and a modern car parked below, we felt like time-travellers who had trespassed into the Middle Ages as we confronted this black-hooded old woman and her donkey against a background of towers. The experience was strangely depressing, and as we returned to the car we felt almost ashamed of recalling Nifákos' cruel but perceptive evocation of the hard lot of women in Deep Mani, which contrasts so harshly with the swashbuckling glamour of the male exploits:

>The women reap and gather sheaves
>   Upon the threshing floors,
>With naked feet they trample them
>   With naked hands they winnow,
>With naked backs they haul the hay
>   And gather close the golden dust
>To save it from the roasting sun
>   That parches dry their panting tongues
>And dries and cracks their hands and feet
>   Encrusted like a turtle's shell;
>And then at night they work their mills
>   And grind their corn and cry.

The hill up which the village struggles is about 300 metres from the cliff-edge, which is clearly recognizable as such from up in the village though not from the road along which we came and which curls back northwards to reach the foot of Koroyiánika round the modern cemetery. All that can be seen southwards from the road itself is a rising, heathery slope with a crude stone building on the skyline, which identifies itself as a church for certain only when you get near enough to see the little scattering of tombs outside. Inside it has remains of an Ascension scene and a Baptism, but though faded and damaged they are nevertheless very interesting for demonstrating the same 'Coptic' influences, particularly in the heads and hands of the characters, that we discerned at St Pantaleḯmon's, Boularií. But it is less for its contents than for its position that this little church is worth visiting. And if you have not first looked over it from one of the highest of Koroyiánika's towers, it comes as a breathtaking surprise to reach it and suddenly find the earth plunging 300 metres to sea-level from before your feet.

We had reached the base of Taïyetos' spine, and in front of us the southern cape bulged like a grotesque pair of hips connected by only a low, narrow isthmus of land. (See Plate 42.) The isthmus itself, which narrows to about 700 metres, divides two bays, Pórto Káyio on the east side and Marmári on the west. Pórto Káyio is a huge, natural, deep-water harbour with a tiny village clustering on the sandy beach at its southern end. Marmári is a double bay with two sandy arcs separated by a rocky headland that juts out into the western sea. Perched on a hill near the centre of the isthmus was a tall, square tower that kept both bays within its cannon range, but though a winding dirt road ran between them below the tower, there was no way for wheels any further to the south. The path to Ténaron, evidently passable only on foot or hoof, could be seen leading south-eastwards from near the tower through the narrow saddle of land that separated the cape's high hills, which are higher and more precipitous on the western side. The whole circumference of the cape looked about 12 kilometres, though it was highly irregular in shape with long promontories separating two more southerly bays on the eastern side and counterbalancing the three conical peaks of increasing height that rise one behind the other on the western. The last of them hid the vertiginous village of Mianés from our sight, the southernmost village of the Balkans beyond which lay the southernmost tip of continental Europe except for Tarífa in Spain.

⚜ 5 ⚜

Kipárissos, Váthia and the Bay of Quails

From Álika the road to Ténaron from Yerolimín descends in a great zig-zag for about a kilometre before returning to the coast at the village of Kipárissos. A river-bed runs into the sea there from a broad, open valley which was once closely cultivated. The river is dry for most of the year, and from where the road crosses it just before a pair of distinctive wayside towers we walked down it for about 200 metres to the pebbly beach over which its winter torrents reach the sea. On the right we passed a large grove of cypresses hiding the tiny monastery-church of the Dormition mentioned by Leake, who spent a restless night there in 1805 after an evening meal of meat on a fast-day invited prompt punishment by a plague of fleas. On the left was a thriving little market garden indicating that fresh water was not far below the surface even in the summer, and then the river-bed lost itself on the beach which shelved steeply into a deep but narrow bay between high cliffs. Today the bay is deserted and the most perfect place for bathing in deep water of amazing clarity with no trace of oil, but in Roman times it was as busy as befitted the most important harbour of the west coast south of Mézapos. There was nothing in those days at Yerolimín or at Yiáli, but here, on and behind the headland that forms the south-east side of the little bay, was a city of such importance that in the first century AD the Elder Pliny could refer to the whole Messenian Gulf as 'the Gulf of Cyparissus, which has the City of Cyparissus on its shore'.

But though Kipárissos is also the modern name of the nearby village, only Pliny among the ancients uses it and it seems to have undergone a change of at least its official name. In the second century Pausanias refers to what is undoubtedly this site as Kenípolis, 'the New City, whose name was formerly Ténaron'. And Procopius says much the same in the sixth century when he refers to Belisarius as having put in 'at Ténaron, which is now called Kenípolis'. But though Pausanias used Kenípolis rather than Ténaron in his list of members of the Union of Free Laconians in his own day, it may well be that Ténaron was still the official name and Kenípolis only the popular or semi-official one (which may subsequently have become official by the time of Procopius). 'Kenípolis' never features on any of the inscriptions that have been found here from the second and third centuries, and where they give any more accurate definition than simply 'The City', it is 'The City of the Tenárians'. But this is not of course the more ancient Ténaron where the temple of Poseidon had flourished, and when therefore an ancient writer refers simply to 'Ténaron' it is not always clear whether the old Ténaron is meant, or Kenípolis, or the cape on which old Ténaron stands, or indeed the whole Mani peninsula, which is also sometimes called after its southern tip. What probably happened is that at some stage Kipárissos took over both the function and name of Poseidon's Ténaron as the chief town of the southern part of the peninsula but was popularly and semi-officially called Kenípolis at least by the second century. This was partly perhaps to distinguish it from old Ténaron and partly in recognition of extensive rebuilding, though it had already come to prominence as the most significant place on the west coast under the name Cyparissus by the time of Pliny, who died observing the eruption of Vesuvius at too close quarters in AD 79. And this original rise to prominence had probably occurred in Pliny's lifetime, since there are no remains that are obviously pre-Roman imperial and there is no mention of any place between Cávo Grósso and Poseidon's Ténaron in Strabo, who finished his *Geography* in 2 BC.

So much for the conundrum of the town's name and the likely date of its development, possibly in the later part of Augustus' principate or under Tiberius or Gaius Caligula. Why it developed there and then are questions less easy to answer. Since it became an important member of the Union of Free Laconians it could have been the Union's creation, though it is hard to see why other member cities should have created a rival to themselves unless perhaps it was designed as a southern bulwark against a Spartan-dominated (old) Ténaron, for the latter is never mentioned as a member of the Union and certainly the island of Kíthira belonged to Sparta. On the other hand it is possible that Kipárissos was a Spartan creation, or rather the creation of one Spartan in particular whose son appears on an inscription as a great benefactor of the town.

This is 'Gaius Julius Laco, son of Eurycles', and for Eurycles to have been the town's developer would be both chronologically and politically appropriate. For Eurycles enjoyed a special relationship with Augustus that gave him the overconfidence to indulge his territorial ambitions. Seeking revenge for his father who had been executed for piracy by Mark Antony, he had led the Spartans to fight for Octavian at Actium in 31 BC, and when the victorious Octavian began turning himself into the Emperor Augustus, Eurycles reaped the rewards of having supported the winning side. He was granted Roman citizenship, official sanction to rule Sparta and the restoration to Spartan control of the island of Kíthira, which became virtually his private possession. But indulgent as he was to Eurycles, Augustus was also careful to recognize the Union of Free Laconians and to keep these cities free of Spartan domination according to the usual imperial policy of 'divide and weaken' where there was no wish to be troubled with direct rule. Eurycles nevertheless sought to recover Sparta's control of them by great benefactions of the sort recorded at Yíthion and Asopós and by encouraging their pro-Spartan political factions. He also internationalized his diplomatic machinations. He visited the courts of Herod of Judaea and Archelaus of Cappadocia, and having played on his special relationship with Augustus to excite dangerous ambitions there, he returned to Sparta with large Oriental funds with which to support his turbulent schemes for reunification of Laconia under his own and Spartan leadership. And it would not be surprising if some of these funds were spent developing Kipárissos as part of his programme. But if so, this politically motivated expenditure benefitted Kipárissos more than Eurycles. His very success in creating party strife in the cities forfeited his last claims to the Emperor's indulgence, and he found himself banished from Sparta as a disruptive influence in southern Greece. His son, however, was more discreet, and having 'rejected all his father's ambitions' he eventually recovered the rulership of Sparta, perhaps in the reign of Tiberius. But though he rehabilitated his father's memory, he was careful not to fall into his father's temptations, and his benefactions to Kipárissos and other Union cities were made without the party political bias that had been his father's undoing.

Thus Kipárissos became one of the most important coastal cities of the Messenian Gulf in the first century AD, and when Pausanias passed by in the mid-second he noted 'a fine *megaron* of Demeter and a temple of Aphrodite by the sea with a standing statue of stone'. And from the second half of that century and the early third we have several grandiose inscriptions dedicated to Roman emperors and their families, possibly in recognition or anticipation of further benefactions. In fact Kipárissos has the largest number of these after Yíthion itself, which was the head of the Union.

A trio of inscriptions datable to AD 166–9 suggests that Kipárissos did well out of the Antonines: one is to 'Divine Antoninus, son of Divine Hadrian', another to 'Marcus Aurelius, son of Divine Antoninus', and the third to 'Lucius Aurelius Verus', co-emperor and adoptive brother to Marcus. The next dynasty and the beginning of the next century are represented by a dedication to Julia Domna, the philosopher wife of Septimius Severus, and by one to her son Caracalla, datable to between 213 and 217, from 'the Ephors of the City of the Tenárians'. And there are two more to the teenage Emperor Gordian, who came to the throne in 238 at the age of thirteen and fell victim in 244 to the ambitions of Philip the Arab, his general and usurper. Then there is silence for more than two centuries to the extent that nothing significant is recorded either at or for Kipárissos, but the town was destined for a moment of glory before fading from history altogether. It was at 'Kenípolis' that Genseric's Vandals landed in 468 from North Africa, and their resounding defeat stifled his schemes for the conquest of the Peloponnese. This had been a critical moment for the Byzantine Empire in Greece; and when Justinian's great general Belisarius was setting out to recover North Africa for the Empire in 533, it was fitting that his unwieldy fleet found safety at Kenípolis after almost coming to grief in unusual doldrums while rounding the cape.

The material remains of all this former greatness are still considerable and not far to seek, but they are not immediately obvious to the casual visitor who might follow the river-bed down to the beach for a swim. And as the bathing is so delightful here he might go away perfectly satisfied without a thought for the Union of Free Laconians, the coming of Christianity or the repulse of Vandal armadas. But it is the great advantage of Greece in general and Mani in particular that natural attractions are so often and so rewardingly combined with historical and archaeological ones, and if the swimmer decided to picnic sitting on the white blocks scattered around a ruined chapel on the beach, he would be literally in touch with the second and third centuries AD. For the blocks are marble and they evidently belonged to a temple before their incorporation into the church. The door jambs are marble too, the lintels pieces of columns, and what he was sitting on could well be a column base from the beach-side temple of Aphrodite mentioned by Pausanias. And when he looked over a low wall and saw a massive inscribed stele in honour of the Emperor Gordian standing like an altar in the ruined apse, the archaeologically minded visitor would be alerted to the possibilities of further exploration.

The obvious place to begin is the headland with a ruined nineteenth-century tower on top of it on the south-east side of the beach. Whoever controlled the beach would certainly have held this commanding height, and even if there turned out to be nothing more ancient up there after all, it would be a good vantage point from which to spot any remains lower down. A promising path, evidently ancient and long disused, zig-zags sharply up the near-vertical slope from the beach from just before the little market garden. The tower itself is about 35 metres above sea-level, and the views from there are very fine, particularly south-eastwards down the coast across the rocky cove on the far side where centuries of erosion have tumbled jagged masses of the cliffs into the constantly enlarging bay: rearing up from the black water at crazy angles they look like petrified dinosaurs and make this inlet as treacherous as the one we have climbed up from is safe. And the archaeologist is not disappointed. The tower itself is surrounded by marbles, its fabric is studded with them and the foundations of another temple are still *in situ* here in a great oblong of marble blocks set into the ground. Perhaps this was Pausanias' *megaron* of Demeter, or perhaps this and not the ruined church on the beach itself was his temple of Aphrodite, since his topographical indication 'by the sea' is not very specific. Or it might have been some other temple altogether either of the same or different date, for Pausanias recorded only the two buildings that he considered most noteworthy at the time of his visit.

Walking out along the headland is not easy because the whole surface is a tangle of waist-high spurges and thorns, but finding two more gleaming stelae like the one on the beach about 50 metres away from the tower rewards the discomfort, for they mark the site of yet another candidate for Aphrodite's temple. The foundations are now overgrown with thorns but still intact, and the stelae at the west end, which made the jambs of the low door when the temple became a rather disoriented church, are covered with still legible inscriptions. One is the dedication to Gaius Julius Laco from the Union of Free Laconians, the other to an 'excellent citizen' named Tanagros from his own 'City of the Tenárians'. Then returning to the tower but looking inland this time gives a bird's-eye view of the ancient town, which resembles an enormous version of Hampton Court maze built in dry-stone walling. Evidently the whole area was once covered with buildings that more recent villagers have tried to clear to make room for their olive trees and patches of corn, with the curious result that tiny plantations are surrounded by walls of anything between 2 and 4 metres in height. That makes them extremely difficult to see over except where they have been built close in parallel lines and over half-filled with stones, in which case you find yourself walking about 3 metres above ground-level and able to see but not get down. And since not a few of these innumerable passages are dead-ends, it can take some time and patience to find what can be so easily spotted from the tower – the arched east end and gleaming marble ruins of St Peter's basilica in the very centre of the labyrinth. (See Plate 44.)

When we finally clambered down a crumbling terrace into the west end we were engulfed in a great crowd of butterflies that had been sunning themselves on the ruins. The jambs of the west door were two great stelae like those on the headland and similarly inscribed, this time to the Empress Julia Domna and to a generous citizen named Lysicrates. (See Plate 45.) No expense had been spared on these elaborate dedications, and their almost perfect legibility after more than sixteen centuries of exposure is a tribute to the excellence both of the craftsmanship and of the stone. The great single apse at the east end has been partly restored, and the whole church has external dimensions of about 22 metres east-west by 19 metres north-south, which make it very nearly as large as the great basilica on Tigáni. But there is less doubt about the date of St Peter's. Whereas Tigáni's church could be as late as the tenth century, this one is definitely late fifth or early sixth, though some of the decorated marbles and column-capitals that litter the site are later work, possibly of the seventh or eighth centuries. Again Professor Drandákis would urge this evidence against the tradition of a pagan Mani until the ninth century, but though his case is impressive, the existence of two Christian strongholds on the coast in the sixth century (if we give Tigáni its earliest possible date) need not mean a significant penetration inland at that date or preclude a backsliding between then and the missionary efforts recorded for the reign of Basil I in the ninth century.

But to probe really deep into Mani's pagan past we must leave the new Ténaron for the old and press on southwards in the tracks of Leake's expedition to Matapán. A low spur separates the open valley of Kipárissos from that of Váthia, which is about 2 kilometres further on. Váthia itself is perched on a peaked height about a kilometre from the sea, but though the present road climbs up this and through the village, Leake's mounted party could take a lower track across the torrent-bed without going so far inland. And in 1805 it was safer to give Váthia a wide berth. Leake's party was held up for five minutes' interrogation by a party of armed men at the foot of the hill, and he records without surprise that the village had been divided into two factions for the last forty years, 'in which time they reckon that about a hundred men have been killed'. It was a typical Maniáte feud, but what is difficult to understand now is how an active war could have continued for so long in so confined a space. A whole generation must have been born and bred in the shadow of enemy towers that are only metres apart. They cluster together on their windswept height as though for comradeship rather than mutual destruction, a bewildering complex of skyscrapers rising from a maze of cobbled streets that often turn into staircases and lose you in a warren of tunnels and arches. It is as strange as exploring the ruins of a Maya city, except that these ruins are still inhabited by about thirty elderly folk under the supervision of their fiercely monarchist mayor. And the sensation of being caught in a time-warp is as vivid here as at Koroyiánika. It was incongruous enough when the mayor's black-cowled wife conjured a cold beer from a vast refrigerator in her otherwise medieval roadside tavern, but only a few metres away we met a ninety-year-old widow lugging a bucket of water into her tower through a door that was scarcely a metre high. Doors were kept low and narrow to prevent their being rushed by enemies, and in the smoke-blackened interior we could see a cauldron hanging over a low fire and the simple squalid furnishings of a war-tower unchanged from Leake's day when its occupants spent their lives belabouring their enemies next door. But in the absence of civil war there was evidence of remarkable longevity among the aged Vathiátes who sit outside their towers every summer evening to watch the sun setting peacefully in the Messenian Gulf. And who is to say they are worse off than their children, sitting on their balconies in the tenements of Athens, gazing through the exhaust fumes at their neighbours doing the same across the street and struggling to hear themselves think in what must now rank as one of the noisiest, most polluted and most crowded cities in Europe?

The road continues to climb a little way beyond Váthia and gives a last, splendid view back over the village and up the whole of the coast to the Cávo Grósso before it disappears round a headland into the dramatic landscape described by Leake. (See Plate 43.) 'We pursue the summit of the cliffs overhanging the sea,' he wrote, 'along the side of a very steep mountain, where are some difficult passes, one in particular formed by a wilderness of immense masses of rock, which seem to have fallen from the brow of the mountain.' The present road follows a ledge that has only recently been cut from even higher in the side of Leake's 'very steep mountain', and though our journey is easier than his, it is no less exciting. Travelling northwards has the comfort of hugging the cliff-face, but the southbound motorist teeters alongside a precipitous drop to a long narrow plateau whose far side plunges into the sea down great cliffs. Or rather it is more a valley than a plateau, for it rises again before the sea-cliffs to a variety of heights, the greatest of which is a vast jagged crag climbing sheer from the seaward side but dragging several crazy tiers of terracing up from the valley to where a ruined tower clings dizzily to the side of its naked peak. (See Plate 48.) It dominates the deserted valley like some forgotten but tenacious ziggurat, lashed by the winds and shattered by lightning but still hanging there to provide an eyrie for the ravens whose black plumage and mournful voices make them appropriate occupants of a Maniáte tower.

Just beyond this place, which is called Pírgi after the towers, the coastline curved eastwards towards the isthmus and we were above Pórto Marmári, the ancient Achíllion, whose two sandy inlets are two half-cups separated by a high promontory. Beyond them rise the three conical peaks that we spotted from Koroyiánika on the western side of the cape; and to our left, on the highest point of the isthmus, the tower of Chárakes whose commanding position had been a bone of contention between the lords of Deep Mani ever since it was first fortified in 1829 by the Grigorakiáni of Kítta. Conceiving Independence as the freedom to do as they liked without Turkish interference, this expansionist family decided to take control of the southern cape, but the Michalakiáni of Váthia and Láyia were not prepared to be cut off from their possessions there without a fight, and declared war. The result was a victory for the Grigorakiáni, but the two families then patched up their quarrel, and the Michalakiáni were not only allowed to pass freely across the isthmus but were entertained at the tower when they did so. But still it rankled with them that their free passage was a privilege and not a right, and one day, when a visiting party of Michalakiáni found themselves outnumbering the hospitable garrison, the temptation proved irresistible: they turned on their hosts and took over the tower.

Needless to say the Grigorakiáni immediately declared war, and a great new battle began on 25 June 1829, just in time to incommode the French scientists of the *Expédition Scientifique de Morée* whose vessel put into Pórto Káyio, the eastern bay, on that very day. 'We had scarcely anchored at . . . the bottom end of Pórto Káyio,' records their leader, 'when balls came whistling over our heads, and the tower of Chárakes, which they pointed out to me on a nearby crest, was the cause of the battle.' He then describes how they climbed to the fortified monastery on the cliffs at the northern end of the bay to visit the Bishop in the hope of securing his assistance in their work, but that worldly hierarch, evidently not wishing to be involved in the squabbles of his flock, had already left on an ecclesiastical visit to Kalamáta. His substitute was a fat, lazy monk whom the scientists found sitting cross-legged on a mat outside the gate while five or six ill-dressed but well-armed Kakovouliótes guarded the walls. 'He did not move at all at our presence, and receiving with indifference, if not disdain, the friendly greetings which I gave him through the interpreter, he asked laconically what I wanted.' But he soon remembered his manners when the interpreter took it upon himself to convey the quality of these guests: 'Why did you not get up and greet with appropriate reverence this great effendi who does you the honour to climb up to your nest – the effendi who is the friend of the Prime Minister himself.' This weighty name had scarcely dropped when the priest was on his feet, kissing the scientist's hand and exuding such oily helpfulness that it was scarcely more attractive than his former indifference. But the writer took it all in his stride, and with a detachment more scientific than Gallic he records seeing some young warriors coming down to join the battle *en famille*: their wives staggered ahead with all the luggage piled high on their backs; the men carried nothing but their weapons, and even a boy of eight was armed with an ancient pistol.

Again the Grigorakiáni were victorious, and the tower remained in their hands with even greater security after 1834 when John Grigorakákis became one of the first clan chieftains to break the anti-royalist coalition and accept a lucrative commission under King Otho from the wily Feder. And with the money that came to him from this source he destroyed the old tower in 1852 and built the splendid new one that stands there today, though the rival families took the opportunity to have one last attempt at regaining control of the isthmus. But the Grigorakiáni won yet again, perhaps not least because of the death of the great leader of the enemy coalition, Michael Gounelás, whose highly cathartic *mirolóyi* suggests that there was no one of much calibre to take his place:

> O brave Micháli Gounelá,
> How could you die and leave us so?

> That pig Berdésis, gulping swill,
> Now thinks to take the leader's place,
> Or incense-swinging good-for-nought,
> Our useless priest all plucked and shorn,
> Or thick Mourkákis, feeble loon,
> Or foul Yiatrós with matted hair
> And stinking breath that kills his lice,
> Or nostril-bulging Vangelákis,
> Herding cows that bear his likeness –
> O brave Micháli Gounelá,
> How could you die and leave us so?

Two roads cross the isthmus from Marmári to Pórto Káyio, whose ancient name was Psamathoús but the Venetians called it Porto Quaglio from the vast numbers of quails that used to be netted there on their annual migration and salted for an export market that was surprisingly extensive. The first road creeps round the mountainside to the monastery and castle at the northern side of the bay. The second crosses near the tower and winds down to the sandy beach at the southern end, from where the northward view is like the view from the stage up into the auditorium of some vast ancient theatre. The almost complete ring of sea forms the circular *orchestra*, beyond which the cliffs of the northern side rise like steep tiers of seats to Koroyiánika's cliff-edge church, which is appropriately in the gods. The great castle and monastery share the grand circle half way up, separated from each other by a near-vertical aisle formed by a steep gorge whose sides are wonderfully terraced and thick with cypresses. Clearly there is no shortage of water up there, and when you take the little road to the monastery, the luxuriance of its hanging gardens is quite extraordinary.

When Leake spent the night there in 1805 his experience was evidently more favourable than that of the French scientists twenty-four years later in the days of liberation. He was treated to 'by far the most agreeable lodging I have met with in Mani', and he recorded with relish an excellent salad for dinner and the choicest Maniáte honey. Today there are no monks, let alone a bishop, to worship the Virgin of Pórto Káyio, but the monastery buildings are still inhabited by a farmer and his wife, and they will show you her church which stands huge and forlorn in a magnificent position overhanging the bay. They also tend the terraces, and just beyond the monastery you will find the source of such unexpected luxuriance in a roadside fountain of the most delicious water. It gushes everlastingly from a cleft in the rocks in the shade of a fig tree, and after filling a cistern bubbles merrily under the road to the terraces full of cypresses, oranges and olives in the gorge. The walls of the castle rise stark and forbidding on the far side, and when you stand on its parapets and look down into the deep, blue bay, it requires little effort of imagination to see the historical pageant unfolding on the stage below.

It was in 1570 that the Turks first decided to make Pórto Káyio a naval base and build a castle to defend it. It was not only to strengthen control of recalcitrant Mani for its own sake but a preliminary to the conquest of Cyprus which, like Crete, was still in Venetian hands. And a glance at the map shows how perfectly suited a base here would have been for intercepting the Republic's line of communication and supply to Cyprus and the Levant. But no sooner were the Turks building their castle and unloading its cannons than a message was on its way from the Maniátes to the Venetian admiral at Chaniá. The governor of Crete was not slow to acknowledge the mutual advantage to the Maniátes and the Republic of a pre-emptive strike. On 29 June 1570 twenty-four galleys flying the Lion of St Mark were streaming into Pórto Káyio bay, and with the help of the Maniátes who attacked simultaneously by land, the Turks were defeated, their cannons captured and turned against them, and their fortress blown up by mines.

It was a brilliant success for the Venetians and their Maniáte allies, and though it failed to save Cyprus from the gigantic naval and military power that the Sultan brought against it, Pórto Káyio at least remained free of a permanent Turkish presence for exactly a hundred years. But when the Grand Vizier Kuprili finally wrested Crete from four and a half centuries of Venetian control in 1669, he decided to secure Mani against Venetian interference in what had always been the Achilles' heel of the Turkish empire in the Peloponnese. He offered an amnesty to all those Maniátes who had fought for the Venetians in Crete, cancelled arrears of tribute and appointed a Greek as Bey; but he was not relying on good will and diplomacy alone to secure Mani's future tribute and suppress its piracy. He also established permanent garrisons to control the two critical bays of Ítilon and Pórto Káyio, and thus the present-day castle of Pórto Káyio is a contemporary of Kelefá. But even now the Turkish garrison did not last more than fifteen years at Pórto Káyio, if that. In 1685 Mani was quick to rise in support of Morosini's conquest of the Peloponnese; and whether or not the castle was taken over by the Venetians, like Kelefá, or disused like Passavá, the bay will have seen more of the Lion than the Crescent for the next thirty years until the returning tide of Ottoman power swept the Venetians out of the Peloponnese again and even Mani returned to Turkish rule.

Another century goes by, and the scene is set for the brief drama of Major Lámbros Katsónis, the piratical patriot or patriotic pirate whose monument stands on the mole that all but encloses the bay. He was one of many Greeks commissioned in the Russian army as future agents of Catherine's imperial ambitions, and as long as Russia and Turkey were at war from 1787 to 1792, his piratical operations against the Turks were sanctioned by the Russian flag and at least partly financed by Russian funds. But when the Empress made peace with the Sultan in 1792 and lost interest in the Levant, Katsónis proclaimed that he would continue the liberation struggle alone and made Pórto Káyio his base. He built a gun battery to the southwest of the old castle, and having collected eleven ships and a large number of similarly redundant desperadoes, he sallied forth to terrorize the shipping lanes of the Mediterranean and Aegean. But though he was undoubtedly brave and energetic, it is hard to see him as the modern Themistocles whose mantle he bears in the mythology of the long struggle for independence. His main concern was to continue in the only position of power and lucrative employment he knew, and when he found it impossible to maintain his ships and crews by attacking only infidel vessels, he did not scruple to attack the shipping of any nation that offered the prospect of easy profits. But when he attacked and sank two French ships near Náfplion in May 1792, it was the beginning of his end. The French ambassador in Constantinople sent the information to the commander of a French naval squadron in the Levant, which promptly joined forces with the Capitán-Pashá and sailed with him to smoke out the pirates' nest. On 19 June Katsónis watched with dismay as the Turkish fleet began streaming into the bay with the support of a French destroyer, *La Modeste*, which demurely destroyed his batteries. His crews fled, his empty ships were carried off in triumph to Constantinople, and he saved nothing from the wreck of his fortunes but his life by fleeing into the mountains, from where he eventually made his way to the Ionian islands.

To have watched the Katsónis episode from the old castle would have fulfilled the war correspondent's dream of being on top of the action without danger to himself; but it might have been more nerve-racking to be here on occasions in the Second World War when aeroplanes had added a third dimension to naval battles and made even a bird's-eye view unsafe. On 29 March 1941 the British fleet from Alexandria confronted an Italian squadron off the coast of Matapán with such devastating fire power that five of the enemy ships were destroyed for the loss of one British aeroplane; but heartening as it was to the Allied cause, the Battle of Ténaron did nothing to retard the fall of Greece to the Axis powers a month later, or even the loss of Crete a month after that. The Allies had no option but to withdraw their forces ahead of the German advance, but it was a messy business which went on long after the German occupation and involved dangerous attempts to take off stranded British troops from remote harbours in southern Greece, one of which was Pórto Káyio. And in Kítta we met a man who had then lived at Pórto Káyio and had himself watched one of these rescue attempts from within a stone's throw of where we were standing on the castle walls.

The evacuees had been waiting on the sandy beach at the southern end of the bay since midnight, but the destroyer that was to take them off arrived only a little before dawn, and it was already light before the embarkation was complete. As the last of the men were scrambling aboard, the ship was spotted by a Stuka which immediately circled and began its run-in from the south while the destroyer hoisted anchor and prepared for action. The call to action stations, the clanking of the anchor chains and the first rattle of flak were only heard for a moment before all other sounds were engulfed in the thunderous roar of the approaching Stuka, the explosion of its bombs in great fountains of spray and the scream of its engines as it banked steeply to avoid the cliffs while a pursuing hail of bullets peppered the castle walls. Our eyewitness ducked involuntarily as he told the story. He had been sent back wounded from Albania, and when the bullets started spattering his home too, he thought his number was up anyway. But the destroyer was now steaming full speed out of the bay making smoke, the Stuka drew off after a second attempt and our friend lived to tell the tale as only a Greek can do, for there is no more war-loving nation on earth. And as his companions now vied to cap his war reminiscences with their own, we recalled the incredulity that greeted some American 'draft-dodgers' who fetched up in a remote Cretan village where we were staying in 1968. For a long time the locals simply refused to believe that these young men actually preferred not to fight; when they were finally convinced, they all manifested the most withering contempt except for one splendidly moustachioed old warrior who produced his own, more credible theory. 'Of course they wanted to fight,' he confided in a stage whisper, 'but they were not allowed to. They have flat feet, perhaps, or bad eyes. They do not look strong. And they have come here to hide their shame, the ill-fated children.'

But no stage could have had a less warlike setting than the Pórto Káyio that dozed in the still heat of the June afternoon when we last visited its castle. The church shimmered silently across the hanging gardens in a halo of haze, and there was no movement anywhere either of man or beast except a few butterflies fluttering lazily among the cypress trees and a white-sailed yacht gliding slowly to anchor off the sandy beach at the far end of the bay. Its destination was irresistible, and having refreshed ourselves deliciously at the monastery's fountain we drove back to the Marmári road, took the second of the branches that cross the isthmus, and wound our way up and over past the Chárakes tower to the inviting beach where the evacuees had waited for the destroyer in 1941. Undoubtedly Pórto Káyio is one of the most beautiful bays in the whole of Greece; and having bathed in its translucent water, which is so happily free of the oil that mars the perfection of the Marmári beaches on the western side, we were ready to face the stiff walk down the cape to find the ancient Ténaron, the Temple of Poseidon and the cave where Heracles dragged up the hell-hound Cerberus from the Underworld.

6

Poseidon, Ténaron and the Sunward Coast

From the highest point of the road that connects Marmári and the southern end of Pórto Káyio a short offshoot leads a little further south down the centre of the isthmus to a cemetery on a hill opposite the hill of Chárakes, and this is as far south as a car can go. The little bay in which Poseidon's temple stood is fifty minutes' hard walk south-eastward from here along a mule track which first crosses a little valley containing a nineteenth-century church so huge that it could scarcely be filled by the whole of Inner Mani's present-day population, let alone the handful of people who still live on the cape itself. The only houses in sight are the straggling towers of Páliros to the east, a hilltop eyrie like Koroyiánika with only about ten inhabitants left to enjoy its tremendous views northwards over Pórto Káyio bay and southwards over that of Vathí, which is the next inlet on the eastern side.

We saw Vathí bay as we emerged from the first valley – a gleaming strip of sand with two little ravines running down to it from north-west and south-west, the north-westerly one sporting an improbable cluster of planes on the otherwise treeless slopes. Páliros was now over our left shoulder, Pórto Káyio out of sight, and we were walking on a gently descending path along a scarp that rose increasingly steeply from the bay on our left to the high masses of the western side of the cape. A fork to the right would have taken us sharply up the side of the scarp to the village of Mianés, now deserted but for a few hardy bullocks that the Palirótes take up there to graze and enjoy the westward view. The lower track continued more or less southwards to the shoulder of the great promontory of Livádi which forms the bottom end of Vathí Bay, and as we climbed over its low saddle we looked down to the Bay of Asómati where Poseidon was worshipped for over a thousand years.

'There is a temple situated in a grove,' wrote Strabo towards the end of the first century BC, 'and nearby a cave through which mythology maintains that Cerberus was brought up from Hades by Heracles.' Today there is neither temple nor grove, but the cave is still to be seen alongside the pebbly beach below the little ruined church of Asómati that gives its name to the bay. It is roughly oval in shape, mainly open to the sky but with a few smoke-blackened caverns at the north-west side and a few slabs of masonry inside. It is only about 3 metres deep and perhaps 9 metres long, and with a leafy tree growing out of it – the only tree in the whole neighbourhood – it hardly satisfies the terrifying expectations of Vergil's 'Tenarian jaws', especially as we were able to confirm Pausanias' disappointed observation that 'there is no passage leading down through the floor'. But there is no doubt that this was the famous cave, and the traces of an extensive religious complex are still visible all round. The sunken foundations of a large, oblong building are still to be seen running into the sea on the beach adjoining the cave, and this is a more likely candidate for the temple itself than the church, which stands on a little height about 30 or 40 metres away. But the church too, if not the main temple, is almost certainly on the site of an ancient building that formed part of the complex. (See Plate 46.) As Leake observed, its partial disorientation from the usual east-west axis suggests that it was not in origin a Christian church, and the huge, squared blocks of its northern wall could well be ancient masonry *in situ*, especially since they admit an external door near the altar that shows no trace from the inside and was possibly walled up in the process of converting the pagan structure into a church.

Although the church is the only prominent feature of the present-day site, which is superficially unimpressive, there are many less obvious traces of an extensive ancient city to be found, particularly to the south-west behind the deeper inlet than the one containing the cave. Columns and fine masonry can be carted away and the mud-brick walls of houses soon disappear, but their rock-cut foundations are still traceable over a surprisingly large area. There are numerous cisterns, which give the bay its other name of Pórto Kísternes. There are smooth, broad steps leading up from the sea, and there are remains of a mosaic floor whose colours can still be revived by a bucket of water. And if Poseidon's extraordinary prosperity and importance in this remote and inhospitable place were inspired by a dingy cave barely 10 metres deep, one can only wonder what such ancient commercialization would have made of the Caves of Díros.

But Poseidon may not have been the first occupant of Ténaron, for though he was well established here in Thucydides' day in the fifth century BC, the Homeric *Hymn to Apollo*, possibly of the seventh, refers to it as:

> 'The sea-girt town of Helios, the gladdener of mortal men,
> Lord Helios whose fleecy sheep forever feed and multiply
> Rejoicing in his gladsome land. . . .'

Presumably Poseidon made a take-over bid for Ténaron before the classical period began, but the common features of dolphins and serpents here and at Delphi suggest an amicable arrangement between the powers of sea and sun. The Homeric hymn has Apollo entrusting himself to Poseidon's element in the form of a dolphin which proceeded to divert a ship-load of Cretans bound for Pylos to Delphi, where he made them priests of his new oracle there and called the place after the beast whose form he had assumed. Hecataeus believed that Ténaron's 'Cerberus' was not a dog at all but a serpent like Delphi's Python. And when the golden-voiced minstrel Aríon was returning loaded with money from a successful singing tour of Italy and the evil crew of the ship he had chartered made him walk the plank, it was to Poseidon's Ténaron that Apollo brought him safely to land on the back of yet another dolphin.

According to Herodotus, who tells the story of Aríon in one of the numerous digressions that make his history so delightful, there was a small bronze monument of a man riding on a dolphin at Ténaron in his own day, though whether the monument commemorated Aríon or the Aríon legend was located at Ténaron on the strength of the monument is another question. It is not absolutely inconceivable that a seafarer was rescued off Ténaron by a dolphin. It is well known that a sick or dying dolphin will be raised to the surface on his comrades' backs to help him breathe, and it is possible that they would respond to a drowning man in the same way. Or was the monument commemorating not a sea rescue but the sort of games that are common today among the staff and inmates of modern dolphinaria?

In one of his less tedious epistles than the dreary administrative correspondence with the Emperor Trajan, Pliny the Younger gives a well authenticated story of a similar but short-lived tourist attraction of the first century AD at the Roman city of Hippo on the North African coast:

> The favourite sport of the local boys was a swimming race in which the greatest kudos went to the one who swam furthest from the shore beyond his colleagues. One day a particularly brave boy went very much further than any of his friends. A dolphin came up to him and began playing all round him, then suddenly dived underneath him, raised him on its back, toppled him off, took him up again and carried him terrified even further out to sea before turning round and bringing him safely back to land and his companions.
>
> The story spread through the town, and all the people gathered to stare at the boy as a prodigy and to ask him questions and retail his replies to their neighbours. The next day the beaches were thronged with people watching the sea while the boys swam out again, though more cautiously this time. The same boy was among the swimmers. The same dolphin punctually reappeared and came towards him, and when he fled with the rest, it jumped and dived and swam round in circles as if inviting him to play and calling him back. The same thing happened the next day, and the next and for many more days until these people, who are born and bred to the sea, began to feel ashamed of being afraid. They went up to the dolphin, played with it and called it. It even allowed them to touch and stroke it, and their courage grew with their experiments. In particular the boy who had first had experience of it swam up to it in the water, jumped on its back and was carried out to sea and brought back again. He believed that it recognized and loved him, and he loved it. Neither feared nor frightened the other, and as the boy became more confident, the dolphin grew tamer. Some of the other boys used to go out with him on either side, shouting encouragement or warnings. And the dolphin was accompanied by one of its own kind (which is also a remarkable thing), but this other one only watched and kept company: it did not do the same things or allow itself to be played with but only escorted its friend to shore and out to sea again as the other boys did with their own friend.

It is incredible, I know, but as true as the rest of the story, that the dolphin who carried and played with the boys even allowed itself to be dragged out onto the beach, dried in the sand, and rolled back into the sea when it had become hot. It is also generally agreed that the governor's legate, Octavius Avitus, prevailed upon by some misguided superstition, poured scented oil on the creature as it lay on the beach, and the strange sensation and smell made it take refuge in the open sea. Only after many days was it seen again, looking languid and gloomy, but it soon regained its vigour and returned to its former playfulness and its usual tricks. It was a sight that attracted shoals of local officials, whose arrival and sojourn in the little town began to be an expensive burden, and eventually the place quite lost its quiet and retired character. It was therefore decided that the public attraction should be secretly destroyed.

Besides pointing an interesting contrast between ancient and modern attitudes to tourist attractions in Mediterranean seaside resorts, this sad story suggests novel lines of speculation on the origins of Ténaron's dolphin rider. If this could happen at Bizerta in the first century AD, something similar could have happened at Ténaron six or seven centuries earlier, and with even greater effect on superstitious minds than on the fatuous Octavius Avitus. But to return from speculation to fact, Poseidon's temple repeatedly reappears in classical and hellenistic times as a place of refuge of remarkable sanctity, particularly for those who found themselves suddenly *personae non gratae* in Sparta in whose territory it lay.

One of the earliest recorded suppliants for Poseidon's protection was a go-between entrusted with treasonable correspondence from the Spartan regent Pausanias to the Persians in the aftermath of the Persian Wars. In 479 BC Pausanias had commanded the Greek armies that destroyed the Persian hosts at Plataea, but the victory had gone to his head. Having driven the Persians from Byzantium in the following year he began behaving more like a liberated Spartan than a Spartan liberator, affected Persian dress and manners, and gave every sign of having belatedly found the only way to live and of making up for lost time. Although recalled to Sparta to answer charges of pro-Persian intrigues, he behaved no better on his return and was recalled again after the Byzantines had themselves expelled him from their city with Athenian help. But still it was difficult to find evidence that would convict a member of the royal family, not to mention the victor of Plataea, until one of his messengers, ordered to take a secret letter to the Persian satrap in Phrygia, 'was suddenly struck by the thought that none of the previous messengers had ever returned from there', whereupon he opened the letter and read why.

It was not very pleasant to see a treasonable letter ending with an instruction for its bearer's death and the unhappy man took it to the Spartan ephors, but they were still reluctant to order an arrest 'without hearing something from Pausanias' own mouth'. They therefore decided to set a trap for him and chose Ténaron as the best place to spring it. They ordered the messenger to go as a suppliant to Poseidon's temple where he could confront even the regent in safety, and when Pausanias duly pursued him to find out why he had gone there instead of to Phrygia, they were waiting in an adjoining room to overhear the conversation. It gave them all the evidence they needed, and when Pausanias was safely back in Sparta, they set out to catch him unawares in the street and arrest him. 'But when he was on the point of arrest, the face of one of them as they approached him betrayed their purpose, and another who was friendly warned him by a barely perceptible nod.' He ran for refuge to the temple of Athena of the Brazen House, but though he got there before his pursuers and gained the goddess's sanctuary, the ephors walled up the doors and took off the roof so that he was left both incommunicado and exposed to the elements. And there he stayed until he had starved to the point of death, when they brought him out unresisting to expire on unsanctified soil.

What had really been feared from Pausanias was that he would create a revolution in Sparta itself. As regent rather than king in his own right he knew that his constitutional authority would end with his ward's majority unless he first took control of the state by a *coup d'état*, which would require both external and internal assistance. The outside support could come from Persia, not in the form of men but of money. There were all the men he might need already on the spot, for the vast majority of the population of Laconia and Messenia – the wretched helots – were perpetually ripe for revolution against the small dominant class that had totally militarized itself to keep them in subjection. But in the event it was not Pausanias but Poseidon himself who precipitated the wholesale revolt that was every Spartan's nightmare, and he did it, so many Spartans believed, as a direct consequence of their having once violated his sanctuary at Ténaron.

The story comes in Thucydides' description of the propaganda battle that preceded the outbreak of the Peloponnesian War between Sparta and Athens in 431 BC. The Spartans sought to discredit Pericles' political leadership at Athens by demanding the expulsion of his family as being tainted and accursed ever since his ancestors had violated the sanctuary of Athena: they had dragged a suppliant from her altar and put him to death after a failed *coup d'état*. The Athenians replied with similar charges. For the Spartans to accuse the Athenians of offending Athena when they had done the same in the case of Pausanias was a classic case of the pot calling the kettle black, for she had not been impressed by having a suppliant starved to the point of death on her premises even if the Spartans had technically not removed him violently from her sanctuary or allowed him actually to die there. On the other hand they had already made expiation both architecturally and financially on the instructions of Delphi, and the Pausanias card was a weak counter to that of Pericles' ancestors. The strength of the Athenian hand in this particular game was their demand that Sparta should expel 'the curse of Ténaron, for the Spartans had on one occasion caused some suppliant helots to leave their refuge in the temple of Poseidon at Ténaron, and had led them off to death'. Even helots were sacrosanct at Ténaron, and when a great earthquake shattered Sparta in 464 BC and provided the opportunity for the servile rebellion that then preoccupied her for ten years, the Spartans themselves attributed it to Poseidon the Earthshaker taking his revenge.

Sparta recovered from her chastening and won the Peloponnesian War, which brought her to the zenith of her power and oppressiveness at the end of the fifth and the early fourth centuries until nemesis struck again in 371 BC, this time through the agency of Thebes. The Battle of Leuctra finally shattered the reputation for invincibility that Sparta's infantry had enjoyed for so long. Messenia was freed after some two and a half centuries of Spartan domination. Spartan institutions had proved incapable of adapting to the pressures of new wealth and empire, and the decline continued with little alleviation until well down in the next century when two idealistic young kings, Agis IV and Cleomenes III, tried to recreate Sparta's military power by recreating its economic and social base.

Their ideal was an army combining the professionalism of mercenaries with the patriotism and economic self-sufficiency of citizens. This had been the source of Sparta's greatness in classical times when enough Spartans had had enough land and serfs to free them from any productive distractions from the practice of arms; but most of the land had long since been concentrated into the hands of a few families, the citizen body was now tiny, and the majority of the small landowners who remained were mortgaged to the hilt. Only redistribution could recreate the ideal, and when the other king, Leonidas, opposed this as the champion of vested interests, Agis procured his deposition and replacement by his reformist son, Cleombrotus. But the existing citizens' enthusiasm for his redistributory scheme extended no further than the cancellation of debts that was its prerequisite, and Agis returned from an expedition to find himself and his fellow king totally discredited by the friends who had failed him in his absence. No redistribution had taken place, and since no one is less popular than the raisers of false hopes, both he and Cleombrotus found themselves fleeing for their lives. Agis fled to a temple in Sparta, Cleombrotus more sensibly to distant Ténaron, and it was there that he received news of his sentence of exile and of Agis' death.

King Leonidas was back with a vengeance, but the reactionaries' triumph proved short-lived when his second son, Cleomenes, came to the throne. Leonidas had married Cleomenes to Agis' widow for the sake of her vast wealth, but her estates were only part of the inheritance that came to her new husband. He was infected by her reformist ideas, and after biding his time to consolidate his strength he took Sparta by *coup d'état* and made sure that the redistribution was carried out by doing it himself and by including his own mercenaries in the share-out. The result was dramatic. In no time at all his citizen armies had all but recovered Sparta's old hegemony of the Peloponnese, and if an embittered rival had not called in the might of Macedon against him, he would have kept it.

In an attempt to play off one of Alexander's successor kingdoms against another, he approached Egypt for help against Macedon; but when King Ptolemy demanded his mother and son as hostages for a lucrative alliance, he was in two minds until the courageous old lady overcame his reluctance with a vigorous reply: 'Make haste and put me into a ship,' she cried, 'and send this frail body where you think it will be of most use to Sparta before old age destroys it sitting idly here!' And Ténaron was the port from which she sailed. She was escorted down the length of the Mani peninsula by King Cleomenes and his whole army in glittering array, and when she was about to embark, Poseidon alone witnessed her private farewell to her son. 'She drew him inside the temple by himself, and after embracing and kissing him in his anguish she said firmly, "Come, O King of Lacedaemon, when we go forth let no one see us weeping or doing anything unworthy of Sparta. For this lies in our power, and this alone; but as for the issue of the future, we shall have what the gods ordain." ' But the gods sided with the bigger battalions in the end, and though Cleomenes put up a brilliant struggle against Macedon, he lost the last great battle on which he had staked everything and fled to a miserable death in Egypt, where he eventually killed himself in the streets of Alexandria after failing to incite revolution among an uncomprehending populace 'who ran away from freedom'.

To envisage Cleomenes and his army taking leave of his mother and son at this deserted, barren little bay needs a much greater imaginative effort than reliving historical episodes at Tigáni or Passavá or Pórto Káyio with their impressive and evocative remains, but in fact far more needs to be envisaged here than Poseidon's temple and a harbour town to serve his pilgrims. Its central position on the sea routes between Italy and the Levant and between Greece and North Africa made Ténaron a thriving market town, and the commodity in which it specialized was mercenaries. In 303 BC, for example, when the Greeks of Tarentum were at war with Rome and sent money to Sparta to buy a general and an army, the general who was chosen went straight to Ténaron and hired five thousand mercenaries on the spot. Little wonder then that the bare hills of this remote cape with now only a handful of inhabitants were once terraced to conserve every fraction of cultivable soil. And since the interests of mercenaries are not confined to religion, Ténaron must have provided good business in hellenistic times for other professions too, particularly the one that is even older than that of arms. But the mercenary market declined with Rome's conquest of the eastern Mediterranean in the second century BC, and in the first we hear of Ténaron among the numerous coastal sanctuaries that were plundered by pirates during the Mithridatic Wars. King Mithridates of Pontus fostered these ancient pirates for his own purposes as effectively as the Ottoman Sultans employed Barbary corsairs in more recent times, and they virtually paralysed trade throughout the Mediterranean until Rome sent Pompey the Great against them in 67 BC and his huge fleets swept the seas clear in an amazing campaign of only a few months' duration. Then Ténaron revived and continued to attract pilgrims to Poseidon's temple at least until the second century AD when Pausanias recorded his disappointment about the lack of a passage through the floor of the cave, though its importance as a city had evidently been transferred to Kipárissos early in the century before.

It was exciting to follow the telegraph poles that march southwards for another kilometre to the lighthouse at the southernmost point of the Balkans before turning back to retrace the steps of Cleomenes as his mother and son sailed off to Egypt and he returned alone to pit Sparta against the might of Macedon. But we followed him only a little beyond Kipárissos, for he and his army no doubt continued up the easier west coast route down which we had come. We had yet to see the whole of the east coast between the Bays of Pórto Káyio in the south and Skoutári in the north. At Álika, therefore, we turned right and retraced the road that we had previously taken on our way to Koroyiánika. We enjoyed again the spectacular views over Váthia and up the west coast as far as the Cávo Grósso before we crossed the watershed and came into sight of the eastern sea. But this time we ignored the right turn to Koroyiánika, and after 3 more kilometres reached Láyia, the main town of south-eastern Mani, about 400 metres above sea-level and some 2 kilometres from the sea.

Though much decayed and depopulated this gaunt town still flourishes its former greatness in some exceptionally fine towers, one of them tapering from a broad base in the style of the very much older Anemodourá tower, which we saw at Boularií. (See Plate 47.) It was evidently another great stronghold of systematized belligerence; and with its easy access to both eastern and western Mani, it was an appropriate centre for Mani's most famous doctor, whose business was brisk in a land of endemic civil war and blood feud which attracted little professional competition. And this was no charlatan like Leake's extraordinary Frenchman, the 'fugitive from justice' who set up a quack practice at Tsímova, cured psychosomatic ailments with a pinch of snuff and was even credited with powers of prescience until he failed to predict the ambush in which he was waylaid and murdered for his ill-gotten gains. On the contrary, Láyia's Dr Papadákis was a very professional man, a physician and surgeon whose manuscript casebook of fifty pages still survives from the period 1715–63. Often his patients came to him and he was of course on the spot to attend Láyia's own feuding families, but he also seems to have visited many other villages as far north as Ítilon whenever local wars produced worthwhile concentrations of casualties and prospective fees. Indeed his casebook is almost a catalogue of civil wars, with different pages for different villages and gruesome lists of heads mended, bullets extracted and wounds bound in geographical arrangement. The entries are often illustrated with cartoons of bandaged heads or wounded legs, and among the seven hundred or more entries there is a bloody sprinkling of priests who were evidently in the thick of the fighting among their wolf-like flocks, for example:

Láyia:	Father George: stiletto through foot
Láyia:	Father George: rock on head
Kítta:	Father Kokkorákis: bullets in thigh
Tserová:	Father Zevyolátis: bullets (2) in thigh, straight through; severe sword wounds
Boularií:	Father Dikeólias: musket-wounds in shoulder

Only the good doctor himself was sacrosanct, for he was always neutral and far too useful to all sides to be offended: he lived long and well, and his family were still doctors in Láyia until early in the present century.

But for the hiker who enjoyed the stiff climb to Kítta's Áyii Asómati, Láyia is best approached from Álika not by driving over the motorable pass but by walking from the aerial village of

Moundanístika that towers above it at a height of 623 metres above sea-level. The road up to Moundanístika is incredibly steep but beautifully surfaced because it also leads to a mountain-top installation of the Greek Telecommunications Service whose sign, 'OTE', marks a sharp turn left immediately after leaving Álika on the Láyia road. Moundanístika's towered houses were the crenellations on the distant ridge on which we looked down from Áyii Asómati, which is about 2½ kilometres as the crow flies north-north-west, and the views are magnificent in both directions – northwards to Áyii Asómati and south to Cape Matapán.

The size of the village at this altitude and – until the advent of telephone and radar – inaccessibility is astonishing; and though it is totally deserted now in winter, the barren escarpment up which the road winds is so covered with ruined terraces that you feel as though you are climbing to the gods in a vast Roman theatre through hundreds of tiers of seats. Yet even this wuthering height is urbane compared with the ruined villages of Óros that you will see in the five-hour hike from Moundanístika to Láyia, which begins with a roughly paved path that leads south-east from the far end of this linear village. Again it is not something to be undertaken in the glare of a summer's day when the rocks crack in the heat, the ruined villages shimmer like a mirage and one has to keep a sharp eye out for snakes. The landscape is lunar, and how or when people lived here and built their forlorn terraces and tiny single-celled houses and churches is as much a mystery to the present-day Maniátes as to the rare visitor from elsewhere. Indeed the place has such a sinister reputation for being haunted and generally ill-omened that they tend to shrug their shoulders when asked about it and change the subject. But if its history is unknown, it was evidently a long one to judge from the composite church of St Eustratius that you will meet about a kilometre from Láyia. It consists of two barrel-vaulted chambers side by side, of which the southerly one forms the narthex for the present church, which has been added as an extension to its east end. But the difference in the external fabrics indicates the original church, which could be as old as the tenth century; and as the variations in the exterior are matched inside by different layers of frescoes, it could be worth while attempting to restore the earlier ones.

Deep in the mountains about 3 kilometres north-west of Láyia are the rich quarries of Mani's famous *antico rosso* marble, which was so highly prized in antiquity. Traces of the ancient workings can still be seen near the more modern ones, together with indications of a rock-cut road down which the great blocks were manhandled to the coast for export. But there are no antiquities at Láyia itself and few along the whole of the east coast from here to the foot of the Kótronas-Areópolis pass over 20 kilometres to the north, for reasons that were immediately apparent as we descended from Láyia and got a long view up the coast to the great promontory of Stavrí, behind Kótronas. The small, stony coastal plain of Mani's 'Shadowy' side, which seemed so meagre when we first saw it, is Oklahoma compared with its 'Sunward' counterpart along which the road now squeezed between sea-cliffs of perhaps 30 metres in height and a mountain range rising almost immediately behind them. Apart from one little bulge of green round the harbour of Kokkála about a third of the way to Kótronas there was no softening of the utter barrenness of its waterless landscape, and we would find no equivalent heritage of classical, Byzantine and medieval remains on this side. And yet the Sunward coast has its own harsh fascination, its naturally dramatic scenery intensified by the high-towered villages clinging to its mountainsides behind barricades of prickly pear. They were safer up there from pirates and from each other, and they made up for the lack of fresh water, as on Tigáni and Monemvasía, by constructing cisterns to collect the rainwater that was their most jealously guarded possession. In only one place between Láyia and Kótronas Bay is there an abundance of fresh water, and not surprisingly it is also the one exception to the dearth of important archaeological remains.

The site is nearly half-way between Láyia and Kótronas near the Monastery of the Dormition of the Virgin at a place called Kournós, at the top of a steep ravine about 3 kilometres north-west of Kokkála's little harbour. It is best approached by turning off the coast road to the village of Nímfi about 5 kilometres north of Kokkála, driving as far as possible up the southern side of the valley and then walking up the mule track that climbs steeply round the sea-facing hillside into the Kournós ravine, at the top of which the half-ruined monastery can be seen garlanded by luxuriant trees as at Pórto Káyio. It is also like Pórto Káyio in having no monks nowadays but a farmer and his wife, who happened to have their little grandchild staying with them when we last visited them. We could hear her shrill voice ringing like a bell down the gorge, but we were quite unprepared for her sudden appearance on a donkey galloping towards us down the narrow track up which we were toiling. Encumbered as we were with tripods, cameras and other impedimenta we only just got out of the way as she hurtled past, her little legs flailing at the donkey's side to urge him to greater exertions while she maintained an elegant side-saddle that would have been sensational at a rodeo. 'Sorry,' she cried, 'but I'm late for school.' She was only 7 years old, but she evidently thought nothing of riding to the tiny village school at Nímfi every day on a steep rocky track that took us more than two hours to climb and gleamed treacherously with a greyish marble that her donkey happily found less slippery than we did.

The monastery itself is built on terraces on the mountainside. Delicious cold water is available for passing men and animals from just below it, where a large, circular cistern of marble, probably ancient, is perpetually overflowing under a gushing stone spout. An underground channel brings it here from the fountain that emerges on the upper terrace under the leafy canopy of a huge fig tree in the monastery's private garden. The small, low living rooms are built over storerooms on three sides of a small courtyard. The church forms the fourth side, and while the farmer entertained us to some very welcome coffee and cheese under his fig tree, we could hear his wife frantically sweeping the steps of the already spotless little church before she would let us see it. And though the monastery is not very old, probably seventeenth century at the earliest, its atmosphere and way of life are entirely medieval. There is no concession whatever to the twentieth century, not even a battery radio or a canister of camping gas let alone electricity, telephones and all the other supposed essentials of our own existence. But as the farmer said, they had all they needed, and they were evidently so entirely happy that it was we who felt anachronistic as we said goodbye and began lugging our electronic wizardry even higher up the mountainside and deeper into the past.

Our objective was a high plateau jutting seawards on top of the promontory that forms the southern side of the ravine. As the path began to level out about 400 metres beyond the monastery we found a triglyph set into the corner of a ruined house; and about 100 metres further on we found where it had come from – the remains of two Doric temples on a bleak and windswept height about 550 metres above sea-level. It is a magnificent site. The temples look out over the Laconian Gulf eastwards to the Maléa promontory and south-eastwards to the dim outline of Kíthira. At the southern end of the plateau are great outcrops of rock like Cornish tors; and from there we had a bird's-eye view down to Kokkála harbour and could follow the line of the road by which we had come right back to Láyia, some of whose towers could just be seen swaying in the heat haze on a distant crest. As for the temples themselves, there were ample remains to give us a reasonable idea of what they were like. The foundations are all *in situ*, and the whole site is littered with fluted Doric columns of the local grey marble and several more triglyphs lying half buried under a carpet of cornflowers. The more northerly temple, which faced north-east, was an oblong about 9.2 metres long by 8.4 metres wide and evidently surrounded by columns, seven on the long sides and six across. The more southerly one is adjacent to it but not in alignment. It faces due east, and is set slightly further back than the first. It is smaller, measuring about 7.2 metres by 5.1 metres, and has a very different appearance, not surrounded by a colonnade as was the larger one but with only two columns set *in antis* on the east front. These temples must have looked very fine two thousand years ago, and there are remains nearby of an evidently quite extensive settlement that grew up around them. Traces of what was probably a third sanctuary can be found to the south-west, and there are many foundations of other ancient buildings, together with fonts, cisterns and a rock-cut relief of three panels depicting two badly worn figures. Clearly it was a centre of some importance, and there is far more to see here today than at Ténaron for example; but what was it called, when was it built, by whom and why and how long did it last?

The place is a mystery. Its only names are those given it by the villagers below – Kiónia, 'the Columns', or Vasilikés Pétres, 'the Royal Stones'. No ancient author mentions it, not even

Pausanias, who in fact mentions nothing at all on the whole of the peninsula's eastern coast between Kótronas and Ténaron. There are no inscriptions or sculptures to identify the deities worshipped here, and though the rock-cut relief has been thought to represent a Roman emperor and a Tyche holding a cornucopia, it is too badly worn to be reliable and would in any case be no evidence for the date of the temples. As a guide to how long they lasted it would have been strange, though not impossible, for Pausanias to have ignored them if they had been active in the second century AD, but how long they had been defunct by that time, or how long they had lasted before they became defunct, is impossible to know. Only a proper excavation might produce a reliable chronology for the site as a whole. In the meantime there is little to go on but the style of the temples themselves, which suggests a late hellenistic date for their construction, possibly the late third or early second century BC.

But why was a settlement ever built on so inaccessible and bleak a spot? As far as religious foundations are concerned, the question is based on a mistaken premise, for bleakness and inaccessibility were not necessarily disincentives to the ancients any more than to the monks of the Metéora or Mt Áthos. And even for the worldly-wise this site has two great attractions. One of course is the nearby abundance of fresh water; for the fountain at Kournós never fails even in the height of summer, and this unique resource in so arid a region would not only provide for the local agriculture but for the thirsty herds of more distant settlements that would have to pay for its use. Moreover accessibility is a matter of relativity; and relative to the other mule tracks that lead across the mountain spine between the Kótronas-Areópolis pass in the north and that from Láyia to Álika in the south, the one that leads across from here down to Mína and so to Mézapos on the western coast is the best of a small and difficult intermediate selection. Most of us are simply too soft nowadays to appreciate sites according to the values of hardier ages.

Sinking gratefully into the twentieth-century comfort of our car after the long climb down from Kiónia we continued up the coast road towards Kótronas. The mountains on our left rose steeper and higher and thirstier, they came nearer to the sea, and the luxuriant terraces of Kournós seemed in another world until suddenly, only 6 kilometres from Nímfi, the landscape was transformed as swiftly and dramatically as if we had been spirited from Petra to Padua. Ahead rose the high towers of Flomochóri, but this was no thirsty hamlet clinging to a beetling crag. We saw it with difficulty through a screen of cypresses, olives and figs – a large village spreading prosperously on its evidently fertile and well-watered domain. And to the right lay the pacific expanse of Kótronas Bay with its little island of Skopá anchored just offshore, like Yíthion's Kranaï, by a low, narrow isthmus.

To get down to Kótronas we first had to follow the road past Flomochóri and climb north-westwards towards the pass for about a kilometre before a sharp right turn enabled us to double back eastwards down the southern side of the broad, cultivated valley that sinks gently into the bay. Its northern side rises steeply to more than 500 metres in the great promontory of Stavrí that separates this bay from that of Skoutári to the north and blocks any further progress up the east coast except on foot; and even then it is a long and gruelling climb across a mountainous barrier 4 kilometres thick before you descend into the oak-covered valley where the deserted monastery of St George presides over Skoutári's sandy beach. Kótronas too has a sandy beach and is an altogether delightful little fishing village with a fine view all down the east coast as far as the bulging excrescence near Láyia that cuts off any further view southwards towards Ténaron after about 14 kilometres. It also has a history. Its ancient name was Teuthrone, another member town of the Union of Free Laconians; and the temple of Artemis Issoria and the spring at Naia that Pausanias saw on his grand tour were almost certainly on Skopá, where a sculptured relief of the hunting goddess was discovered early this century and ancient foundations are still visible among the fallen masonry of haunted medieval fortifications. When Colonel Leake visited the site sixteen and a half centuries after Pausanias, he was solemnly informed that 'the sounds of persons tossing over heaps of gold is sometimes to be heard here'; but either our timing was wrong or we were unreceptive, for we listened in vain.

After a refreshing swim in the beautifully clear water of the bay and an invigorating drink in the beach-side café, we drove back up to the pass but stopped to investigate the high village of Loukadiká with its curious citadel called simply the 'Kastro' by the villagers, who could tell us nothing of its history. But it was evidently once fortified, and on the very top is a small, ruined church whose almost north-facing 'east end' suggests yet another adaptation of a pagan site to Christian uses. And it was the perfect vantage point for a farewell view over the Sunward coast, for it gave a bird's-eye panorama from the Stavrí promontory over Kótronas village, the island of Skopá, the towers of Flomochóri, and right down the mountainous coast up which we had driven from Láyia. (See Plate 49.)

Driving westwards from Loukadiká on a warm June evening we were almost intoxicated by the smell of the roadside herbs as we continued through the pass; first among cultivated land interspersed with cypresses and little oak-covered hillocks, then through a slight constriction at the neck of the valley until the pass opened out again about 4 kilometres from Loukadiká into the plateau of Pírrichos. And Pírrichos, like Yíthion or Ítilon, still bears its ancient name. It was Pírrichos in Pausanias' time, and evidently the sources of the vital well that he saw in the market place are still functioning as reliably as ever, 'for if this were to fail, the people would be short of water'. Traces of public baths and other Roman remains can still be seen; and Pausanias noted sanctuaries to Artemis Astrateia and Amazonian Apollo, both connected with a legendary invasion of those single-breasted Sagittarians who turned back here. And it is interesting that he troubled to note that these two deities were 'represented by wooden images, said to have been dedicated by the Amazons'. It reminds us that artistic excellence is no criterion for the veneration in which the statues of deities were held. Artistically the great classical masterpieces of marble and bronze were as much admired by the ancients as by us; but as objects of veneration they were considered far less 'holy' and 'potent' than crude wooden images of mysterious antiquity, which were in fact the ancient counterparts of the thaumaturgical icons and relics of the modern Greek church.

Less than 2 kilometres beyond Pírrichos we had crossed the watershed and were descending to the west coast with a fine view down to Díros Bay where the Amazons of 1826 had thrust Ibrahím's Egyptians back into the sea. When we joined the coast road about 2 kilometres south of Areópolis, we had come full circle in our tour of the Deep Mani. We had travelled through only about 150 kilometres in space but a great many millennia in time. We had seen Stone Age remains in some of the most beautiful caves in Europe; Bronze Age sites in the Cávo Grósso; and the temples and towns of classical Greeks and Romans whose fortunes we could sometimes follow in history. We had marvelled at a Byzantine heritage of extraordinary richness and diversity, and been appalled by a neglect that will not be forgiven by future generations. We had visited the power centres of a succession of would-be conquerors: the fortifications of Franks, Venetians and Turks among the strange towers of the Maniátes themselves whose medievalism endured almost to the twentieth century. But it was fitting that we should end our tour at the war-god's city that had witnessed Mani's finest hour. For when Petróbey raised his standard of rebellion in the square of Areópolis on 17 March 1821, the feuding stopped, the armed might of the peninsula united against the Turks, and the Maniátes were the first army in the field in the great war that ended nearly four centuries of Ottoman domination.

Having reached Areópolis we drove down to watch the sunset from the Mavromichális castle at Liméni; and as the sea turned incarnadine and the snowy peaks of the Pentadáktila streamed blood above the darkening layers of cloud that hung about them like smoke, it was not hard to imagine the lords of Mani marching into Messenia. (See Plate 50.) While their *achamnómeri* and donkeys struggled with the supplies and cannon, the great Niklians rode or swaggered up the pass with their long muskets over their shoulders and their cummerbunds stuffed with pistols and yataghans. They stank, but looked magnificent. With their tasselled fezzes, embroidered waistcoats and huge moustaches dyed as black as their boots, they were dressed to kill; and in the long war that followed, through countless engagements of the sort dramatized in the following verses translated from the French of Leconte de Lisle, they made the names of Mani and Mavromichális almost synonymous with the cause of Independence and the creation of the nation-state in which, ironically, they were themselves almost too independent to integrate:

The Mavromicháles, the eagles of Maine,
Caught three hundred Turks in a narrow defile,
And from dawn to midday from the high cliffs above
Rained bullets and boulders that whistled and sang.

The dry powder flares and spurts with a flash,
Smoke rises in wisps that writhe in the sky,
And flurries of shots that crack in the air
Turn to hailstones of echoes thrown back by the walls.

The sour smell of sweat, foul breath and saltpetre
Comes up from the bends of that narrow defile
As a myriad sounds make cacophanous chaos
And barbarous blasphemies vie with Greek oaths.

'Allah!' 'Christ!' 'Jackals!' 'Foul circumcised pigs!
Spit forth your souls to the fiend's eager hand!'
'Attack! We must not let one robber escape!
The rope and the stake for these Christian giaours.'

'Come nearer my lambs!' cry the Greeks on the hills,
'We'll tear at your sides like wolves in the fold!'
And all of the infidels, cursing and bleeding,
Struggle to climb through the tangle of thorns.

The women of Pírgos in silent delight
From on high feast their eyes on the carnage below
While their sons, all rejoicing, are bent on revenge,
Red lips drawn apart, teeth gleaming like wolves.

Then at last, by the Virgin, the deed is quite done,
The Turks all lie dead, blood and bones, in a heap,
And scavenging vultures now gather to feast
And make themselves fat in a rich charnel-house.

'Now quickly chop off all these infidel heads
And nail them all fast to these walls,' cried the chief;
'Of my trophies of war they will hang as the crown
For the high-soaring swallows to use as their nests.'

Through many long summers and drear winter days
Along his stone ramparts the King of the Maine
Saw all the skin shrivel and then wear away
On each whitening head transfixed by a nail.

Since then all are dead, he, his children and kin,
By shot or by sabre, both victors and vanquished,
But still are young minds inflamed by their names
While their ghosts roam at night round their shadowy towers.

Hard, violent and daring were they while they lived,
All eager for vengeance and proud of their race,
Nor mercy nor favour they begged for nor gave
Secure in the knowledge that heaven was theirs.

Bibliographical Note

The most useful survey in English is Dora Rogan's *Mani*, which lists most of the sites and churches with brief details. Much fuller in Greek are the two volumes of Yiánnis Mantoúvalos' (Γιάννη Μαντουβάλου) *Στὴ Σκιὰ τοῦ Ταΰγετου*, together with Dimítrios Dimitrákos-Mesísklis' (Δημητρίου Δημητράκου-Μεσίσκλη) *Οἱ Νυκλιάνοι*, which is a fascinating compilation of miscellaneous data on almost every aspect of Mani's culture and history. And the English reader who has not already enjoyed it should not miss the magnificent prose of Patrick Leigh Fermor's *Mani*, which is now also available in a Greek translation.

The most useful history of Mani to 1821 is *Ἡ Μάνη καὶ οἱ Μανιάτες* by Dímos Méxis (Δῆμος Μέξης), who also provides an exhaustive and up-to-date bibliography. There is a much shorter history in Greek and English versions by Kiriákos Kássis (Κυριάκος Κάσσης) but the English translation is unfortunately incomprehensible. A more important book by the same author is his collection of *mirolóyia*, *Μοιρολόγια τῆς Μέσα Μάνης*, to which may be added the older monographs of Pasayiánnis (Πασαγιάννης) and Petroúnia (Πετρούνια).

In addition to the surveys mentioned above the archaeologist will find useful monographs on the Díros caves by Petróchilos and Papathanasópoulos (Παπαθανασόπουλος); on bronze age and classical sites by Forster, Móschou (Kiónia, Ténaron), Waterhouse-Simpson and Woodward; and on Byzantine architecture and art by Drandákis (Δρανδάκης), Megaw and Traquair.

For an excellent study of a similar social system involving vendetta and poetic funeral laments (*voceri*), orally composed and sung by women (*voceratrici*) like the sinister heroine of Mérimée's *Colomba*, see Dorothy Carrington's *Granite Island: a Portrait of Corsica*.

Full details of all these works are given in the following list, together with several others whose titles are self-explanatory. To have listed all the modern publications (let alone the historical sources) that have been consulted in writing this book would have required almost another book in itself, but this brief selection will provide some useful starting points for those who wish to explore still deeper into Mani.

CARRINGTON, D. *Granite Island: a Portrait of Corsica* (London, 1971; republished in paperback, 1984).
DASKALAKIS, A. V. (ΔΑΣΚΑΛΑΚΗ, Α. Β.), *Ἡ Μάνη καὶ ἡ Ὀθωμανικὴ αὐτοκρατορία* 1453–1821 (Athens, 1923).
DASKALAKIS, A. V. (ΔΑΣΚΑΛΑΚΗ, Α. Β.), «Ἡ ἔναρξις τῆς Ἐπαναστάσεως καὶ τὰ πρῶτα ἐπαναστατικὰ γεγονότα εἰς τὴν Λακωνία», *Λακωνικαὶ Σπουδαί*, Β' (1975), 5–62.
DIMITRAKOS-MESISKLIS, D. V. (ΔΗΜΗΤΡΑΚΟΥ-ΜΕΣΙΣΚΛΗ, Δ. Β.), *Οἱ Νυκλιάνοι*, τόμ. Α' (Athens, 1949).
DRANDAKIS, N. V. (ΔΡΑΝΔΑΚΗ, Ν. Β.), «Σκαφικαὶ ἔρευναι ἐν Κυπαρίσσῳ», *Πρακτικὰ τῆς ἐν Ἀθήναις Ἀρχαιολογικῆς Ἑταιρείας*, 1958 [1965], 199–219.
DRANDAKIS, N. V. (ΔΡΑΝΔΑΚΗ, Ν. Β.), «Ἀνασκαφὴ ἐν Κυπαρίσσῳ» *ib.*, 1960 [1966], 233–45.
DRANDAKIS, N. V. (ΔΡΑΝΔΑΚΗ, Ν. Β.), «Ἀνασκαφὴ εἰς τὸ Τηγάνι τῆς Μάνης», *ib.* 1964 [1966], 121–35.
DRANDAKIS, N. V. (ΔΡΑΝΔΑΚΗ, Ν. Β.), *Βυζαντιναὶ τοιχογραφίαι τῆς Μέσα Μάνης* (Athens, 1964).
DRANDAKIS, N. V. (ΔΡΑΝΔΑΚΗ, Ν. Β.), «Ἅγιος Παντελεήμων Μπουλαριῶν», *Ἐπετηρὶς Ἑταιρείας Βυζαντινῶν Σπουδῶν*, ΛΖ´ (1969–70), 437–58.
DRANDAKIS, N. V. (ΔΡΑΝΔΑΚΗ, Ν. Β.), «Τοιχογραφίαι ἐκκλησιῶν τῆς Μέσα Μάνης», *Ἀρχαιολογικὰ Ἀνάλεκτα ἐξ Ἀθηνῶν*, IV (1971), 232–9.
FERMOR, P. LEIGH, *Mani, Travels in the Southern Peloponnese* (London, 1958).
FORSTER, E. S., 'South-Western Laconia: Sites', *Annual of the British School at Athens*, 10 (1903/4), 158–66.
KASSIS, K. D. (ΚΑΣΣΗ, Κ. Δ.), *Ἱστορία τῆς Μάνης* (Athens, 1977).
KASSIS, K. D. (ΚΑΣΣΗ, Κ. Δ.), *Μοιρολόγια τῆς Μέσα Μάνης* (Athens, 1979).
KOUYEAS, S. V. (ΚΟΥΓΕΑ, Σ. Β.), 'Ἱστορικαὶ πηγαὶ διὰ τὴν ἡγεμονίαν τῆς Μάνης (1774–1821), *Πελοποννησιακά*, Ε´ (1962), 60–136.
LEAKE, W. M., *Travels in the Morea* (London, 1830).
LEAKE, W. M., *Peloponnesiaca. A Supplement to Travels in the Morea* (London, 1846).

MANTOUVALOS, Y. L. (ΜΑΝΤΟΥΒΑΛΟΥ, Γ. Λ.), *Στή Σκιά τοῦ Ταΰγετου* (Athens, 1975, 1978).
MEGAW, H., 'Byzantine Architecture in Mani', *Annual of the British School at Athens*, 33 (1932-3), 137-62.
MEXIS, D. N. (ΜΕΞΗ, Δ. Ν.), *Ἡ Μάνη καὶ οἱ Μανιᾶτες* (Athens, 1977).
MOSCHOU, L. (ΜΟΣΧΟΥ, Λ.), «Τοπογραφικὰ Μάνης: ἡ πόλις Ταίναρον», *Ἀρχαιολογικὰ Ἀνάλεκτα ἐξ Ἀθηνῶν*, VIII (1975), 160-77.
MOSCHOU, L. (ΜΟΣΧΟΥ, Λ.), «Κιόνια Α'», *Πελοποννησιακά*, ΙΓ' (1979), 72-114.
NIFAKOS, NIKITAS (ΝΗΦΑΚΗ, ΝΙΚΗΤΑ), *Μανιάτικα ἱστορικὰ στιχουργήματα* (Σωκρ. Β. Κουγεά, Ἀκαδημία Ἀθηνῶν - Δημοσιεύματα τοῦ Μεσαιωνικοῦ ἀρχείου, Athens, 1964).
PAPATHANASOPOULOS, Υ. A. (ΠΑΠΑΘΑΝΑΣΟΠΟΥΛΟΥ, Γ. Α.), «Σπήλαια Διροῦ», *Ἀρχαιολογικὰ Ἀνάλεκτα ἐξ Ἀθηνῶν*, IV (1971), 12-26, 149-54, 189-204.
PASAYIANNIS, K. (ΠΑΣΑΓΙΑΝΝΗ, Κ.), *Μανιάτικα μοιρολόγια καὶ τραγούδια* (Athens, 1928).
PETROCHILOS, A. J., *The Diros Caves of Mani 'Alepotrypa' and 'Glyphada'* (Athens, 1970).
PETROUNIA, V. (ΠΕΤΡΟΥΝΙΑ, Β.), *Μανιάτικα μοιρολόγια* (Athens, 1934).
POUQUEVILLE, F. C. H. L., *Voyage de la Grèce*, 2nd ed., vol. 5 (Paris, 1826), Ch. 3, 'Laconie', 519-616.
RANDOLPH, B., *The Present State of the Morea, Called Anciently Peloponnesus* (London, 1689).
ROGAN, D. ELIOPOULOU, *Mani: History and Monuments* (Athens, 1973).
TRAQUAIR, R., 'Laconia: The Churches of Western Mani', *Annual of the British School at Athens*, 15 (1908/9), 177-213.
VAYIAKAKOS, D. V. (ΒΑΓΙΑΚΑΚΟΥ, Δ. Β.), *Μάνη (Μέσα Μάνη)* (Athens, 1968).
WATERHOUSE, H., and SIMPSON, R. HOPE, 'Prehistoric Laconia, Part II', *Annual of the British School at Athens*, 56 (1961), 114ff.
WOODWARD, A. M., 'Taenarum and Southern Maina', *Annual of the British School at Athens*, 13 (1906/7), 238-67.

Index

Achaea, Frankish principality of, 23–4, 49–50, 88, 97
Achaean League, 20
achamnómeri, 36, 161
Achíllion, *see* Marmári
Agis IV of Sparta, 150
Alaric, 21
Albanians, 29–30, 51
Álika, 123–4, 152
Anemodourá tower, Boularií, 111, 153
Areópolis, 32, 57–9, 62, 161
Aríon, 145
Asómati Bay, 143–52
Athanaric, 122
Augustus, 21, 129–30
Avars, 22
Ayeranós, 49, 51, 53–4
Áyia Kiriakí, 84–6, 92, 97
Áyia Pelayía, Mt, 75–6, 85, 104
Áyii Asómati, Mt, 76, 85, 154
Áyios, *for patron saints see under churches or place-names*
Áyios Yeóryios, 100

Baldwin of Flanders, 23
Ballad of Mavroeidís, 89–92
Basil I, 22–3, 134
beaches, 47–8, 53, 127–8, 131–2, 142, 159
Belisarius, 22, 131
Beydom of Mani, 28–33, 46, 51, 53, 58–9, 139
Boularií, 108–23, 153
Bríki, 73–4, 120

Capodistria, 34
castles, *see* Karioúpolis, Kelefá, Passavá, Pórto Káyio
Catherine of Russia, 29, 140
caves, *see* Díros
Cávo Grósso, 73–4, 78, 85–6, 88, 94–106, 123–4
Chárakes tower, 127, 136–7, 143

Charles, Duke of Nevers, 26, 36, 111
Cháros, ballad of, 88–92
Charoúda, 66
Christianity, conversion of Mani to, 22–3, 61, 132, 134
churches
  Apollinaris in Classe, Ravenna, 121
  Apollo, Bawit, 123
  Asómati ('All Saints'), Kítta, 74, 76
  Asómati, Ténaron, 144
  Barbara, Érimos, 71–3, 75, 100, 103
  Barbara, Skoutári, 54
  Basil, Mézapos, 84
  Charalámbos, Tsikaliá, 124
  Dekoúlou, 58
  Dormition, Boularií, 111, 120
  Dormition, Kipárissos, 128
  Dormition, Kournós, 155–6
  Eleoússa, 94–5
  Elijah, Kouskoúni, 56
  Episkopí, 97, 100–2, 117–18
  Eustratius, Láyia, 154
  George, Bríki, 73–4, 120
  George, Kipoúla, 96
  George, Skoutári, 54, 159
  Holy Trinity, *see* Trinity
  John Chrysostom, Skoutári, 54
  Koroyiánika churches, 125–6
  Leo, Bríki, 73
  Loukás, Delfí, 67
  Michael ('Áyios Strátiyos'), Areópolis, 59, 105
  Michael, Boularií, 111–22
  Michael, Charoúda, 66–7
  Michael, Glézos, 66
  Michael, Kouloúmi, 70–1
  Nicholas, Bríki, 73
  Nicholas, Ochiá, 105
  Nicholas, Stavrí, 87
  Odiyítria, 92–3
  Panagítsa, Boularií, 109
  Pantaleímon, Boularií, 111, 120–3
  Peter, Karioúpolis, 55

Peter, Kipárissos, 133–4
Peter, Triandafilliá, 66
Pórto Káyio, Virgin of, 138–9
Procopius, Stavrí, 102–3
Sergius and Bacchus ('Tourlotí'),
    Kítta, 75–6, 100, 103
Sotíras ('Our Saviour'), Charoúda,
    66
Sotíras, Gardenítsa, 103–5, 112
Strátiyos, see Michael
Theodore, Kafíona, 70
Theodore, Kipoúla, 96
Theodore, Vámvaka, 73–4, 77, 104,
    120
Tigáni, 86–8
'Tourlotí', Kítta, 75–6, 100, 103
Trinity, Bríki, 73
Varvára, see Barbara
Vlachérna, Mézapos, 103
Clement VIII, Pope, 26
Cleomenes III of Sparta, 150–2
Constantine VII Porphyrogenitus, 22
Corsica, 27, 31, 57
Crete, 26–7, 139–40
Crusades, 23, 26
Cyparissus, see Kipárissos

Dekoúlou, 58
Digenís Akrítas, 89
Diocletian, 113, 116, 121
Díros Bay: caves, 18–19, 63–5, 145;
    battle, 33, 62–3, 161
Dorians, 19–20, 88
Drandákis, Professor N. V., 87, 134,
    164–5
Drí, 95, 97, 104

Eliá, 113
Élos, 24–5, 30, 44
Érimos, 70–3, 75
Eurycles, 130
Expédition scientifique de Morée, 136

faméyii, 36
Feder, 35–6, 137
Ferdinand II dei Medici, 27
feuds, 36–8, 41, 57, 61–2, 77, 83,
    109–10, 134, 136–8, 153
Filikí Etería, 33, 58
Flamininus, Titus, 21
Flomochóri, 159–60
Fokás, Thomas, 54
France, revolutionary diplomacy of,
    26, 31, 46

Franks, 23–4, 49–50, 88, 97

Galerius, 121
Gardenítsa, 103–4, 112
Genoa, 26–7
Genseric, 21, 131
Geoffrey of Villehardouin, 23
German and Italian occupation, 19,
    25, 38–9, 43, 141–2
Gerontikí, 38
Glézos, 66
Gonzaga, Duke Charles of Mantua, 26
Gordian, inscriptions to, 131–2
Goths, 21, 122
Gounelás, Michael, 137–8
Gregory XIII, Pope, 26
Grigorakiáni (Grigorakákis clan), 106,
    136–8
Grigorákis clan, 30–2, 46–7, 51–4, 59
Grimani, Francesco, 57

Hassán Pashá, 30, 35, 51, 54
Helen of Troy, 19, 44–6, 97
Herodotus (quoted), 39, 145
Herulians, 21
Hippo, 146–7
Hippola, 96; see also Kipoúla
Homer, 39, 49; (quoted) 45, 60, 88, 145

Iatráni ('Medici'), 27, 36, 57
Ibrahím Pashá, 33, 62–3, 84
iconoclasm, 101–3
Ítilon, 19, 21, 25, 27–8, 56–8

Jean, Barons of Passavá, 23–4, 36,
    49–50
Jean de St Omer, 50
John of Austria, 25–6
John I Tsimiskís, 54
Julia Domna, 131, 133
Justinian, 22, 88, 116, 131

Kafíona, 70
Kalamáta, 26, 33
Kalloní, 76
Kakovoúlia, 59–61
Kakovoúnia, 59
Kaouriáni, 77
Karioúpolis, 54–5
Kástro tís Oriás, 88, 97, 124; see also
    Cávo Grósso
Katsimantís, Michael, 107–8
Katsónis, Lámbros, 140–1
Kavallierákis family, 54–5

Index

Kelefá, 50, 56–8, 140
Kenípolis, 21, 33, 128–9, 131; *see also* Kipárissos
Kéria, 104
Kiónia, 157–8
Kipárissos, 21–2, 124, 128–34
Kipoúla, 95–6, 107–8
Kítta, 37, 74–8, 111
Kladás, Korkódilos, 24–5
Kokkála, 155, 157
Kolokotrónis, 63
Koróni, 23, 25
Koroyiánika, 125–7, 135, 138
Kótronas, 21, 158–60
Kouloúmi, 70, 73
Koumoundourákis, Panayiótis, 31
Koúnos, 95, 104
Kourikiáni, 77
Kournós, 155–6, 158
Kouskoúni, 56
Koutífaris, Zanétos, 30
Kranáï, 19, 45–6
Kuesy Ali Pasha, 51, 56
Kuprili, Grand Vizier, 27, 56–7, 139–40

Laco, Gaius Julius, 130, 133
La Crémonie (Frankish 'Lacedaemon'), 23–4
Lákkos, 71–2
Las, 19, 21, 49; *see also* Passavá
Láyia, 19, 124, 152–5, 157
Leake, Colonel, 31–3, 44, 53, 58, 60–2, 77, 128, 134, 144; (quoted) 32, 38, 44, 46–7, 59, 65, 134–5, 138, 153, 159
Leconte de Lisle, Charles Marie, 161
Leo VI, the Wise, 87
Lepanto, battle of, 25
Leuctra, battle of, 20, 149
Liméni, 32, 58–9, 83, 161
Loukadiká, 160
Lysicrates, inscription to, 133

Macedon, 20, 49, 150–1
Maina, Castle *or* 'Great', 22–4, 50, 88, 96
Maléa, Cape, 44, 157
Mantoúvalos clan, 108–11, 123
Marathonísi, *see* Kranáï
marble (antico rosso), 19, 46, 155
marbles (carved), 69, 72–5, 77, 87, 96–7, 100, 104, 119–20
Margaret of Passavá, 24, 36, 50
Marmári, 127, 136, 142

Matapán, Cape, 78, 105, 123–4, 127, 142–52
Mavroeidís, ballad of, 88–92
Mavromichális clan, 29, 32–4, 38, 58–9, 62, 83, 109–10, 123, 161; Petróbey, 32–4, 38, 58–9, 83, 161
Mavrovoúni, 19, 46–7
Medici, 27, 36–7; *see also* Iatráni
mercenaries, at Ténaron, 20–1, 151–2
Mésse, 19, 87–8; *see also* Mézapos
Messenian Mani, 17, 33, 39, 56–7, 62–3, 161
Methóni, 23, 25
Mezalímonas, 93–4
Mézapos, 70–2, 78–85, 87, 97, 106, 109
Mianés, 127, 143
Michael VIII Palaeologus, 24, 50
Michalakiáni, 136–7
Milengi, 24
Mína, 72
mirolóyia, 39–40, 71–2; (translations) 40–3, 51–2, 71, 79–82, 137–8; *see also* ballad, sátira
Mistrá, 24, 50, 88
Mithridates of Pontus, 152
monasteries: Áyia Eleoússa, 94–5; Dekoúlou, 58; Dormition, Kournós, 155–6; Holy Trinity, Bríki, 73; St George, Skoutári, 54, 159; Virgin of Pórto Káyio, 138–9, 142
Monemvasía, 23–6, 50, 86, 88
Moréa, Chronicle of the, 36
Morosini, 26, 28–9, 57, 140
Moundanístika, 77, 154

Náfplion, 25
Naples, 26
Napoleon, 31, 33
Navarino, battle of, 33
Nevers, Duke Charles of, 26, 36, 111
Nicephorus Phokas, 54
Nicholas of St Omer, 36
Nicholas the Grammarian, Patriarch, 22
Nicholas the Mystic, Patriarch, 87
Nikítas the Marbler, 73–4, 77, 120
Nikliáni, 36–7, 107, 111, 161
Nímfi, 155–6
Nómia, 76–7

Ochiá, 104–5
Odiyítria, 92–3

Oetylus, 19; *see also* Ítilon
Orlov, Count Theodore, 29, 51
Óros, 154
Otho (Otto), King, 35–6, 137

Palaeologus, Michael VIII, *see under* Michael VIII
Páliros, 143
Papadákis, Dr, 153
Paris, 19, 44–6
Passavá, 21, 23, 46–53
Pausanias, geographer, 21, 32, 44–5, 49, 88, 96, 128, 131–3, 144, 152, 158–60
Pausanias, Spartan regent, 147–9
Pelagonia, battle of, 24, 50
Peloponnesian Wars, 20, 149
Pentadáktilos, 56–7, 85, 161
Petróchilos, 18–19, 63
Philip V of Macedon, 20, 49
Philip II and III of Spain, 26
Phokas, Emperor Nicephorus, 54
piracy, 26–8, 34, 37, 60, 78–83, 93–4, 140–1, 152
Pírgi, 135–6
Pírgos Diroú, 65–6, 67
Pírrichos, 21, 160
Pliny the Elder (quoted), 128–9
Pliny the Younger (quoted), 146–7
Pompey the Great, 152
population, 37–9, 65, 125, 151–2
Pórto Káyio, 25, 27, 106, 127, 136–42
Poseidon, cult at Ténaron, 18, 20–1, 129, 142–52
Pouqueville, 108
Procopius, 88
Psamathoús, 138; *see also* Pórto Káyio
Ptolemy of Egypt, 151

Randolph, Bernard (quoted), 28
Revolution of 1821, 33, 38, 55, 58–9, 62–3, 79, 161
Ricord, Admiral, 34
Russia, 29, 32, 51, 140

Saints, *for patron saints of churches, see under* churches
St George, cycle of, 101–2
St Nicetas, 122
St Pantaleḯmon, 113, 121–2
San Gimignano, 37
Sássaris clan, 70, 79–84, 93, 109
sátira, of Yerolimín, 106–7

Second World War, 13, 25, 38, 43, 141–2
Selim II, Sultan, 25
Sklavounákos tower, 65
Skopá, 159–60
Skoutári, 51, 53–4, 159
Slavs, 19, 22, 24
Spain, 26, 50
Sparta, 20, 36, 129–30, 147–50
Stavrí, 85
Stefanópouli, 27, 31, 37, 57
Strabo, 129, 143–4
stradioti, 25, 37
Sunward Mani, 17, 44–54, 124, 139–60

Tanagros, inscription, 133
Ténaron: battle of, 141; city of, 21, 128–9, 133–4; temple at, 18, 20–1, 129, 142–52; *for* Cape Ténaron, *see* Matapán
Teuthrone, 21, 159; *see also* Kótronas
Thebes, 20, 36, 149
Theopistus, 101–2
Thucydides, 145, 149
Thyrídes, Cape, 78; *see also* Cávo Grósso
Tigáni, 19, 22–3, 84–92, 97, 134
Tolmides, 20
Tourlotí, 75–6, 100, 103
towers, 35–8, 65, 77, 83–4, 105, 109–11, 125–7, 134–5, 152–3
Triandafilliá, 66
Trissákia, 67–70
Trojan War, 19, 45, 87
Troupákis, Michális, 30
Tsákones, 24
Tsikaliá, 124
Tsímova, 32, 59, 110; *see also* Areópolis
Tsópakas, 67, 71
Turks: indirect rule of Mani, 28–33, 46–7, 53, 139–40; wars with Venice, 24–9, 37, 51, 54–5, 88, 139–40

Union of Free Laconians, 21, 49, 129–33, 159

Vámvaka, 73–4, 77, 104, 120
Vandals, 21–2, 33, 131–2
Vasilikés Pétres (Kiónia), 157–8
Váthia, 38, 124, 134–5
vendettas, *see* feuds
Venice, 23–9, 37, 51, 54–7, 88, 139–40

Index

Vérga, battle of, 33, 62–3
Villehardouin (princes of Achaea), 24, 36, 50, 88

wall-paintings, 117; *see also under* churches, *especially* Dekoúlou, Episkopí, Michael (Boularií), Michael (Charoúda), Odiyítria, Pantaléímon (Boularií), Sergius and Bacchus ('Tourlotí'), Theodore (Kafíona), Trissákia
William I, prince of Achaea, 23

William II, prince of Achaea, 24, 36, 50, 88

Yerakáris, Liberákis, 27–30
Yerolimín, 105–8, 111
Yiáli, 109, 123
Yíthion, 19–21, 30–2, 35, 44–6

Zanetákis, Thodorós, 32
Zarnáta, 50
Zervákos, Konstantís, 32